Hitler's Judas

Tom Lewis

DUPLIN COUNTY LIBRARY SYSTEM
KENANSVILLE NC 28349
MAGNOLIA BRANCH

VP Publishing, LLC
Rocky Mount, North Carolina

Copyright © 2007 by Tom Lewis

All rights reserved. No part of this book may be reproduced or utilized in any form or by any means, electronic or mechanical, including photocopying, recording, electronic copying or transmittal, or by any information storage or retrieval system without permission in writing from the publisher

Printed in the United States
10 9 8 7 6 5 4 3 2 1

Cover by Bill Benners

Interior layout by Delaney-Designs

VP Publishing, LLC
P.O. Box 4623
Rocky Mount, NC 27803

ISBN 978-0-9705793-6-2

First Edition September 2007

Read more about Tom Lewis at www.tomelewis.com

For

James Vick and Ron Pate

Who also believed

Acknowledgments

As usual, there are too many people to properly thank for helping bring this book to print. Still, I must list the names of a few who made special contributions. Among those who freely offered keen insight, timely suggestions and encouragement are: Don and Linda David, Georgia Lewis, Bill Benners, my oldest son, Erik, and of course, my tireless life partner, Ila Grey. All have earned my gratitude many times over.

I should also thank all the wonderful teachers, librarians, and other writers who long ago instilled in me a deep and abiding love of history, along with so many old-time outer banks residents who, from time to time, made small but important suggestions for the entire trilogy.

David French unselfishly gave time and expertise in keeping our computers from going off the tracks at critical moments, and finally, to James Vick and Ron Pate, my patient and faithful partners at VP Publishing, to whom this book is warmly dedicated.

Tom Lewis
Fall, 2007

Book II

The Pea Island Gold Trilogy

HITLER'S JUDAS

"The wars of peoples will be more terrible than those of Kings"

...Winston Churchill, at age 19

"Of all the seven deadly sins, greed is by far the worst"

...Anonymous

PROLOGUE

10 November, 1918—The Eve of the Armistice

Nearing midnight, two officers of the Imperial German Army, both aides to high-ranking Generals and friends since their cadet days, trudged away from the hoarfrost-coated railway car they had been staring at. Neither spoke until they reached the frigid edge of the clearing in the bleak forest near Compiegne. Major Karl Heinz Eppinger offered a cigarette to his companion, Colonel Ernst von Hellenbach. "What will you do after this sad business tomorrow, old friend?"

"Since we will be out of work, I suppose I will go home to Freiburg and try to help my wife raise the twins I have not seen in over a year."

"How old are they now?"

"Almost five. My sons need a father, Karl Heinz. I imagine one in disgrace is better than none at all. And you?"

"Go to Berlin and do what I can to help the Fatherland climb off its knees. This isn't the end of it, you know. One day, we will have to do it all again."

"I hope not, although I think you may be right. *This* war has been a disaster from the beginning. An insanity. And what we Germans have to look forward to after tomorrow will be worse." He turned and faced his colleague, not without sympathy. "But what can you do with only one arm?"

"One arm and one brain, Ernst. Someone will have to salvage what is left of our Army and our country. I'm afraid it will be up to the old men and cripples like me. We're practically all that's left."

Colonel von Hellenbach offered a wry chuckle. "Once a Prussian, always a Prussian, eh?"

"You should talk! Yours has been a family of soldiers longer than mine. Besides, I don't have any family left. I envy you."

"Do you have any more of those cigarettes?"

With his one hand, Eppinger reached into his tunic pocket. "Are you chain-smoking now? You never smoked much."

"I know, but it helps take away the smell of death. The Kaiser has made us pay a terrible price for his stupid pride."

"True. And tomorrow, the French and English are going to make us pay with ours, too, along with everything else we have. You are quite correct, it will be worse than war. A defeated country has no heroes."

Tom Lewis

Both men walked in the cold air for a while in silence. It seemed there was nothing else to say, at least not without choking on their emotions. Not even Eppinger, who had always been a big talker, had any words of either comfort or admonishment when he watched his friend rip the Iron Cross from his tunic, drop it on the ground, and then viciously step on it.

And both men shed unashamed tears when they witnessed the humiliating truce signing the following morning in Field Marshall Foch's *wagon lit*.

There were others, not present, who reacted in different ways once they heard the news of the Armistice:

At a hospital north of Berlin, a decorated young corporal from a Bavarian regiment, recovering from a gas attack, flew into a characteristic rage at the back-stabbing politicians and Jews he was convinced had caused Germany's cowardly surrender, and on the spot made up his mind to go into politics. He had no way of knowing his warped ideas and yet to be developed charisma would eventually propel him to the top of a political regime and a military machine that would come close to ruling the entire civilized world. His name was Adolf Hitler.

Elsewhere, an eighteen year-old artilleryman named Martin Bormann was glad not to be shot at any more, but wondered how he would now earn a living. He was not particularly worried, though, since he had long ago learned how to take care of the one person on earth that really mattered. Himself. Neither did he dream that not too many years would pass before he would design and execute the most brilliant double cross and greatest theft in modern history.

Hitler's Judas

Two young women, one in Stuttgart and one in Munich, were not in the least interested in what was happening in France. They were both in labor, and that night, would give birth to daughters. One little girl would be named Elisabeth Kroll, the other one would be named Edda Winter, and each would later become mothers themselves— of boys who would grow up to play important parts in the drama of Germany's tragic future.

And, thousands of miles west, on a sliver of sand north of Cape Hatteras, North Carolina called Pea Island, totally oblivious to war or anything else happening in Europe, a handsome Negro giant appeared at the door of the Pea Island Lifesaving Station, asking for a job as cook.

None of these individuals had any knowledge of each other.

Not yet. . .

Tom Lewis

CHAPTER I

The Obersalzburg, 2 May, 1941

When not obscured by veils of fast-drifting clouds, the view was beyond magnificent. From the granite patio of the Eagles Nest where he stood with his immediate superior, Rudolf Hess, Martin Bormann could intermittently see shimmering Salzburg in the distance. Bormann, never one to speak first, waited for his boss to explain why he'd suggested a breath of fresh air.

"Can I trust you with a secret, Martin?" Hess finally said.

Bormann felt like laughing at the question. With the exceptions of Goering and Himmler, everyone closest to the Fuehrer trusted their secrets to him. Even Eva Braun. "Of

Hitler's Judas

course you can. I'm the best secret keeper in the Third Reich. You know that."

Perhaps having second thoughts, Hess still hesitated. Shuffled his booted feet. His face looked even more cadaverous than usual. Bormann had the sudden, comical thought that Hess was already a dead man; a cardboard-cartoon corpse held upright only by the *rigor mortis* of his slavish love for Adolf Hitler. Bormann was also quite aware of the nicknames he and Hess had acquired in Hitler's inner circle— not to mention the General Staff. Hess was "the beetle" and he himself was "the mole." Bormann knew Hess was ultra sensitive to their behind-the-back whispered condescension while he, on the other hand, was only too happy to suffer their undisguised snobbery. It suited his purposes just fine that collectively, they thought no more of him than they did Hitler's chauffeur. Bormann knew he had the Fuehrer's ear, far more than any of the others realized, and what was infinitely more important, Hitler trusted him as much as he did his faithful Hess.

"So, what is this great secret? You have a girlfriend on the side?" Bormann was in a particularly good mood, and couldn't resist the jibe, which had its intended effect. Hess colored, then looked sharply from beneath the black hedgerow of the single eyebrow that ran from one side of his head to the other. "Don't be silly. No, what I want to tell you is that—"

"Ah, so here you are. I was looking for you."

Both men came quickly to attention as Hitler approached. As usual, Hess was too slow to respond with an excuse, so Bormann decided to save his bacon. He extended his arm out toward the valley. "We wished to treat

Tom Lewis

ourselves to one more glimpse of all this before you start the next conference, my Fuehrer."

Just as Bormann had hoped, Hitler's gaze followed the path of his outstretched, swastika-banded arm. With a deep breath, the Fuehrer replied, in almost a child's voice, "Yes. Truly stunning, isn't it?" Hitler walked to the edge of the parapet railing. "Only the bravest of eagles fly here, fearing nothing."

"And only you could have designed and built this nest for the bravest eagle of all, Fuehrer."

"*Ach*, my dear Bormann," Hitler said with a smile, "You are too kind. I only wish I could spend more time up here, especially in weather like this, and not have to think of nasty things like war, or nasty, fat people like Churchill. I simply do not understand that man. Why doesn't he listen to my reasoning? He knows well and good that I harbor no hatred for the English people. They are, by and large, from sturdy Nordic stock, and not yet too contaminated by Jews. I actually admire them. You've both heard me say that more than once."

He turned and faced his underlings, an impish twinkle in his eyes. "You know what Canaris told me last week? Churchill has a double! Some unfortunate fellow they found who looks remarkably like him, and whom they use to disguise his movements. Can you believe it? Herr Churchill must be frightened that one of his own countrymen might assassinate him. Canaris even suggested I find one for myself. I laughed until I cried. Can you imagine my doing such a preposterous thing?"

Again Bormann reacted first. "No, my Fuehrer. Your people love you too much. There would be no need."

Hitler beamed. "Exactly so." He turned back to the majestic panorama stretching nearly into infinity and sighed, clasping his hands behind his back. "But I still don't understand why they don't face facts. They are so unlike the French, who realize, when all is said and done, they are good at painting and cooking, but not at fighting. The English don't seem to know when they are beaten, but America will not keep them afloat much longer. Doenitz's young sharks will take care of that problem. I, on the other hand, have a much bigger problem. One that must be taken care of now."

He turned back once more. This time his face showed the familiar set of jaw. "I have to go back inside and light a fire under that spineless batch of jellyfish who call themselves Generals." He took a step, then stopped, apparently having thought of something else he wished to add. He wagged a finger at Hess. "Rudolf, since Dunkirk, they and all the world think I am going to invade England, and while they hold their breath waiting for me to do it, I am going to de-claw and then destroy the Russian bear before his teeth get too long. Are you coming in?"

Hess finally found his voice. "Certainly, my Fuehrer, but please give me another half minute. There is an important party matter I need to mention to Martin. We'll be right in."

Hitler nodded, turned, and went inside. Hess, whose tortured face was now even more pale than before, grabbed Bormann's sleeve. He lowered his voice to a whisper. "Did you hear that? He's going to invade Russia! Listen, I have to be quick. I mean to fly to England and try to make peace."

Bormann's mouth flew open. "What? Are you *insane?*"

— 18 —

Tom Lewis

"No. I have already tried three times, but bad weather forced me to turn back each time. I don't expect you to understand my motive, but you must believe me when I tell you I need desperately to do my part to help the Fuehrer with the English problem, and I believe I can. I have a certain Scots friend, who... Never mind, we must go in now. If I get another chance, I will explain all to you."

Bormann followed Hess's quick step into the room where Hitler was already holding forth. He allowed his gaze to wander over the faces of the audience. Most of the Generals were scowling. Bormann knew why, too. It was patently obvious that not one of them thought there was a remote prayer of crushing Stalin's Russia the way Hitler was outlining it in rough terms. Among those present, however, Goering and Goebbels, sitting as if under the hypnotic spell of white-hot religion, blatantly showed fervor that bordered on the orgasmic. Hess was staring at something on the floor.

Bormann had no doubt Hess would follow through with his mad plan. Or at least attempt it again. The poor simpleton was in a state of worsening depression caused by his acute feelings of abandonment. As Hitler had reached unprecedented heights of glory, carrying all his followers with him on the crests of each wave of his amazing success, Hess, whose sole responsibility was as party chief, had practically nothing to do. Hitler had become an all-powerful dictator, and no longer had any literal need for his figurehead party. Rudolf Hess was now nothing more than a ceremonial and largely forgotten icon, far overshadowed by the likes of "that obese toad Goering, that scheming chicken farmer Himmler, and that rabid rodent Goebbels"

Hitler's Judas

as he bitterly called them. There was precious little prestige Hess could claim or enjoy despite holding the lofty "office" of Deputy Fuehrer, which in his frustrated brain now meant nothing more than being a highly paid ribbon clerk.

Besides, Bormann himself was already performing nine tenths of Hess' mundane duties. If he had been compassionate, he might have felt some pity for the fool. But Martin Bormann was not a compassionate man. No, Bormann felt no pity at all for his pathetic colleague. But he would keep Hess' secret. He knew Adolf Hitler affectionately cared for his "right hand man", and simply was too busy to take time enough to show it. Nor did Bormann have the slightest doubt about who would succeed Hess when it was discovered he was gone. He allowed himself a hidden smile. Things were looking better. A lot better. No matter if Hess actually managed to reach England or died in the attempt, which was far more likely, Bormann would soon be in a position that he could eventually turn into real power. Power enough to accomplish his secret ends.

No one was paying him the slightest bit of attention when, over his upper lip, he blew out a surreptitious sigh of vast relief. No one who had taken the time to seriously read what Hitler had written in *Mein Kampf*, should have any reason not to believe he would try to someday wipe Russia off the map, and in so doing, would fail. He would succeed only in destroying Germany— and himself. Bormann could foresee that easily enough, and suspected most of the General Staff could as well, though none would dare say so to Hitler's face. But whether Hess made good his daring attempt to fly to England or not, or whether the

— 20 —

Tom Lewis

coming Russian catastrophe would spell the end of the Third Reich far sooner than Hitler's thousand-year boast, Bormann would make sure he survived— and not as a pauper either.

Hitler ranted on and on for three hours, then abruptly dismissed his Generals. Goering, Goebbels, and Himmler left as well, each having his own pre-planned agenda. Automatically, Bormann and Hess stood to follow them out but Hitler called them back. "No, don't leave, you two. I have a little surprise planned for tonight, and you're both invited."

Bormann and Hess stopped in their tracks and turned around. Bormann, strictly observing protocol and rank when in the presence of the Fuehrer — or any others superior to himself — glanced quickly at Hess, as if to prod the man into some sort of response.

"Surprise, my Fuehrer?" Hess said.

Hitler was apparently also in good humor. He leaned forward over the map table, smiling. "Yes. A small dinner party at my house. After all this talking, I need a little diversion." He winked at Bormann. "Leni is coming with some movies. Perhaps she will bring another of the *Kultur* films, too."

"Wonderful, Fuehrer!" Bormann replied, meaning it. He shared Hitler's deep admiration for famous movie actresses, although not the same types. Hitler loved the long-bodied beauties like Dietrich and the haughty Garbo, while he liked the more natural, well-rounded pretty girls who were always in the background, sometimes nearly nude. Besides, they were often available, and many of them were not any taller than himself. Bormann, who was only

Hitler's Judas

five foot six, couldn't stand having to look up to see a woman's eyes. He grinned broadly at Hitler and nudged Hess. "We'll have a lot of fun tonight, eh, Rudolf?"

Hess' face instantly showed his embarrassment, and Hitler could not resist his own barb. "Oh, come, Rudolf. You're always stiff as a constipated priest. If I can relax for a little while, surely you can."

"*Bestimmt*, Fuehrer. I shall do my best," Hess stammered.

Hitler and Bormann laughed. Both knew Hess would be uncomfortable and self-conscious in such company as was likely to be present. In such an atmosphere, he could no more relax and unwind than he could strip his uniform off and dance naked on the table.

"Nine o'clock sharp," Hitler said, still laughing.

Both men clicked heels and fired off stiff-armed salutes.

"*Jawohl*, my Fuehrer," they barked simultaneously. Hitler raised his right arm and hand part way up in answer, and bent again over his maps. Dismissed, both men walked to the elevator that took them hundreds of feet straight down the gullet of the mountain to the tunnel that had been bored out of solid rock and which led to the entrance and the winding road to Berchtesgaden. Cars and drivers were waiting. They shook hands, took separate cars, and left; Hess, who was already complaining of a migraine, to his quarters to rest, and Bormann to the village, specifically to the *Gasthaus Limmer*, where he would fill up on good sausages and beer, having little appetite for the bland, overcooked vegetarian slop he knew Hitler's cook would serve up.

— 22 —

Tom Lewis

At nearly two in the morning, he found himself standing next to Leni Riefenstahl behind the projector. "Martin," Leni whispered, "Would you please get me another cup of tea?" In the half-light, Bormann saw she was smiling over a silver flask she held up next to her cup, and quickly hid.

"Certainly." Bormann took her cup and moved quietly to the large linen-covered table that stood close to the door leading to the hall— which held a large urn of Hitler's only social drink as well as his favorite cakes and chocolates. He poured; one for her, and one for himself, but only half full. He made his way back to the dark corner where Leni now stood and held out the cups. From the flask, Leni filled both. The Russian vodka was, *Gott sei dank*, odorless, which was absolutely necessary at any of Hitler's parties.

"This helps, but I'm dying for a cigarette," Leni said.

"So am I, but we'll have to wait."

Leni nodded, and both looked down the mote-filled beam of light that ended on the large screen, which was filled with Greta Garbo's classic face. The movie was *Wild Orchids*, one of the earlier Garbo films Hitler never tired of watching. "Whoever told that skinny bitch she could act?" Leni whispered, half to herself, half to Bormann. "I'm glad she went to America."

"She must be making lots of money," Bormann said. "The other one, too."

"Dietrich? Of course she is. She's even a worse bitch, but at least she knows something about acting, and she's a far stronger woman. She will outlast Garbo by far."

"No matter. You're still here and still the Fuehrer's favorite, Leni. Mine, too."

– 23 –

"*Ach*, Martin, you always know the right things to say, don't you. How's your... tea?"

"Good. Excellent, in fact. Thanks for bringing the flavoring."

"You're welcome. I've also brought a film I know you'll want to see."

"Really? Which?"

"One you haven't seen before, but you'll have to be patient. The Fuehrer wants to watch *The Mysterious Lady* first."

Bormann sighed. Silently biding his time was not a problem for him. He'd had a good deal of practice. Years of practice. Another hour or so was nothing, especially if the vodka in Leni's flask held out.

This time his patience would be rewarded in an unexpected way. The extra movie Leni Riesenthal had brought was another of Hitler's favorites; the highly successful '*Kultur*' film, *The Ways to Strength and Beauty*, in which there were artistic scenes of nude women cavorting about in 'natural' physical exercises. Bormann, who wouldn't have recognized art if it slapped him in the face, was aroused by the movie and in one scene, couldn't remove his eyes from one girl who was somewhat shorter than the others. When she moved, he caught himself holding his breath, knowing he was getting an erection.

He nudged Leni. "Who is she?"

"Who, the little blonde? Her name is Jutta Winter. Extraordinary body, mediocre talent."

"I have to meet her. Please, Leni, you have to arrange an introduction."

"Why, Martin Bormann, you old dog, you're a married

man with half a dozen children."

Bormann smiled at her gentle, mocking tease, but knew she wouldn't dare refuse his request. After all, she had done the same thing before. More than once. He looked back at the screen. "She's gorgeous. What a body!"

"Martin, that film was made in 1925, and she's now well over forty. But if you think Jutta was something special then, you should see her daughter now."

At this remark, Bormann tore his eyes from the screen and stared at Leni for a long moment. Then he said, "I'll call you in Berlin day after tomorrow. Will you have some more of the Fuehrer's good tea?"

CHAPTER 2

Off the coast of New York City, 15 January, 1942

"Down periscope. Surface." Lieutenant Heinrich Fortner's command was given softly. Fortner seldom raised his voice unless he was in the engine room. Beneath their feet, the entire crew of the U-119 soon felt the boat's upward movement. Lying in their narrow bunks, not one single man of the off-watch was asleep. In spite of the heat, the stench of oil, and their own sweat, every man felt a cold, tingling exhilaration from the knowledge that they would soon breathe some fresh air, plus the natural excitement each felt from knowing (because their Commander never kept secrets from them) exactly where they were. It was like a double shot of adrenaline.

Tom Lewis

First Officer of the Watch Horst von Hellenbach felt it, too. He hadn't experienced that kind of weakness in the knees and knotted stomach muscles since Scapa Flow back in '39. Moments later, he followed his Commander up the ladder and through the hatch to his station next to him in the tower. Neither man needed his powerful binoculars.

"My God," Fortner said. "It's a Christmas tree!"

Horst von Hellenbach was totally speechless.

Before their eyes was the largest city on earth and one of the biggest and busiest harbors, ablaze with light and activity. "Don't they know they are at war?" Fortner said, unable to quite believe what he was seeing. He glanced at Horst. "Is it from impunity, stupidity, or sheer arrogance?"

"Sir," von Hellenbach said, "With your permission, the crew needs to see this, that is, if we can spare the time. It would be good for morale."

Fortner turned back to his second in command, shaking his head, his voice low and sympathetic. "I can't chance it, Horst. This place is a beehive. We had best get the hell out of here, but you are right, they do need to see this. Take one last look yourself."

He gave his orders and soon the U-119 slipped back under the surface of the dark water, but only to periscope depth. As the boat cruised slowly away from the harbor, one by one, starting with the officers and the Chief of the Boat, the entire fifty-five man crew lined up, momentarily fixed one eye to the awesome prism picture, then silently went back to his post. There would be plenty to talk and write about until they got home, whenever that might be...

The following night, the U-119 rounded Long Island

Hitler's Judas

and crept up the coast toward Boston. She was one of the five boats Admiral Doenitz had dispatched to the American coast soon after Hitler had declared war on the United States. Their mission was to first probe, report, then attack. Within ten days and nights, Fortner's crew got unbelievable looks at northern towns and harbors before reversing course and heading down the eastern coastline toward Cape Hatteras. Everywhere it was the same. The officers and crew of the U-119 were absolutely astonished, and were anxious for action.

Submerged off the Virginia coast, cruising slowly and waiting for darkness, Fortner and von Hellenbach sat in the Captain's small 'cabin', talking quietly. "It's amazing," Fortner said. "I remember reading about what von Nostitz and Koerner did with the old U-151 back in 1918. It was exactly like now. No blackouts in the towns, ships with all running lights on, radios blaring their positions, all just as in peacetime. Incredible carelessness. What do you make of it, Horst?"

"They seem to be just as stupid now as they were then, and if that is so, they will not be using convoys up and down the coast. I think we should have good targets practically anywhere in the shipping lanes we choose."

Fortner nodded. "You are a fine officer, Horst. You keep a cool head when the going gets rough. The men all like and respect you, as I do myself. I wouldn't be surprised if Uncle Karl gave you your own boat after this patrol. I have already sent that recommendation to him."

"Thank you, sir, but I'm in no big hurry for it. I enjoy serving with you, and have learned a great deal from you."

"As much as you did with Prien?"

— 28 —

Tom Lewis

"More. Plus, I feel, well, a great deal more comfortable with you. You're a human being as well as a leader of men. With you, the crew always comes first. Prien was a fanatic. I don't mind admitting I was scared to death at Scapa Flow. Prien drove himself as much or more than his crew. I think he never saw any of us as living men, only uniformed machines. Like robots. Keep them oiled and greased, they'll perform." Horst caught himself about to say something more, then said, "I shouldn't talk of the dead like that. I'm sorry."

Both men fell silent, each thinking the same thoughts. Prien, Kretschmer, and Schepke, the famous three aces, and Doenitz's favorites, were all dead, lost within days of each other in the same battle. Their loss had been such a terrible blow to the Admiral, the Fuehrer, and the U-Boat Command, Hitler had refused for a while to announce their deaths, even cruelly keeping the news from Prien's wife.

"Right!" Fortner said, stretching, "Uncle Karl and the Fatherland need a pick-me-up, and we're it. Ready to go to work?"

"I'm quite ready!" von Hellenbach replied. "Where shall we start?"

Fortner pursed his lips. "You know, the old-time sailing men used to say the three most dangerous passages in the world were around the Cape of Good Hope, Cape Horn, and Cape Hatteras, and because that's where the cold Labrador current collides with the warm gulf stream, Hatteras was the worst, and still has the most shipping. I think we will go a-hunting there. If you have people you want to write to, you'd best do it now. After tonight, I doubt if you'll have time."

— 29 —

Hitler's Judas

"Aye, sir." The young officer stood, saluted, and turned to go, but Fortner called him back. "Wait a second, Horst. One quick question. Have you or any of the rest of the men noticed anything wrong with the food lately?"

"No, sir, not counting the usual mold on everything and the potatoes that are sprouting arms and legs. Why?"

"Just wondering. My belly has been hurting like hell for two days now. I've been abusing my turn in the head but nothing's happening. My bowels are locked up tighter than the Chief's tool locker, and I was looking to blame the cook. Never mind, go write to your girl— what's her name again?"

"Elisabeth."

"Ah yes, your Elisabeth. Is she pretty?"

"She's very pretty, Herr Keleun."

"She would be. Well, when you get a chance, bed her but don't marry her. Remember what happened to Prien. Germany has enough widows, and our Service has produced more than our share of them. Now, get out of here and go take the con. I've got to go try to shit again. Damn, I'd give a thousand Reichmarks for a box of salts."

Heading aft, Horst ran into Oskar Knapp, the burly Chief of the Boat. "Chief, have you noticed the Skipper is under the weather?"

"No, sir, I haven't, but then, he always shows that poker face, don't he? Especially under pressure. He could get both legs blown off and be walking around on stumps and still show that face. Calm as the surface of a trout pond. You think he's sick?"

"He's complaining about cramps."

"I wouldn't worry about it. Think we're going into action soon?"

—30—

Tom Lewis

"Yes, very soon. Everything with the boat all right?"

"Yes, sir. Right as rain."

Horst returned the Chief's informal salute, and went to his own tiny nook for a rare moment of solitude. He reached under the mattress he shared with the third officer for his notebook, which was full of letters from Lizzle he had saved, along with one long one he had written to her, knowing he could not post it until they were back at Lorient. He removed the single photograph of her he had carried with him on every patrol. In the steamy artificial light, he could hardly make out her features. Whether the U-boat was running on or below the surface, the lights stayed on all the time, making it difficult to tell whether it was day or night outside their iron coffin, as some of the crew called the boat.

He lay back on his bunk and pretended he was talking to her on the telephone. "My darling, I have come cruising to America! I am the quietest of tourists, but not for long. If only this voyage here was under different circumstances, and that you were with me. How I miss you!! Do you see my worthless brother from time to time? I commanded him to look out for you while I am gone. Does he? Does he bring you a flower and say it is from me? He had better! I think our Captain is sick, and we have no one in the crew with any real medical knowledge. Too bad Harald is not aboard. He would know what to do. He was always the brother with the brains, and I'm sure he is already the finest surgeon in..."

—Battle Stations! The horn, which sounded so much like an old Mercedes automobile horn—only magnified by ten—sent every man rushing to his post. Horst shoved his

Hitler's Judas

tablet back under the mattress, grabbed his leather coat, and climbed to the tower next to his Commander, automatically raising his binoculars to the west. The raw-cold night was moonless, the sea unruly, but the boat was surprisingly stable.

"Two of them," Lieutenant Fortner said. "Looks like tankers coming out of Norfolk, loaded to the rails and lit up like the *Reeperbahn*. So! Let's invite ourselves to their party."

In his understated style, Fortner gave brisk orders. "Helmsman, come left. Make your course ninety degrees."

"Nine-oh degrees, Aye, sir."

Feeling the boat turn, Fortner, without taking his eyes from his distant prey, told Horst, "What luck they're sailing out together! They can't be more than five hundred meters apart, and in perfect tandem. Range?"

"Range five thousand meters, sir."

"Bearing?"

"Bearing 360 degrees, sir."

Fortner took a deep breath and turned to Horst. "You already know what I'm going to do, don't you?"

Horst smiled. "I think so. You've already given them the smallest target possible. When they come within range, you'll turn and shoot; one from the bow tubes and one from the stern tubes."

Fortner laughed. "Right. It'll be like shooting a pair of fat, sleepy pigs with a rifle that has a barrel on both ends. Almost too easy."

Both officers fell silent. Waiting. On such a moonless night, their narrow silhouette would be almost impossible to see. They didn't have long to wait, either. Within twenty

Tom Lewis

minutes, both tankers were almost abeam, on both their port and starboard sides. Fortner gave his orders. "Come right to one-eighty degrees."

"One-eight-oh degrees, Aye, Captain."

Again feeling the boat turn beneath their feet, both men stared at the plodding tankers, steaming ahead at about ten knots. Fortner glanced at his watch. "Range?"

"Both vessels coming up on two hundred meters, sir."

"Set torpedo depth to run at six meters. Stand by to shoot."

The voice of the Chief came through. "Ready here, Captain."

Fortner counted seconds, his lips moving, but without sound. Then, still quietly, he ordered, "Fire one." He allowed himself a three-second pause. "Fire three." He winked at Horst. "At this range, there's no way could we miss." He leaned over the conning tower and shouted, "Man both guns!"

Horst realized he had been holding his breath. He also began counting seconds. The first torpedo struck the south tanker on her port side, and within the space of half a minute, the U-119 was sandwiched between the walls of Hades.

Half an hour later, they were steaming away at full speed to the east, leaving behind two gigantic fireballs surrounded by oil-covered, screaming and dying men. The U-119 had spent only two torpedoes and eighteen shells.

"Don't look back, Horst," Fortner said. "Never look back. You will stay sane longer."

At that moment, already well into the next morning

Hitler's Judas

in Stuttgart, Elisabeth Kroll heard the discrete knock she had been listening for. She slid out of bed, slipped her robe on, not bothering with her nightgown, and went into the small sitting room, closing the bedroom door behind her. Pulling her long blond hair back behind her ears, she padded across the carpet to the door of the small suite, opened it, and pointed to the table where she wanted the porter to leave the room service tray. Averting his eyes, the old man— who had known her all her life and had performed the same service for her several times before—did so, bowed, and left as quietly as he'd entered, knowing he would collect a generous tip later. Elisabeth sighed contentedly, poured a cup of coffee from the heavy silver pitcher, added one lump of sugar, stirred, and retraced her steps to the bedroom.

Propped against both pillows, Harald von Hellenbach was sitting up, pulling the coverlet over his body to his waist, not so much to hide his thin physique—or exposed genitals—as his feet. To be more accurate, only his left foot.

Herr Doktor Harald von Hellenbach had been born with a clubfoot, which had caused him lifelong humiliation, and which he kept hidden as much as possible from view, even from Elisabeth. Especially from Elisabeth. "Ah, my blond angel has brought me coffee. *Danke.*"

While he took his first sips, Elisabeth reached for the cigarettes and lighter on the nightstand. She lit two, and handed one to her lover. Harald inhaled deeply, then blew the smoke out upwards, so as not to blow it directly into her face. Harald would never do that. Horst might, just for the fun of it, but Harald wouldn't. He would never tease the woman he had loved since he was a child. Since they all three had been children.

— 34 —

Tom Lewis

Elisabeth smiled at him. What was he thinking just now? Well, she could guess. He was probably wondering how many times she had brought coffee to his twin brother like this. In this very same room. Very same bed. She knew each twin suspected she had slept with the other, but she also knew neither man would ever bring it up. Distant cousins, they had all known each other since they were six years old. Had played together as children, were an inseparable trio in school, and had remained close when Horst and Harald had gone away; Horst to Officer Cadet School and Harald to the University at Tubingen. Elisabeth looked away, using the excuse of extinguishing her cigarette. She knew Harald thought Horst had taken her virginity, and vice versa, but the fact was, neither had. It had been some slow-witted, intoxicated soldier she had taken to her room for half an hour one night three years ago specifically for just that purpose, so she wouldn't have to choose which of the von Hellenbach twins would be her first.

They were not identical. A stranger would not guess they were even brothers, let alone twins. Horst was the older, by about eight minutes, which was one of the things that rankled Harald. Son-and-heir, and all that. The other, of course, was his lame foot. Ironically, Harald was the better looking of the two; taller even than his brother, with slender, aristocratic features, dark, wavy hair, impeccable manners, while Horst, like his father, was blond, with cobalt-blue eyes. He had a rather plain, yet ruggedly handsome face, and an athlete's sturdy, well-shaped body. Horst smiled more often, and generally didn't take himself so seriously. That is, he hadn't until he'd come back from his last two patrols. Then, he had seemed to have changed.

Hitler's Judas

He was quieter, often lost in thought. Almost distant at times. Elisabeth wondered which of them she would marry. That she would wed one or the other twin had been a foregone conclusion since she was ten, and since then had still not been able to make up her mind. What a pity she couldn't marry both of them!

Her widowed mother, ever the practical, hard-working proprietress of the *Hotel und Gasthaus Kroll*, naturally favored the younger brother. ("He is highly intelligent, and a fine physician. *Der* Horst is a daredevil gambler who wanted desperately to please his father by choosing the most dangerous of all military careers. *Kriegsmarine* officers live about as long as unfed goldfish, Elisabeth. He will make you also a widow in less time than you can make his first baby!")

This was all true, Elisabeth thought, reaching for yet another cigarette, but Horst was more *fun*. He knew how to laugh and also, more importantly, knew how to make her laugh. In bed, he'd pull her hair teasingly, and call her Lizzle, the nickname he'd given her when they were children frolicking on the lake beach in the Tyrol where both families took annual vacations. Then he'd make love to her passionately, even fiercely, like there was no tomorrow. Harald, when she was with him, performed the sex act much the same as she imagined he executed an operation; tenderly, certainly, but somehow detached, and with a meticulous surgeon's skill. She'd never had the slightest doubt that both brothers loved her equally. And, the one trait they both shared—as far as she was concerned—was that both were tacitly willing to give her whatever amount of time she needed to make up her mind.

– 36 –

Tom Lewis

Neither had actually proposed, and she was certain each was waiting for the other to, and be either accepted or rejected. Elisabeth knew, way down deep inside her, that Horst would survive this war, and, she knew, had known for a long time, that she would have to make her choice one day, and that she would have to be the one to say the words.

Harald broke into her thoughts. "I must go, Elisabeth. Turn your head while I dress."

Elisabeth frowned, got up and walked back into the sitting room. She poured herself a cup of the strong coffee which was getting harder and harder to get these days, and waited. After a few minutes, Harald came out of the bedroom, dressed, as always, like a well-to-do-banker, complete with the Nazi pin in his lapel. The special shoes he wore almost disguised his limp, and made him even taller. "Must you go? Really?" she said.

"Yes. I have to catch the noon train to Berlin, then back to Leipzig. Our wounded can't wait for me to have long love affairs."

"It's bad, isn't it?"

"It's war. But the Fuehrer will be victorious. Of that I am sure."

Elisabeth stood to kiss him goodbye. "Will I see you soon?"

Harald donned his greatcoat and hat. "Not soon. I don't know when I shall be able to get away again."

"I understand." She held the door for him. "Don't forget to say goodbye to Mutti when you get downstairs, and, thank you for the flowers."

Harald turned and smiled at her. "You know they're

– 37 –

Hitler's Judas

from Horst. A promise is a promise."

Elisabeth smiled back at him. She knew of the 'pact' the brothers had made at the outset of the war. Whichever of them saw her first, he must bring flowers from the other. "Be well, love. And think of me."

"Always. *Wiedersehen*, Elisabeth."

Elisabeth closed the door when he was gone, went back to the table and sat down. She cried for only a few minutes, then made up her face and got dressed.

There was, after all, a hotel and restaurant to be run.

CHAPTER 3

Inside the huge fort of a building in Frankfurt, Bormann followed the two men on whom he had sprung a surprise visit down a long corridor. One was Walter Schackt, Hitler's sweating Finance Minister. The other man was Kurt Flammer, the *Direktor General* of the German National Bank, and a high ranking officer of the Treasury. They entered a private elevator that dropped them four stories down, deep underground and opened into a cavernous vault. A uniformed guard handed all three men white smocks, which they slipped on over their suits.

Everything was spotless. Not a speck of anything that could be construed as dirt or dust was to be seen. Silent, unseen humidifier fans produced a cool breeze throughout. Bormann had never seen anything like it. "It looks and

Hitler's Judas

feels like a hospital!"

"Indeed," said the rotund banker. "Come, let me show you something interesting." He led the way into another large room to the left. Bormann had to bite his lip to keep from reacting like a child on his first visit to a circus. From floor to ceiling were neatly organized stacks of paper currency from practically every country on earth, including Francs, Pounds, and American Dollars of every denomination. "Billions?" Bormann said.

"More than billions," the *Direktor* smugly confirmed, "In this vault plus four more like it."

Bormann whistled softly through his teeth. He felt a distinct chill permeate his body from the soles of his feet to his collar. His quick mind wasn't slow to react, however. He could easily guess where a great deal of all this money had come from. It represented the lion's share of looted national treasuries from every helpless country Germany had overrun. *To the conqueror belongs the spoils of war.* "It's... It's very impressive," he managed an echoing whisper, trying hard to keep his awe from being discernable.

Schackt, anxious to impress further, clucked like a mother hen. "True, but there is something in the next vault even more so." He nodded at Flammer who turned and led the way through an arched passageway to a massive stainless steel door. It was so well engineered and balanced, Flammer only had to shove it gently with his left hand to open it. Bormann felt his sphincter tighten. He blinked rapidly at the sight. It was a cavern—a *large* cavern--full of gold! Dull-yellow bars of solid gold, each twenty-pound ingot boasting a molded, encircled imprint of the swastika showing on its top side. *"Gott in Himmel!"* Bormann's voice

Tom Lewis

was close to cracking.

Flammer snickered, enjoying himself. "Yes, heaven would be a good description of this place, that is, for any ordinary man less than God. However, do not be fooled." He gestured by throwing both arms out from his sides as if helpless. "Most of this comes in and goes out on a regular basis. War costs a staggering amount of money, and this war is cash-hungry. Unfortunately, Germany does not fight on credit."

Bormann found some vocal control. "But, why is it all here?"

"I beg your pardon?" said Flammer.

"I mean, why is it all in one place? Wouldn't it be more advisable to store it in more than one location? What if this spot was bombed?"

Flammer arched an eyebrow. "We believe it is quite safe here. The physical protection is state-of-the-art, including the guards, who are ranking SS men, committed to their duty. Besides, neither the English nor the Americans have bombs strong enough to reach down here. Trust me on that."

Bormann kept his face neutral. *I trust no one about anything, you fat fool.* "Of course. You are quite correct." He straightened, to signify he was satisfied with the 'inspection' tour he had requested on such short notice. "The Fuehrer will be pleased with my report, I'm sure. Thank you, Flammer. Down here, everything appears to be quite *in ordnung.* Herr Schackt, do you perchance have some coffee in your office upstairs?"

Just as Bormann suspected, in his private office, the wily Minister of Finance had a good supply of the best coffee,

— 41 —

Hitler's Judas

which he brewed and poured himself, along with generous dollops of 'requisitioned' French brandy. "Your visit here today comes as something of a shock, Herr Bormann," he said. "Forgive my curiosity, but I was not aware our Fuehrer thought there might be some kind of problem in our department. To be blunt, he has rarely shown much interest in how we administer the Fatherland's money."

Bormann showed another poker face. Schackt was right. Hitler knew next to nothing about economics. So little in fact, that even his own personal finances would have been in shambles had Bormann not taken charge of them some time ago. The truth was simply that, unlike Goering and a not a few others, Hitler was not greedy when it came to the personal wealth his conquests had made possible. His official, considerable income came solely from sales of his book. *Mein Kampf* had long since supplanted the Holy Bible in every household in Germany, since every single German citizen was required to buy a copy. Extra money was not important to Hitler. He had far more pressing things on his mind. Bormann had taken quick advantage of that, and had set himself the formidable task of learning where the Third Reich's money came from and where it went. He had also organized the Adolf Hitler Endowment Fund, effectively blackmailing Krupp, Theissen, von Bittnerhof and most of the other big shots of German industry who were getting war-rich into 'contributing', and which Bormann himself doled out to party members and Hitler's entourage in regular tax-free payments.

"This is excellent coffee," he said. "I wish I knew your private source for it."

Schackt's face turned beet red, and Bormann leaned

Tom Lewis

forward to drop the hammer. "The Fuehrer's mind has many compartments, Schackt. And none of them are empty. I assure you he wants to know the Fatherland's treasury is safe and unassailable. As I said, I will give him a favorable report."

Schackt allowed himself a short breath of relief.

"However," Bormann went on, "I am positive he will disagree that all this wealth should be kept here. All the eggs in one basket? No, I think not. Perhaps we should transfer some of it to Switzerland, especially much of the gold. I shall discuss it with him in detail and let you know his decision."

Bormann sat back and sipped his coffee. He knew that Schackt had no way of knowing he was lying through his teeth. Hitler had not sent him there at all, but would without doubt listen to and agree with his logic, then probably say something like, 'Good idea, Martin, take care of it immediately.' And Bormann would waste no time making a discreet visit to the German Embassy – and a few certain banks - in Zurich, Lucerne, and Geneva.

Pleased with his morning's work, he glanced at his watch and stood. "You will excuse me now, Minister. I have a luncheon engagement. Rest assured I will tell the Fuehrer you and Flammer are doing a very good job." He offered a hand, which Schackt grabbed and pumped like a reprieved prisoner. Bormann then turned on his heel and left, laughing to himself. *What an imbecile. It was easy. This is all going to be so very easy.* Bormann checked his watch again. He hated being late for anything, even if it was a simple lunch with his younger brother, which was business. His mind was already on another lunch date in Berlin the

— 43 —

Hitler's Judas

following day, which definitely was not business.

Leni Riefenstahl sat impatiently in the dingy *Bierstube*-cafeteria just inside the entrance of the gigantic complex of the UFA film studios. She had more important things to do than play matchmaker for sugar-daddys and actresses, but there was no way she was going to chance getting on the bad side of Martin Bormann. Ever. Nervously, she lit another cigarette and waited, thinking of how that stupid cow Eva Braun had described the scene when the Fuehrer found out about the lunacy of Rudolf Hess' defection. Hitler had worked himself into a fine lather, cooled off enough to organize some hasty—and largely ineffective—damage control, and then had screamed, *"Where is Bormann?"*

Leni's mouth turned up into a sardonic smirk. Well, old Martin hadn't been far away, had he? Not likely. Leni blew a smoke ring. Ha! She had known some crafty, devious people in her time, especially in the film making industry which was chock full of small intrigues, but Martin Bormann was by far the slickest operator she had ever known. She knew only a little about him, which was probably a lot more than ninety-nine percent of Germany's population did. He'd been a young soldier in the Great War, had jumped on the Nazi bandwagon early on, and had served as an elected member of the Reichstag, (this after also serving a year in prison— for murder, no less!) Though he disguised it well, Bormann was far and away the smartest of the motley gang of thugs Hitler had surrounded himself with, and was not one iota less evil. She had not been surprised as he had quietly but steadily worked himself into a position of power that no one could afford to ignore.

— 44 —

Tom Lewis

Of all the men she had known, Leni thought, Bormann—because he had absolutely no conscience—was the most dangerous, and although she enjoyed a close and unique relationship with Adolf Hitler, all that could change drastically if she ever crossed the man who had taken Hess' place.

She stubbed her cigarette out when she noticed the two women approaching her table. *Finally!* She gestured for Jutta Winter and her daughter to sit. "You are late. He will be here in five minutes."

She eyed the mother and daughter professionally. Jutta's fresh Bavarian looks, which had stood her in such good stead for years of playing barmaids and farm-girls, were on the verge of fading, and she was gaining too much weight now. Edda, who had inherited her mother's healthy complexion and high-breasted figure along with her actor-father's fine bone structure, dark hair, and light blue eyes, was just now blossoming into what would be one of Germany's great beauties. Plus, Edda Winter had twice her mother's brains, three times her cunning, and four times her acting talent.

"Are you working now, Edda?" Leni asked, though she knew the answer.

"No, Fraulein Riefenstahl, but I hope to land something else soon. Can you tell me, I mean us, more about this Bormann person? He's been sending me flowers and Swiss chocolates every day recently, and I've never even seen the man. At least not that I know of."

"I can tell you this much, Edda," Leni said, "In my opinion—and don't forget, I'm in a position to know—he will soon be the second most powerful man in all of Germany

— 45 —

Hitler's Judas

if not already."

"But how does he know me?"

"He has seen the two films you have made so far." Leni didn't tell the women she had sent Bormann the prints herself. "I think he is quite taken with you. In fact, I am sure of it, and he wants to meet you personally, which is the reason for this lunch today."

The street-smart, experienced Jutta sneered. "He only wants to lay her, that's all. I've heard about his fooling around with more than one actress."

"Mother!"

Knowingly, Jutta glanced sideways at her daughter. "Don't play the innocent *ingenue'* with me, you ambitious little slut. I know you're far from a virgin any more. You'd sleep with anybody who could advance your career, but you'd better watch out for this one. He could hurt a lot more than your heart— or your future."

"Oh, please," Leni said, "Spare me the family wash. I've heard it all— *Ach*, here he comes now. Listen quick, Edda, a little advice. If he takes you out somewhere, wear something long, and no high-heeled shoes."

Leni wasted little time performing perfunctory introductions, then said, "Oh, by the way, Jutta, can you spare me a few minutes over in my office? There's a role in Lanning's new film I'd like to talk to you about."

"*Naturlich*," Jutta said, standing up and offering a hand to Bormann. "A pleasure to meet you, Herr Reichsleiter."

Leni took Jutta by the arm and led her out into the street. "Don't worry, Edda will be fine. She's already a damned good actress."

— 46 –

"I know. Better already than I ever was or will be. But she had better watch her step with that one. I've heard he is quite the stallion."

Leni snorted. "I've seen a few horses that were better looking, but my guess is that Bormann will move mountains to boost Edda's career."

"More than Goebbels could?"

"Far more."

"That's surprising, Leni. Why do you think so?"

"Because, my dear Jutta, I think for the first time in his life, Martin Bormann may be in love!"

CHAPTER 4

Petty Officer 2nd Class Hans Rath looked up at his First Officer. "I believe it is his appendix, sir."

Horst stared hard at the only man aboard who had any kind of rudimentary medical training. "What can you do?"

The hapless Petty Officer, whose face was nearly as contorted as that of his beloved patient, shook his head, his voice a mere whisper, "I gave him morphine. That's all I *know* to do. I'm not a doctor. I can lance boils and pass out aspirin, but the Captain needs an operation. If I tried to cut him open I could kill him, and I don't think I could bear it either."

"What happens if you don't try to operate?"

Rath's face plainly showed his anguish. "The appendix

Tom Lewis

will burst, and he will surely die an agonizing death. The pain would be more than all the morphine..."

"How long?"

Rath shrugged. "Who knows? A day? Maybe two? I'm not sure."

Horst clapped him lightly on the shoulder. The poor man was helpless, and in his helplessness, totally miserable. But something had to be done. And soon, too. The last words Lieutenant Fortner had said before the morphine took hold were to beg Horst to give him a pistol! Horst spoke softly to the man, "No need to blame yourself, Rath. Go see if you can find the Chief. Tell him I need him here right away."

Happy to be excused, the young crewman scurried off. Horst squatted down next to his Commander who was curled up in a fetal position on his bunk, now blessedly unconscious. Having sunk four ships in four days, and trying, unsuccessfully, for the last two of those to hide his condition from the rest of the crew, he had doubled over in extreme pain more than twelve hours ago, leaving Horst in command. Through clenched teeth, he had said, "Keep on attacking, von Hellenbach. It's a turkey shoot up there."

"You sent for me, sir?" The husky Chief of the Boat had apparently been standing just outside the curtained cubicle.

"Chief, do you have any recommendation?"

Chief Engineer Oskar Knapp looked down at his sleeping Commander, then back at the young officer who had not lost his cool in this unforeseen, tragic emergency, which by now was common knowledge throughout the boat. "No, sir, unless the morphine can help him die without so much pain. If we run out of it, then yes, hand

Hitler's Judas

him his pistol. Better to die like that than—"

Battle Stations! The klaxon went off again, sending both men to their stations on the double. Horst took over from the nervous Second Officer, who reported, "She's a large tanker. Biggest I've ever seen, and all alone, low in the water and steaming north at no more than 9 knots." Horst turned his cap around backwards, stuck his eye to the periscope eyepiece for a long moment, swinging the scope around the compass to make sure his junior officer's assessment was correct, then ordered, "Down periscope." The huge tanker was indeed alone, and not even making as much speed as the U-119 could submerged. An idea began forming in Horst's head.

He turned to the fuzzy-cheeked officer, whose eyes were big as full moons, and the other equally young boys silently watching him, waiting for him to give the orders to attack.

My God, we are a boat full of babies. In a low voice, he said, "We will follow her until dark."

"But she's all by herself, First Officer. We could kill her with—"

"You heard me," Horst snapped at him. "We'll wait until night."

An hour after sundown, cursing both the clear weather and the stupidity of the American Navy's reluctance to herd ships like his in a convoy, which made it necessary to duck into pre-chosen, protective ports every night, Captain Alfonse DeLeone was just coming on the darkened bridge when the shrill cry from the lookout came: "Submarine off the port bow!" Automatically, he turned to his port side

Tom Lewis

window, raising his glasses in time to see a flash of orange, followed by the bark of a single cannon shot.

Jesu, how could they have missed? They are so close! Then he instantly realized the sub had simply fired a shot across his bow. Why the warning? He was about to give an order when something else caught his eye. Signal lamp. *Signal lamp?*

The International Morse Code flashes came rapidly:

STOP

DO NOT USE RADIO OR WE WILL SINK YOU

DO YOU HAVE MEDICAL DOCTOR ABOARD

ANSWER BY SIGNAL LAMP

REPEAT IF YOU USE RADIO WE WILL SINK YOU

The sixty-two year-old DeLeone had not reached his high rank in the Venezuelan Merchant Marine Service by being either careless or foolish. In the blink of an eye he assessed his situation: There was the unmistakable slender shape of a German submarine not more than a hundred meters off his port side, pointed bow on, deck gun manned and torpedo tubes undoubtedly loaded and ready to let loose what would turn his laden vessel into fiery hell itself within minutes. And at that range, *they could not possibly miss.*

First things first. "All stop!" He thundered. "Man the signal lamp. Tell them we are heaving to and will not use the radio."

The signalman jumped to it and followed his Master's orders with a steady hand. While he was sending, Captain DeLeone called down to the radioman. "Don't touch that radio, whatever you do. Stand by for orders. No, belay that. Leave the radio room, lock the door and bring the key to the bridge. On the double." He leaned over the console, peering out the thick

Hitler's Judas

plate glass of the port side bridge window. *Mother of God. And only three hours out of Wilmington!*

The sub flashed again:

DO YOU HAVE DOCTOR

And again, Captain DeLeone responded. "Tell them yes."

YES

He watched as the sub's lamp flashed:

SEND BOAT OVER NOW

NO FURTHER MESSAGES

In half a second, several more thoughts flitted across the mind of the experienced Captain: The submarine obviously had someone aboard with a severe medical problem, and her commander knew, or guessed, that because of the inherent danger from the cargo she carried, a loaded tanker the size of his ship would probably have a doctor in her crew. If he played his cards right, he just might escape with his ship *and* his cargo.

It didn't take him long to decide. "Lower a boat, and be quick about it," he ordered. He turned to his First Mate. "I want Doctor Gonzales standing by the davits in one minute, dressed or not. You take over here. I'm going with the boat." He started to leave the bridge when he had an additional thought. He turned back to his Mate and said, "If you want to ever see your wife and children again, don't do anything crazy, and don't let that radio operator out of your sight. If he puts his paws back on those knobs, we're all dead men. All of you sit tight until I get back."

"Can we trust them not to shoot?" The Mate asked.

"We don't have much choice, do we? Do as I told you."

"Aye, Captain."

–52–

Tom Lewis

In the U-119's conning tower, glasses to his eyes, Horst stood next to Chief Knapp. "They're lowering a boat. Good."

"You think they are telling the truth about having a sawbones aboard?"

"They had better be. Otherwise, they'll soon be crispy *pomme frittes*, frying in their own oil."

Knapp scratched his beard. "You're taking a big chance, First Officer. If their radioman has a nervous finger, we'd hear him sending all right, but close as we are to the coast, we could have the whole damned United States Navy up our backsides before we get fifty clicks away."

Horst didn't answer. He watched the enormous tanker's tender pull away, and turn toward them at top speed. He was thankful the Atlantic was not misbehaving tonight. Only two-foot swells to worry about. The transfer would not be difficult. He turned to the Chief. "Go below and bring Lieutenant Fortner up. Use the forward hatch, and be as gentle as you can."

It only took a few minutes for the tender to reach the lee side of the U-119, which was rocking slightly in the swells. Horst decided not to use the megaphone. Instead, he slid down the ladder to the slippery deck, and hailed the approaching boat, at the same time signaling his men to stand by with lines. "Who is in charge?" he shouted, in English.

A short, chubby man with four stripes on his sleeve stood in the tender's sternsheets and answered in kind, "I am. Captain Alfonse DeLeone, master of the *STANDARD ISABELLA* out of Caracas, bound for New Jersey." He pointed to a thin, balding man who was not wearing a uniform. "We have a doctor here."

– 53 –

Hitler's Judas

The ship's boat came alongside, and was fendered and snubbed, the coxswain and the rest of its four-man crew silently eyeing the conning tower machine gun which was pointing its ugly snout directly at them. "What is the nature of your problem, sir?" DeLeone yelled.

At that moment, Chief Knapp and another crew member eased the unconscious form of Lieutenant Fortner out of the forward hatch and carefully carried him down the over-washed teak deck strakes to the boat.

"We think this officer has appendicitis," Horst said. "In need of an immediate operation. If you agree to save his life, you will save your own. You have my word on it. Take him aboard your vessel, and continue on your way. We will not shoot. Can we trust that you will not use your radio to give our position?"

Captain DeLeone straightened to his full height. "Rest assured we will do all we can for your man. And I will not betray your position. I have held a Master's ticket for twenty years, sir, and you have *my* word on it."

Horst nodded. Orders were given in three languages, and the inert form of Lieutenant Heinrich Fortner was transferred with strong but caring hands from his own boat to the tender. "Go quickly, Captain," Horst said, saluting, "And good luck."

The Venezuelan officer gave orders to cast off. As his boat moved away, he also saluted, and yelled, "Thank you. Don't worry about this man. He will soon be recovering in a soft American hospital bed, pinching pretty nurses, and in less than a month will be playing baseball and eating hot dogs. Good luck to you, too. *Vaya con Dios.* I won't forget you."

Tom Lewis

Horst climbed back into the conning tower, Chief Knapp right behind him. For a minute or two, both men, not even trying to hide their tears from each other, watched the tender making a straight line to her mother ship. Horst cleared his throat, and gave orders to turn east at flank speed. Then he turned to his Chief and said softly, "He always told me not to look back, Oskar. Come on, we have a war to fight."

There was genuine respect in the Chief's voice when he answered, "*Jawohl*, Herr Kaleun. Only. . ."

"Only what?"

"Was he serious, that Spanish Captain? Do Americans make their prisoners of war eat dog meat?"

Alfonse DeLeone stared down at the pale, blond-bearded face, then looked into the sad eyes of Dr. Heitor Gonzales, who was pulling his mask down. Gonzales returned his Captain's glance, and looked down as well. "It's a damned shame. I have two sons older than this boy."

"I know. So do I. He never had a chance did he?"

"No. If I could have gotten him a few hours sooner. . . Well, at least they had pumped him full of morphine before we brought him aboard. He died without pain. He was their Captain, wasn't he?"

"I think so. Otherwise they would never have taken such a risk. His crew must have loved him. They obviously considered his life more important than sinking a hundred ships like us. I would have done the same thing."

"What will you do now, turn his body over to the port authorities?"

Captain DeLeone frowned. "No. We won't make

Hitler's Judas

Wilmington for at least another hour. Time enough to give this young warrior the sea burial he deserves. And when we make port in New Jersey, you and I will have to write a report about all this, and maybe take it to the Argentine Embassy."

"Why them?"

"The Peron Government is somewhat sympathetic to the Germans. They will make sure our report gets to this boy's service command."

Gonzales nodded soberly. "I'll make the necessary arrangements for the burial right away, Captain, but I'll tell you something else, I hope to God we never see that other one again. That other German officer, I mean. Did you see his eyes?"

"Yes. Like twin ice cubes. A leader and a killer if I ever saw one. We are lucky to be alive. Now, hurry. We don't have much time."

CHAPTER 5

Fifty-one year old Admiral Karl Doenitz allowed himself a rare smile. It was a sight that never failed to lift his spirits; one of his boats coming home, kill-pennants flying. Her crew was proudly standing on deck at attention, bearded, but washed, and wearing uniforms cleaned with perhaps the last drops of the fresh water on board. Unmindful of the freezing temperature, all of them—officers and men—were grinning from ear to ear, listening to the march music of the blaring, out-of-tune brass band, squinting to pick out a pretty girl from the dozens cheering and waving flowers from the quay. Straight as a flagpole, Doenitz stood on the platform at the head of his carefully orchestrated welcoming ceremony, which was so critical for morale. He, along with his two chief operations officers, Schnee and

Hitler's Judas

Godt, returned the salutes from officers in the conning tower of the U-119. He turned to Godt. "Do you have enough medals?"

"Yes, Admiral. Two trays full; one Iron Cross First Class and fifty-five Second Class, plus Patrol Badges for each man."

"Good. It would be embarrassing to run out of them." It was his intention, as always, to personally pin the medals on, and to shake the hand of every crew member, knowing that such a small but personal touch further cemented the already close bond between himself and those brave *Junge* who served the U-Boat arm and the Fatherland so well.

Following their Admiral's example, Godt and Schnee remained at attention until all the boat's lines were made fast and engines shut down. Then the three of them crossed the narrow gangplank to the deck. Employing the proven psychological practice of starting with the cook, Doenitz began pinning medals on the tunics of each crew member along with a firm handshake and working his way up to the officers, saving the boat's Commander until last. Looking Horst von Hellenbach in the eye, and in a voice loud enough for all to hear, he said, "Congratulations. You are hereby promoted to the rank of Lieutenant, and it is my honor, in the name of the Fuehrer, to present you with the Iron Cross, First Class."

He hung the ribboned medal around Horst's neck, shook his hand warmly, leaned forward slightly, and in a lower voice, he said, "Faced with a difficult decision, under pressure, you did the right thing, son. Have your party tonight, and report to me at nine tomorrow morning. Sober, please."

Tom Lewis

"Yes, sir!" Horst knew he was blushing. "And thank you, Admiral."

When Doenitz stepped back to formally salute, the crew erupted in a spontaneous cheer. The band struck up another march, and more boisterous cheering broke out all along the quay as Doenitz and his staff departed.

As soon as Admiral Doenitz and his entourage were out of sight, Horst gave an order dismissing the crew, then watched in amusement as officers and men alike bowled over each other hurrying below to collect their kits. He stood by the gangway and personally said good-bye and good luck to each man who left the boat, heading for the Personnel Office to collect their leave papers, many of them needing to be physically supported until they slowly regained their land-legs.

Chief Oskar Knapp remained behind. "Like kids just let out of school for holidays, aren't they? Hell, they *are* kids!"

Horst turned to the Chief of the Boat. "You're not leaving yet, Chief?"

"No, Herr Kaleun, not for a few more days. They will be moving our boat into the pens within the hour. I want to go over her carefully with the repair crew. Make sure they do the job right. I know every inch of this old girl like a husband knows his wife's warts, and I want to make sure she's shipshape and mechanically sound when we go out again. I don't like surprises. Don't worry, I'll get my time off, my beer, and maybe a woman, too. How about you? You going home to see that pretty girl of yours?"

"Yes, but I'm going to Bremen first, to see Lieutenant Fortner's family. It's the least I can do." He gave the burly

Hitler's Judas

Chief a light punch on the shoulder. "Right now, though, I'm going to find a hotel that has hot water and take the longest bath in history, then I'm going to go party at the One-Eyed Whore and wash my insides out with some of that good French champagne."

"That's the ticket, Lieutenant!"

"Where will you go? Home to Hamburg?"

"Nah. I ain't got nobody to go home to. If it was summer, I'd wind up down at Le Treshier with most of the crew. Old Uncle Karl spares no expense for our R and R spas. Good chow, good booze, plenty of sun and beautiful women. But since it's the middle of winter, I expect many of them will go to the Alps to ski. Not for me. I'll probably just hang around here, shooting the bull with other chiefs and petty officers. Mainly, I want to watch out for Kirchner. Make sure he stays out of the brig. When he's drunk, he gets into fights. Long as he's sober, he's the best cook in the Kriegsmarine and I don't want to take a chance on losing him."

Both men lapsed into an awkward silence, each trying to put into words the similar thoughts they were having. At last Horst said, "Chief, Heinrich always preached to me that if I ever got my own boat, to make sure I never sailed without a great Chief and a good cook. If that should ever happen, well..."

Red-faced, Knapp placed his big paw on Horst's shoulder. "No need to say it, sir. All of us would be happy to serve under you. Anytime. Anywhere. Now get going, I got work to do."

Back in his warm headquarters office at Kerneval, Doenitz reached into his desk drawer, and to the surprise

Tom Lewis

of his two assistants, extracted a bottle of peppermint Schnapps. "Schnee," he said with an uncharacteristic wink, "It's after duty hours. See if you can find three clean glasses." Adalbert Schnee, himself a highly successful U-boat ace and now the ever dependable staff officer, hurried out of the room. His immediate superior, and Doenitz's right hand man, Rear Admiral Eberhard Godt sat down across from the desk of his boss and remarked, "Well, sir, it seems we have a potential new hero, although Lieutenant Fortner will be missed. He was a good man."

"A very good man. He will be sorely missed. I miss all of them that don't come back. But I agree with your assessment, von Hellenbach showed he has what it takes. His tonnage after sending Fortner away with that Venezuelan tanker was outstanding. Eight ships, 60 thousand tons! He earned his promotion and decoration, no question about it."

"Are you going to tell him about the report we got through the Argentine Consulate?"

"Certainly. I don't believe in either lying or sugar-coating the truth."

Schnee came back in with the glasses. Doenitz poured. Glasses were raised. "To Commander Heinrich Fortner. God rest his soul," intoned Schnee.

"And to the, what did they call it? The turkey shoot?" Godt added.

"The turkey shoot," Schnee said, "And to the Good Time." They drank again. Doenitz and his staff had reason enough to celebrate. During the past year and a half, which they informally referred to as the "Good Time," Doenitz's young sharks, as Hitler called them, had sunk a staggering

— 61 —

amount of tonnage. This was all the more impressive because Doenitz never had more than a fraction of the three hundred U-Boats he had begged Hitler for on patrol at any given time, and in spite of the loss of so many good men like Fortner, Prien, and the others.

As if reading his mind, Godt said, "Lieutenant von Hellenbach is typical of the bright fellows flocking to the Kriegsmarine service, Admiral. If the Fuehrer would only give us enough boats, we could actually win this war for him."

"We are getting more boats, but the shipyards can build them only so fast, you know," Doenitz replied, his voice sounding an optimism he really didn't feel. Hitler, or for that matter, the entire General Staff had absolutely no faith in sea warfare, let alone the already proven U-Boat arm of the Navy. To them, skirmishes, battles, and wars must be decided *only on land.*

To change the subject, he said, "Schnee, don't you want to go to von Hellenbach's victory party? If so, you had better get a move on."

The intelligent junior staff man instantly took the hint. "Oh, I do indeed, my Admiral. There will be a full house at the One-Eyed Whore tonight, that's for sure." He stood, saluted, and left, not uneager to get to the infamous waterfront café where the officers would already be toasting the newest member of the growing Iron Cross fraternity.

"So," Godt said, "After his leave, which wolfpack will you assign von Hellenbach to? I presume you're going to give him a boat."

"Oh, yes. I'm going to give him a boat, all right. The one he brought in. But I'm not going to assign him to a

Tom Lewis

regular sector. I have other ideas for that boy. You mentioned he could be a potential hero, and God knows the Fatherland needs one. No, Lieutenant von Hellenbach is going to be our lone wolf. Here, let me pour you another drink."

At precisely nine o'clock, Horst presented himself at the Admiral's door. He knocked.

"*Komm.*"

Once inside, Horst saluted and was told to have a chair. He sat on its front edge, hardly able to hide his anxiety. Doenitz steepled his fingers and looked over the tips of them with thin lips. "Young man, there is something I want you to know, if you don't already. I have both a son and a son-in-law in our service. I would hope that given the same set of circumstances, they would have performed exactly as you did. For that, I am proud of you, but I must tell you that through our foreign contacts, we have learned that in spite of your efforts, Lieutenant Fortner perished before the tanker reached port. The report said he was given a proper burial at sea. I'm very, very sorry."

Horst managed to keep his composure. "Yes, sir. So am I. I admired him a great deal. I'm sure he would have done the same for me, and that tanker's Captain was a true man of the sea."

"Yes, quite. Well, now down to business. You have two weeks leave coming. My advice is to take it somewhere far away from here. When you come back, you will take command of the U-119. You will then put to sea immediately, with sealed orders. Dismissed."

Elated beyond words, Horst stood, saluted smartly, then turned to go. He had taken only one step toward the

– 63 –

Hitler's Judas

door when Doenitz called him back. "Just one other thing, Lieutenant. I have a present for you."

He reached into a large leather briefcase resting on his desk and from it, removed a new white cap that only U-Boat commanders were allowed to wear. He handed it over and said, "Wear this well, von Hellenbach. I happen to know your father, and I believe he would also be very proud of you today. Incidentally, how is he?"

Horst took the cap, and scarcely able to keep his voice under control, replied. "To be honest, sir, I don't know. The last I heard, he was somewhere in Russia with Field Marshall Paulus' Sixth Army."

"Ah. The eastern front. Rough duty indeed. Well, my personal regards to him when you are in touch."

"Thank you, Admiral, I will."

"*Ja*. Now, go. I'm a busy man."

Brigadier General Karl Heinz Eppinger had never been so cold in his life. It had taken him four days to reach the Sixth Army Headquarters, riding in a squalid troop/supply train, wasting most of his precious leave time traveling through Poland (or rather, what used to be Poland) and western Russia toward the stalled front, on the pretext of gathering first hand intelligence information for his boss, Admiral Canaris. His real mission was to manage, if possible, to sound out his old friend, Ernst von Hellenbach on a secret matter of grave importance.

Directed to a log hut at the center of a clearing, he trudged over packed snow, against the howling wind that bit clear through his greatcoat and wool scarf, his gloved hands clutching his briefcase already numb. He ducked into

— 64 —

Tom Lewis

the small door. There was no heat in the hut, but out of the wind, it felt twenty degrees warmer.

When Colonel von Hellenbach, who was not expecting him, looked up, Eppinger was shocked to see how his best friend had aged. He looked like an old man! The two men hugged each other fiercely. "Karl Heinz!" von Hellenbach finally said, "What the hell are you doing here?"

"The *Abwehr* wishes to know first hand how things really are out here. Are we alone? Can we talk privately?"

"Yes," von Hellenbach said, pulling the ratty blanket back around his shoulders. "Anybody of any importance is over at Headquarters, burning the office furniture to stay alive. I wish I could offer you a drink, but I have nothing. Anything that would make a man warm inside or outside has long since been used up, including heating fuel. All has to be saved for the Fuehrer's tanks and trucks, which can't move one meter anyway."

Eppinger noted the bitter sarcasm in von Hellenbach's voice. "No matter. I've brought something." From his briefcase, Eppinger fished out a bottle of brandy.

"Napoleon brandy? Really? I have died and gone to heaven!" Both men took long pulls. "*God,* that's good," von Hellenbach said, wiping his mouth with the back of a filthy hand. "Haven't had anything that delicious since before we started out for Moscow, and you know what's happened since then. How's everything back in Berlin?"

General Eppinger shook his head. "What would you think? People are worried. Disillusioned. It is hard for them to believe our invincible Army has suffered defeat. Moscow was a worse military debacle than Verdun."

Von Hellenbach spat on the floor. "What did that crazy

Hitler's Judas

little son of a bitch think? That he could do what Napoleon couldn't? And now, I hear he's going to make us try again come spring. We'll never make it, Karl Heinz. I doubt if we will get past Stalingrad. Look around. I am supposed to be this Army's assistant quartermaster. I don't even have enough overcoats to pass around to the officers, let alone the men. It's practically hopeless *now*, and you can imagine what it will be like the next time he yells, 'Attack. No man retreats!' And he will. You can count on it."

Both men drank from the bottle again.

"I'm afraid I have worse news," Eppinger said.

"What could possibly be worse?"

"We, the *Abwehr*, I mean, are fairly certain the Allies are planning to invade. Most likely Italy first, then probably across the English Channel. And, maybe as soon as next year. Hitler is going to have to fight on two fronts."

Von Hellenbach sighed. "Why does that not surprise me? Anyway, just look at you. A General! Only active General with one arm at that, I'll wager. Congratulations."

"Thanks. You would have been a General long ago yourself if you hadn't waited so long to join the party."

"Shit! I would never have joined that gang of criminals if it hadn't been for my son Harald. Such a brainwashed fanatic. Threatened to denounce me one time when he was in the Hitler Youth. He'd have done it, too. That's when I finally joined. I was sick to my stomach for a month."

"Well, it all turned out all right. Your other boy is making quite a name for himself in the Kriegsmarine. Won the Iron Cross recently. The real one."

"I didn't know that."

"Ernst, are you well?"

Tom Lewis

"Had a bout with pneumonia recently. I'm better now. But I'll tell you something, old friend. There are a million men out here getting ready to piss in the wind when the little Corporal says go. Most of them will die. If what you say about the Allies is true, the few supplies we have will dry up like tears in Rommel's desert. Those men will die for nothing, this war will be lost if it hasn't been already, and Germany will cease to exist. Plus, I'm hearing things about Himmler's SS vermin you simply would not believe. I'll be honest with you, Karl Heinz, I don't believe I will survive this next push either, but I don't care. I don't even *want* to live in a country like ours has become. How could we have let it happen? How could we have let *him* happen? He's a mad man. No, I take that back. He's not a man, he's a mad dog."

"And you know what we do with mad dogs."

Von Hellenbach narrowed his eyes. "What are you saying, my friend?"

"You are not alone in your disgust. Not by a long shot. Do you still trust me, Ernst?"

"Of course I do. Why have you really come here, Karl Heinz?"

"There are a few of us, quite a few actually, who are plotting to get rid of the mad dog, sue for whatever kind of peace we can get, and start over. That's the reason I came out here. I'm here to enlist you, Ernst. That's it. Now, you can call somebody and have me shot for spreading treason, or you can have another drink and listen."

"Pass the bottle and tell me about it. All about it. "

CHAPTER 6

Berlin, 15 July, 1943

The *Zweiter Zeit* was not what it once had been. In the past, Bormann had enjoyed taking women there, where the atmosphere was subdued, the food good, and the staff professionally discreet; one of Berlin's finest bistros. Formerly, the only military types who frequented the elegant restaurant two blocks east of *Unter den Linden* were General Officers. Now, it was nightly full of mostly lower ranks, all swilling Dutch courage, loudly belting out beer-blurred words of the *Horst Wessel* and other patriotic war tunes they only half believed in any more, knowing there were a lot more of them going off to battle than there were coming back. Besides, the quality of both food and service

Tom Lewis

had slipped badly. On the whole, Bormann now found it depressing, and wished he hadn't brought Edda there, but she liked to be taken to fancy places where she could show off the expensive gowns and jewels he spoiled her with.

As if responding to a cue, she teased, "How do I look tonight, Martin?"

Bormann showed her half a smile. "Like a Countess."

"I feel like one, too, thanks to you. What's the matter? You've had a sour face all night long. Have I upset you somehow?"

Bormann sighed. "No, my darling. It's just that I've been working very hard lately, and this place is tiresome. Boring. Not like it used to be."

"Nothing is like it used to be."

"That's true enough. To tell the truth, I miss the wonderful old cabaret spots. They were fun. Decadent as hell, but fun."

Several moments passed before Edda, narrowing her eyes, leaned over the table and said, "If you promise me you won't tell any of the Fuehrer's cronies about it, I'll take you to one that's still a lot of fun."

"Where?"

"Promise me first."

"All right, I promise, but why such secrecy?"

"Because if certain people in your circle knew about it, people who work and go there could be in a lot of trouble, including me."

"I see. What is this mysterious place?"

"A nightclub. Kind of like the private clubs they had back in the twenties. We call it 'The Hole'."

"Sounds interesting. Why not? It can't be worse than this. Let's go."

— 69 —

Hitler's Judas

Edda had Bormann leave the car in the vast parking lot of the UFA Studios, and led him three blocks down a narrow side street to the back part of the lot and to the rear door of a broken-down warehouse. An elderly night watchman shone his flashlight into their faces, recognized Edda, and wordlessly allowed them in. Inside, a hundred or more naked light bulbs hanging from single wires revealed to Bormann that the decrepit building was full of theater props. Lifting the hem of her gown up off the dusty floor, Edda led him down a flight of rickety stairs to the basement, where they were confronted with yet another door; a very solid one, replete with peephole and sliding face-plate.

"Is this some kind of American-style speakeasy?" Bormann asked. "Do we need a password?"

"You'll see," Edda replied, with a mischievous glance. She knocked twice, the panel slid open, and Edda said, "Edda Winter and trusted friend. Heil Hitler!"

The door opened, and Bormann couldn't help himself from grinning with delight. Allowing his eyes to adjust to the dim, smoke-saturated room, he saw that 'The Hole' had been aptly named. Nothing had been done to hide the old brick masonry of walls and structural support columns, plumbing pipes, or electrical conduits. The floor was no more than planks laid over dirt, and was sprinkled with several dozen uncovered tables the size of One-Mark coins, all nearly filled with noisy people in formal dress. Bormann's quick eye also took in the slim figures of the hat check girl, the cigarette girl, and three cocktail waitresses. All of them were dressed in pastel-colored, diaphanous costumes, belted and draped over one shoulder, each revealing one bare arm and

– 70 –

Tom Lewis

one exposed breast, nipples painted the same color as the garish shades of their lipstick. In a second glance, he noticed a bar, a sizable dance area, and at the end of the room, a tiny stage. From one side of it, music was coming from only two musicians; an accordion player and a gypsy-style violinist. Several couples clung to each other on the dance floor, including one pair of women who were grope-dancing far too intimately to have been sisters!

Bormann sucked in cellar-dank air through his teeth.

"Is this decadent enough for you?" Edda said, laughing.

"*Jawohl*," he replied. "This is more like it. Brings back a lot of memories."

"I'll bet it does. Remember your promise. Come on, let's see if we can find a table."

They located one in the far left corner, near the dark hallway leading to the toilets and backstage area. "Drinks are hideously expensive here, Martin, especially champagne," Edda said, "But why don't we have some anyway, since you— *Ach*, look over there!"

"Where?"

"There. The third table over. It's my mother."

"So it is. Your favorite person."

"Don't be so mean. She's just a little jealous. Why don't you order us a bottle. I'm going over and say hello. Back in a minute."

Bormann watched her sway through the tables even as one of the *ersatz* Grecian goddesses approached his. He could see right through the gossamer material of her backlit dress. Approvingly, he glanced first at her small, blue-tipped breast, then at the pretty face surrounding the blue-tinted smile that was returning his own. "Your pleasure, sir?"

– 71 –

Hitler's Judas

"I'll settle for a bottle of your best."

"Right away, sir."

Jutta Winter checked her makeup in the cracked mirror in the women's room. "So. Did you bring him here to show off your good fortune or just your newest frock?"

Edda ignored her mother's jibe. "He's not in uniform tonight. I doubt if anyone here actually knows who he is."

"Let's hope not! Well, in all fairness, I have to hand it to you. Two excellent parts and a lead role coming up. Your own furnished apartment, too. Not bad for one year's work on your back."

Edda let that one go by as well. She frowned. "Parts? Two of Goebbel's smarmy propaganda films. Not exactly Hollywood. But don't you worry, I'll get there one day."

"We will have to win this war first."

"I don't give a happy damn who wins it, us or them. Martin will get me there one way or the other, and I'll be a star, too. Mark my words, Mutti. Listen, I'd better get back. He doesn't like me to be gone long."

Jutta snorted. "I'm sure. Tell me, how did you do it? You've been his mistress twice as long as anyone ever has, from the gossip I hear."

"How? Easy. He adores me. What's more, he loves the things I do to him." Edda winked at her mother. "It's a matter of technique. Fraulein Riefenstahl loaned me some pornographic movies made back when you were getting started. Thank God you weren't in any of them. Or were you? Anyway, I'm a quick study."

"You're nothing but a whore and a bitch."

Edda thought of saying something about the pot calling

– 72 –

Tom Lewis

the kettle black, but said instead, "Maybe, but compared to before, I'm a much richer bitch, and someday soon I'll be as famous as Dietrich and those others who were lucky enough to get away. Besides, I really do care for Martin. He treats me like a Princess."

"Hmpf. Is it true what they say about him? You know, the stud horse?"

"Wouldn't you like to know. Ta-ta, Mutti. I'm going back in. By the way, who is that undertaker you're with tonight? You have to give him bedtime injections?"

"Wouldn't *you* just like to know! *Damn* you!"

Waving to friends, Edda made her way back to the table and sat. Bormann had already poured glasses, and handed her one. He lit her cigarette and asked, "Edda, who are all these people? I don't recognize anyone here."

Edda sipped. "Mostly theater people. A few musicians and painters. Artistic types. Those serving girls you keep staring at are would-be film actresses, hoping to get a leg up. They all—"

She was interrupted by a wave of shouts and applause that began at the tables nearest the little stage and moved back through the room.

"What's going on?" Bormann yelled over the noise.

"It's Klaus. Wonderful! We're in for a treat," Edda yelled back at him.

The people around them began standing, clapping and stomping in time, and in one voice, chanting, louder and louder, "We want Ber-ger, we want Ber-ger, we want Ber-ger." Edda, paying absolutely no attention to her lover, sprang to her feet and joined in. Bormann, more from curiosity than irritation, stood slowly to see who this Berger

— 73 —

Hitler's Judas

person was, but being so short, he could not see over their heads.

Suddenly, from the direction of the stage, a booming voice cried out, "Silence, sheep! Silence! Sit your Nazi asses down!"

Like trained seals, the crowd instantly obeyed, their noise reduced to a twitter or two of laughter. Bormann was totally bewildered. Edda placed a hand on his arm and quietly said, "He does mime. Improvisational skits. Remember your promise, Martin, please."

Perplexed, Bormann shifted his eyes to the stage and nearly strangled on the champagne he was swallowing. A more than portly man, decked out in a white uniform—covered from collar to hem with medals—had sauntered onto the stage, a glass of champagne in one hand, a bottle in the other, and walked toward the only set pieces; a small sofa with an end table and lamp. Made up, the fat actor looked remarkably like—*Hermann Goering??*

Bormann watched, first in shock, then mild amusement as the man snapped his fingers, and from the audience, two good looking, well dressed women jumped onto the stage to sit down next to him. One held his long cigarette holder. The other lit it for him. Then they began kissing him and running their fingers through his hair and all over his corpulent figure. When Bormann heard the audience begin to laugh, he squinted, trying to figure out what they were laughing about. Then he saw it. As each of the women 'made love' to him, 'Goering' deftly removed their earrings, necklaces, and the very brooches from their dresses, and tucked them neatly beneath the cushions. Then he sent them away, and two more took their places— with

— 74 —

Tom Lewis

the same results. The audience rocked with laughter, and Bormann couldn't help but emit a chuckle or two himself, especially when the actor-Goering flung away his glass and bottle while his uniform jacket popped several buttons, revealing a pillow that had been painted like a belly with an enormous navel. 'Goering' snapped his fingers again. This time, there were softs oohs and ahhs from the audience as a small oriental figure entered, bowing and scraping in, with what had to be an opium pipe. The Chinaman waved the pipe once under his nose, and the obese character fell off the sofa, and on hands and knees like a salivating dog, followed the pipe-bearing midget offstage.

The applause and laughter, as the curtain closed, was thunderous. Edda gave Bormann a nervous glance and was relieved to see that he was also laughing. "Clever man," he said. "And funny."

He hardly had time to say more before the curtain opened again, this time revealing an office scene and desk, behind which sat a much thinner Klaus Berger, dressed in the uniform of the Minister of Propaganda. Fascinated, Bormann watched and listened as short, recorded bits of Hitler's broadcast speeches wafted over the audience, and after each, the actor jumped up and directed various supporting cast members; a reporter, a cameraman, and, of all people, Leni Riefenstahl, who hurried offstage to follow his 'orders'. Berger, obviously as Goebbels, flapped his arms and moved his mouth in sync with the recorded voice of a rooster, running in circles around his desk!

Bormann, unable to hold back, joined in the guffaws and catcalls. "Terrific stuff!" he yelled at Edda. "This guy's really good. Pour me another glass."

Hitler's Judas

Then came the third act. The curtain opened on a scene that provoked five minutes of continuous cacophony. There was nothing on the stage except the actor, now wearing a black SS uniform and Heinrich Himmler's famous *pince-nez*. He was holding a handful of typed pages, and pants around his knees, was sitting on a huge white chamber pot! To successive peals of laughter, he strained, read from the sheets, pointed at random people in the audience, crooked his finger, and from the wings, a supporting actor dressed in unmistakable Gestapo raincoat and slouch hat appeared, drew his revolver and mimed shooting at the unfortunate targets. Invariably, those individuals, men or women, played their parts and fell off their chairs. After each victim hit the floor, 'Himmler' tore off part of his list, and strained mightily again. The performance was hilarious, and Bormann found he had tears in his eyes, just as caught up in all of it as the others when the actor's rubber face finally showed the tremendous satisfaction of final relief. He then 'used' the last sheets of the list behind him, stood, pulled up his trousers, and peered down, frowning, into the chamber pot. Wrinkling his nose, he started to walk toward the wings, but turned, came back, and with his foot, turned the chamber pot around. On it was painted a large Star of David. With a last gesture; an evil glare, 'Himmler,' as if on sudden impulse, picked the pot up and flung its contents—of confetti—at the shrieking, ducking audience, then stalked off the stage.

Not the instantaneous standing ovation nor the sustained applause and laughter could bring Klaus Berger back. "He never takes curtain calls," Edda explained. "He's Germany's greatest actor, comedy or drama, stage or screen, but he never takes bows. It's a personal quirk."

— 76 —

Tom Lewis

"Strange," Bormann said, wiping his eyes, "Anyway, I'm glad we came here tonight. I can't remember laughing so hard. Edda? Edda, why are you looking at me like that?"

She was slowly shaking her head, her brow furrowed. "I swear, I never noticed it until now, but you know what, Martin? If Klaus wasn't bald, and weighed a few more pounds, he... Well, he looks a lot like *you*."

"You think so? I didn't notice that. Incidentally, I'm also a bit curious, Edda. Why didn't he include me in his parodies?"

"Oh, that's not hard to figure out. Nobody in Germany knows much about what you actually *do*. You're like the Fuehrer's second shadow. It's also possible Klaus may have known you are here tonight. Mutti may have told him."

"Take me backstage. I want to meet him."

"What? And scare him half to death?"

"You don't have to tell him my name. Just say I'm your boyfriend."

Edda bit her lip. "That isn't what I'm concerned about. Listen to me, Martin, Klaus Berger is, as I said, Germany's finest actor, but he hasn't taken a role, not even a bit part, in over five years."

"Why not?"

"Because he's homosexual. You more than anyone should know how the Fuehrer feels about queens. The poor man walks on eggs every day of his life. If he showed his face on screen again, he'd be arrested in a heartbeat."

"Well, I made you a promise, didn't I? I won't cause him any trouble. I only want to meet him face to face."

And so, less than ten minutes later, Martin Bormann

was shaking hands with a man who, except for lack of hair and girth, was exactly his own height, had the same color eyes, appeared to be about his own age, and whose face could have been that of a twin brother! Something flashed in his memory. Something Hitler had said back in '41 just before Hess had flown the coop. *'Canaris told me Churchill has a double...'*

The friendly words of praise he was bestowing on the surprised actor froze in his throat. He suddenly turned on his heel and said, "Let's get out of here, Edda. You drive."

CHAPTER 7

Bormann punched the intercom button and told his secretary he was not feeling well. "No visitors and no telephone calls unless it's the Fuehrer."

"Yes, sir."

He leaned back in his chair. Part of what he'd just told the efficient Fraulein Kemper was true; he did have a slight headache, but the two aspirin he'd taken earlier would take care of that. What he needed was a quiet morning to rethink his plan, which until last night, had been practically complete, lacking only a final timetable for its execution. Now it might have to be altered.

He had not been able to sleep more than a few minutes at the time the night before in spite of Edda's expertise. *Churchill has a double! Churchill has a double!* Hitler's

Hitler's Judas

words sang in his ears and that actor's eyes had kept staring at him in his fitful half sleep-half dreams all night long. Would the fantastic idea he'd had last night *actually be possible?*

He puffed out his cheeks. So much brain work done already, and now, this other possibility. Well, there was nothing for it but to start at the beginning and work through it all again. It was cerebrally taxing, but he had never, *never* committed anything of it to paper, nor would he now. Anything written down within the Third Reich (where everything was inevitably copied with Germanic thoroughness in bureaucratic triplicate) always left an incriminating, possibly deadly trail. No, better by far to weave this new thread into his plan with the loom of his mind.

He had been able to do that all his life. Martin Bormann's highly perfected organizational skills were no accident. His physical discipline, imparted genetically at birth and enforced personally at an early age by his Prussian Sergeant-Major father, was nothing compared to the mental regimen he had taught himself. As a small boy, his favorite pastime had been tearing all the family clocks apart and putting them back together again, knowing even then that it was not mechanical aptitude he was practicing, rather, the development of extraordinary mental powers and infinite patience it took to deduce where the randomly scattered parts and springs should logically fit. Every clock had eventually worked again, good as new.

Like a careful navigator in uncharted waters, he gave himself two hours of meticulously measuring, adding, calculating, fitting, each molecule of this new equation to

Tom Lewis

see how—or if—it would mesh into the overall fabric of his original scheme. When the time was up, he was satisfied that, theoretically at least, it could work. The adjustments were major ones, to be sure, but *it could work!* It would set his timetable back a few months, but that part had always been the most flexible anyway. What did a few more months matter?

He reached for the telephone.

"*Ja?*"

"Edda, I'm coming over early. Right after lunch."

"But Martin, I was supposed to start work on the new film today."

"Call them and cancel. Postpone it until tomorrow. Tell them you are, what, 'indisposed'? Isn't that what temperamental actresses do?"

"Is anything wrong, Martin?"

"Nothing your fingertips can't fix. I'll see you around two."

He hung up, then redialed.

"*Amt Drei*, Bormann speaking."

"*Ach*, little brother, you sound officious as hell."

"Oh, it's you, Martin. One tries one's best, you know."

"Are you free for lunch today?"

"I could be, why?"

"Meet me at the Tiergarten Restaurant at half past twelve. Upstairs."

"All right. Are you buying?"

Bormann hung up, with a sour grunt. *Trust a Bormann to pinch a penny.*

He looked up Leni Riefenstahl's number and dialed again. This time, he smiled with satisfaction because she

Hitler's Judas

didn't make him wait.

"Martin! How good to hear from you. I saw you last night at The Hole. Did you enjoy yourself?"

"More than you will ever know, Leni. Actually, that's why I'm calling. Can you locate in your UFA archives any of the films the gifted Herr Berger made?"

"Certainly. We have prints of all of them here. Why, if I may ask?"

"I would like to see some of them. Privately. Can you arrange it?"

Leni's voice quickly revealed her concern. Some hesitation. "Martin, old friend, please tell me you are not planning some trouble for an out of work actor."

Bormann laughed. "No, no. No trouble. I don't give a damn whether he sleeps with boys, nuns, or even farm animals. I simply want to see a few of his movies. Not any of the comedies, only two or three of his best dramatic films. I'm curious to see if he does serious roles as well as he does funny ones." Relieved somewhat, Leni said, "That's good to hear, and I know just the films you should see. I can arrange for a projection room as early as tonight if you wish."

"Tonight would be perfect. Edda and I will meet you at your office at eight, and thank you, Leni. I won't forget the favor."

Bormann hung up, leaned back and lit a cigarette. So far so good. And, so far, Fraulein Kemper was also doing her duty in the outer office. He prayed Hitler would not call him for some silly reason. He stubbed his cigarette out and reached once more for the telephone and dialed a number not even known to Himmler or Canaris.

Tom Lewis

"Skorzeny here."

"Otto, this is Bormann. The Fuehrer asked me to call," he lied. "We have a little job for you. No, two of them. Meet me day after tomorrow at the same place as before. Ten o'clock."

"*Jawohl*, Herr Reichsleiter. Same place, same time. I'll be there."

Bormann hung up, highly pleased that the morning was going so well. He punched the intercom button again. "Fraulein Kemper, I'm feeling a lot worse. I'm going home to rest."

"Yes, sir. I hope you will be feeling better soon."

"Thank you, I shall probably be all right by tomorrow. Send Glas home. I'll drive myself."

"Yes, sir."

Bormann flipped the toggle switch off, put his coat and cap on, and left by the back door.

In one of the private second floor rooms of the Tiergarten restaurant, Bormann and his younger brother polished off lunches of oxtail soup, bratwurst, and potato salad, washing it all down with some good Danish beer.

"This is quite a treat, Martin," Helmut Bormann said. "But I know there is no such thing as a free lunch, and, I know you! What's on your mind?"

Bormann belched behind his napkin and eyed his brother. Helmut was not the brightest star in the Nazi galaxy, but he was reliable, and, he was *family*. Like all the Bormanns, he was a great deal smarter than he looked, and knew how to keep his mouth shut. Moreover, as with every other job he'd had, he owed his current middle-rank

— 83 —

Hitler's Judas

position in the Gestapo (which also made it easier to spy on Himmler) to his older brother to begin with, and Martin knew Helmut's loyalties to Himmler and even to the Fuehrer came only after those to him. Always had and always would. "You did a good job with that neat investigation of my girlfriend, Helmut, and I'm grateful."

"Thanks. It wasn't easy. Himmler has a long nose."

"Yes, one he's likely to cut off in spite of himself someday, the slimy weasel, but, yes, I do know how hard it must have been to destroy all the copies of the file you gave me."

"So how is the beautiful Edda?"

"She's fine. About to start work on her new film. And, it's film people I want to talk to you about. I need a similar favor."

"I knew it! Anybody in particular?"

"Yes. A homosexual actor named Klaus Berger. Hasn't worked actively for a few years, but he lives here in Berlin, probably off the generosity of his friends. Without his knowing it, I want you to find out everything you can about him; his habits, his background, his lovers, his politics, everything. And just as you did with Edda, keep it quiet, and out of Himmler's reach. One file, my eyes only."

"I can do that. When do you want it?"

"Yesterday."

Helmut laughed. "You don't ask for much, do you?"

Bormann laughed, too. "I know. Nevertheless, I'm depending on you. How's your bank account right now?"

"Fair, thanks to you."

"Well, if I have my hands on that file by the first of next week, I promise you it will become a lot fairer. Say,

— 84 —

Tom Lewis

around five thousand Marks fairer?"

Helmut whistled softly through his teeth. "Why don't we have another beer? On me."

Edda looked up from her magazine as Bormann came in, already pulling his tie off. "Would you please draw me a bath, little one? I need a hot soak."

Edda immediately got up and headed for the bathroom. After so many repetitions, she knew the routine by heart. When Martin asked her to fill the tub, what he really wanted was another of her erotic, full-body massages. It took her nearly an hour to do one, which usually culminated in quick sex. After that, he would rapidly fall asleep— and talk. Like right now, Edda had often wondered what Bormann would do if he found out he jabbered in his sleep. *Probably figure out some way to keep from sleeping— and murder anyone else who knew!* Still, with the way the war was going now, she knew he was close to making his move, and she was determined to be part of it, even if it meant risking her future, gambling that he loved her enough to want her with him when he did.

Humming the melody of a popular sing, Edda turned the taps on, adjusting the water temperature just so. Hot, but not too hot. She poured some of her bath bubbles in and gently stirred. Bormann's timing was always perfect. The moment the tub was filled to the right level, he came in and lowered his thick body in. "Ahhh. *Wunderbar.* And how's my little sparrow this fine day? Not too upset at old Bormann for keeping you home, are you?"

"No, Martin. I'm glad you came early. Shall I wear one of my new outfits?"

Hitler's Judas

"Sure. The red one. And, make your sweetheart a drink, would you?"

Edda poured the whiskey first, brought it to him, then went into the bedroom and changed into the lacey, transparent negligee, taking time to carefully touch a dab of perfume here and there. She also laid a blanket over the bed so the almond-scented oil she used for her massages wouldn't stain the coverlet. She was curious why he had come early, an unusual thing for him, and why he seemed in such a good mood.

Naked, he came into the bedroom and stretched out on the bed. "What is your pleasure, O Sultan?" Edda asked, in her most sultry voice. "Shall I do your front or your back first?"

"My front. I want to watch you. Besides, I haven't finished my drink."

Edda began with his stubby toes, slowly working her way up. When she reached his calves, she said, "You don't seem so tense today. Your muscles feel very smooth. Relaxed. Have you had some good news?"

"I feel good about a decision I made this morning."

"Anything you can share with me?"

"Edda, one thing I love about you is that you never pry."

Edda took a deep breath. If there ever was going to be a time, this was it. "I don't need to."

"What do you mean by that?"

"Because you tell me a lot anyway."

"I do? How?"

Edda's fingers never hesitated, reaching up to his inner thighs. "You talk in your sleep. Every night you're here."

Tom Lewis

She instantly felt his thigh muscles tighten up. Holding her breath, she applied more pressure.

"What kinds of things do I talk about?"

Edda called upon all her acting skills not to betray her fear. In a light voice, she replied, "Oh, never more than bits and pieces. Mostly ordinary things. Sometimes you talk about your wife and kids."

"What else?"

"How like a child the Fuehrer is, and how much he depends on you. And how much the others hate your guts."

"What others?"

"All of them. Goebbels, von Ribbentrop, Goering, especially Himmler. None of them can get through Hitler's door without going through yours. Next to him, you're the most powerful man in the Reich..."

"And?"

This was the moment of truth. Now or never. Keeping her voice even, her fingers steadily moving, she said, "Well, I know you believe the war is lost, and you're planning to get away from Germany before it's too late, possibly to Argentina, and that you are planning to steal a fortune in gold. That's all."

Her fingers reached his scrotum. She made her voice like velvet. "But you know me like a book, Martin. You know how much I love you, and you also know that I would never breathe a word of anything you ever told me to a living soul."

She felt his left hand suddenly reach over hers, stopping their movement. His right hand seized her face and pulled it roughly to within an inch from his own, forcing her to look directly into cold eyes. "Oh yes," he hissed, his

Hitler's Judas

whiskey breath hot on her face, "I do know that. And I know with absolute certainty you would never utter one single peep. There are two reasons why, my clever little detective. One, I know all you want out of this life is to get to America someday, specifically to Hollywood, and I'm your only ticket there, whether it's by way of Argentina or Hell itself. And secondly, you know that if I ever found out you opened your mouth, I would cut off these perfect breasts and carve your pretty face to shreds before sending you to a certain camp in southern Poland where the only acting you would ever do would be to pretend you wanted to live."

Slowly, he released the pressure of his fingers around her jaws and hands. His face showed a malignant sneer. "You are right about one thing. This war was lost two years ago, when Hitler decided to attack Russia. If I stayed here, either the Russians, or the English and Americans who are probably going to invade soon, would have me shot or hanged. I have no intention of waiting around for that to happen. Also, I have become accustomed to having money. I like the power and comfort it can be used for. If the plan I have works, and I now have every good reason to believe it will, I will escape this rotting country with enough gold to *buy* Hollywood. If you are smart as I think you are, and tight-lipped as the Sphinx , I just might take you with me."

There was a long moment of silence between them. Then Bormann reached forward and ripped the flimsy garment she was wearing to pieces, viciously grabbed her, threw her onto her stomach, and did something to her she had hoped he'd never do. It hurt like the devil, causing her to cry out, but she bit her tongue and bore a pain which was not nearly so severe as the humiliation. Mercifully, it

Tom Lewis

was over in seconds. He rolled off of her, turned over on his side and was soon asleep.

She got up, walked gingerly into the bathroom, and settled slowly into the tub which was still full of warm water, adding to it with tears almost as warm. It helped a little...

When he awakened, realizing he was hungry, Bormann got up, stretched, dressed, and walked into the living room. Edda was lying on the couch, her nose in another of the dozens of American film magazines she somehow managed to collect. Bormann guessed they were smuggled in, probably through Italy, and circulated, hand to hand, by her fellow actors. As if nothing unusual had occurred between them he said, "Get dressed. We're going out."

"Really? Where?"

"First to an early dinner. Then I'm taking you to see some movies."

Without a word, Edda got up and walked into the bedroom. Borman sat down at the old fashioned desk, reached for paper and a pen, and for the fifteen minutes it took his mistress to dress, he practiced, over and over, signing Adolf Hitler's signature. He had, with his normal diligence and attention to detail, learned how to forge it perfectly months ago, but had set himself the task of dozens of repetitions every night before sleeping, just to be sure, even keeping pace with the changes in it caused by Hitler's growing hypertension. Bormann could copy it when he was fresh, when he was tired, even when he himself was nervous and irritated. When he was satisfied he had done enough for one night, he burned the papers in the wastepaper bin, carried the ashes to the bathroom and flushed them down

– 89 –

the toilet.

He walked back into the bedroom just as Edda, sitting before her vanity, was finishing her makeup. He peered over her head into the mirror. "You look lovely, my darling. Radiant even. Shall we go?"

Edda smiled at him in the mirror. "I'm ready."

Bormann laid his hands on her bare shoulders. "Oh, and Edda, I'm going to be away from Berlin for a few days. Will you miss me?"

"I'll be very busy on Goebbels' newest piece of shit, but naturally I will miss you. Where will you be going?"

"You want me to tell you now, or find out when I fall asleep tonight?"

Edda managed a tiny laugh. And why should she not? She was still alive!

CHAPTER 8

"Fire one." Horst began counting seconds as the deadly torpedo streaked toward its prey. Too many passed, however, with no result. Softly, he cursed, gritted his teeth and turned to his First Officer. "Either a dud, or we've missed completely."

Both men strained forward, practically grinding their binoculars into their eye sockets. The slow freighter ahead of them steamed on, apparently unmindful of how lucky they were. Just as quickly as it had soured, Horst's mood brightened. "They're not turning! Didn't see the torpedo's wake. Unbelievable! That fish must have passed right under her bows. We get a second chance. Fire two." He glanced at his watch, again counting aloud, "Seven, six, five, four, three, two, one, *Now*, damn you!"

Hitler's Judas

The explosion briefly lit up the night sky. The second torpedo had struck the freighter just aft of midships. Horst didn't wait to see if the hit would break her hull in two, or even slow her down. In his next breath, he ordered, "Hard left rudder. Come to one-nine-five. All ahead full."

Acknowledging the order to turn, then speed away from the stricken freighter, First Officer Rudiger Heidt was incredulous. "But *Captain*—"

Horst scowled at his Junior Officer's stifled objection. "That was our last torpedo, Heidt. It's time to go. There are British warships in the general area. You *know* that, and I have no intention of tangling with them." He inclined his head backwards, toward the freighter. "Yes, we could use our cannon to make sure she sinks, but that would take up precious time. We could possibly get caught in a nasty firefight with only our two little popguns. No, a good run is far better than a bad stand. General Custer of the American Indian Wars proved that."

The ever-correct First Officer was either ignorant of the military history of Custer's last stand at the Little Big Horn, or his sense of humor was sadly lacking. Horst decided it was probably both. "Go below and set our course for the rendezvous co-ordinates. We can't afford to miss our meeting with Mama milk cow."

Heidt saluted and obeyed without another word, and his place in the tower was immediately taken by Chief Knapp, who took one look at the smoke enveloping the freighter and said, "Pretty. Herr Kaleun, you know we have no more fish, and we're low on fuel. Really low."

Horst nodded. "I know, Oskar." He scratched his chin, deep in thought. After a minute he called down for his

Second Officer, who was in charge of all radio communications. The young officer scrambled up the ladder at once. "Sir?"

Horst frowned at him. "Change of orders, Schmidt. Send this message to headquarters: U-119 will be forty-eight hours late for scheduled rendezvous with milk cow."

Twenty year-old Gerhart Schmidt said, "Aye, sir. That's all?"

"That's it. Send it right now, while we're on the surface. We'll be diving soon."

"Aye, Captain."

As soon as Schmidt disappeared below, Oskar said, "He don't have no idea why you're sending that message."

"And you do?"

"I think so, Herr Kaleun. For the past three months, we've been weaving our way through all the passages of the Azores, the Madeiras, and the Canary Islands. We've even snuck down to the Cape Verdi group a time or two, and all the time right by ourselves. Old Uncle Karl has to be damn proud of the tonnage we've picked off. You're his Lone Wolf all right. That British cruiser was a real plum."

"Yes, she was," Horst had to agree. "And each time, we showed them our backsides in a hurry. But this time—"

"Let me guess, Oskar interrupted. To save fuel and keep us from running into trouble, you're just going to run on the surface at night at slow cruising speed, and submerge and lie still during the day hours."

"Right, Oskar. Deep as this old sewer pipe can stand it. I'd take her straight to the bottom if I could. And, we have to be quiet, too. Card games and chess matches are fine, but no singing contests. No noise at all. Not even a

Hitler's Judas

quiet fart. Also, I want you to tell Kirchner I'll make sure he gets the Iron Cross First Class if he outdoes himself in the galley these next few days. I want the crew rested, well fed, and happy."

"They're in good shape anyway, Herr Kaleun. Morale has never been better."

"They have all grown up a lot these past few months, haven't they?"

"Yes, sir. It's been remarkable. You know what they're starting to call you, don't you?"

"No, what?"

"The Wizard. I've even heard Heidt call you that."

Horst laughed lustily. "Really? I'll bet he followed it up by clicking his worn-out heels and yelling 'Heil Hitler' to the top of his voice, too."

Oskar showed yellow teeth. "Well, something like that. You think we killed that freighter?"

Horst shrugged. "If we didn't, she'll be very late delivering her cargo. In any case, we'd best make tracks fast as possible for the next two hundred kilometers. We'll dive just before dawn. You might as well go on down and pass the word."

"Aye, aye, Captain."

"Oh, and Oskar?"

"Sir?"

"Do you have any more of those rotten Dutch cigars left?"

Oskar stuck his tongue in his cheek. "Only one," he lied. "I'll send it up with a cup of Kirchner's best coffee."

Horst turned to his Chief in honest surprise. "Coffee? Real coffee? Where the hell did Kirchner get it?"

– 94 –

Oskar showed his gapped teeth again. "There are a few things even a Commander needn't know, sir. I'll send him right up."

"Excellent. If it *is* the real thing, tell him I said he gets Oak Leaves with his Iron Cross."

Five minutes later, Horst enjoyed a smoke and the purloined coffee as well as the beautiful night sky and warm temperature. To his starboard side lookout, whose glasses never dropped from his eyes, he gently said, "Rather like a pleasure cruise, isn't it, Sautermann?"

"Yes, sir," the rating answered. "Like a canoe on the little lake at Wannsee in Berlin. Only thing missing is—"

"A girl. I know."

"Aye, sir. A girl would be nice."

Horst allowed himself one fleeting thought of Elisabeth, and then threw the stump of his cigar overboard. "All right, everyone below. Prepare to dive."

Two days later, a hundred and fifty kilometers southwest of the Azores, Horst gave the order to surface. From long habit, he hurriedly scoured the sky and the horizon. All was clear. Like a polished mirror. And, not more than three hundred meters off their port side, wallowing in the swells, lay the huge tanker-tender. "Heidt," Horst said, "Break out the flags and tell them to dive. We'll make the transfer at dusk."

"Sir," the First Officer replied, "Why not just use the radio?"

Horst felt his cheek muscles tighten. "I have my reasons. Do as I told you."

The message was dutifully sent, and the answer came

Hitler's Judas

swiftly by the same method:

NEGATIVE. WE ARE ALREADY TWO DAYS LATE. STAND BY TO TRANSFER FUEL AND STORES NOW.

Horst cursed under his breath. "Damn fools. Well, hop to it then. All off-watch hands turn to. We can't waste a second up here like a sleepy goose. Heidt, I want the four best pair of eyes up here on the double. If any one of them takes his eyes away from his glasses, I'll keel-haul him."

Nervously, Horst watched the transfer of precious fuel lines being snaked over from the milk cow to his own vessel. Soon, the smell of diesel fuel permeated everything, but with typical German thoroughness, combined with outstanding engineering, the tanks of the U-119 were rapidly guzzling fuel like life saving plasma. Simultaneously, torpedoes, wrapped in life jackets for extra buoyancy, were floated over, hauled aboard and loaded through the hatches. The crews of both vessels worked hard and silently, shirtless, and sweating profusely under the near-tropical afternoon sun.

The haughty Captain of the milk cow hailed Horst with his megaphone. "Captain, we brought you plenty of bread that isn't moldy, some new potatoes, and a lot of fresh lemons."

"Thank you," Horst shouted back. "Sorry we had to make you wait for two days. It was necessary. Did you bring us any good movies like the spoiled American sailors get?"

Both skippers were enjoying the joke. "Sure," the tanker's Captain retorted. "All gangster movies. Next thing you guys will want is a boatload of whores! Half blondes, half brunettes."

"What, no red-heads?"

"No, they are all in concentration camps."

— 96 —

Tom Lewis

Horst frowned at the connotation. "Have you brought any eggs? We are down to our last—"

"Captain!" the port lookout shouted, pointing. "Airplane. Two o'clock!"

One fast look was all Horst needed. He yanked the megaphone up to his lips and yelled at the tanker's Captain. "Cut all lines. Now! Dive. Meet us back here in this same spot exactly three hours from now." He didn't wait for a reply. Chief Oskar Knapp was already supervising the severing of lines connecting the two boats. "Done in half a minute, Herr Kaleun," he shouted.

Horst yelled at his crew. "Get below, all of you. Close hatches. All ahead full. Emergency dive. Emergency dive!"

The enemy plane had come straight out of the sun and was now bearing down on them with terrible speed. Horst prayed they would make it. The bows were already under water when the first strafing bullets stitched the water on both sides of his hull. The last thing he saw before slamming the hatch cover down over his head was a pair of cylinders fall from beneath the planes wings. He knew they were depth charges.

Once below, he yelled at Chief Knapp, "Take her down all the way, Chief. One-three-oh meters!"

Every man's mouth was clamped tighter than a vise, and every one of them knew a hundred thirty meters was far in excess of the boat's maximum dive rating. But none voiced any protest, not even First Officer Heidt. Every man grabbed what he could to keep from falling forward on the steeply pitched deck, and every eardrum, already popping at the change of pressure, was blasted by the awesome metallic sound of the depth charges exploding on both sides

Hitler's Judas

of them— not more than forty meters away. Every man prayed openly to both God— and the Wizard. Each had but one single, secret thought about how the men in the slower milk cow were faring. Each was mumbling to himself, "If it has to be, let it be them, not us."

Thankfully, it only lasted minutes. The single plane had only been carrying four depth charges, but Horst kept the U-119 under for another two and a half hours just to make sure. Chief Knapp turned to his friend Kirchner, the cook, who was standing next to him, his arms folded with stoic patience. "I hope those guys in the milk cow realize what a brilliant move the Captain made."

"What move?" Kirchner said. "We ain't gone nowhere."

Knapp rolled his eyes. "That's just it, stupid. If you were the pilot of that plane, what would you have done?"

Seeing the blank look on the cook's face, Knapp went on. "You would have noticed that when we started our dive, we were heading south. The milk cow was headed north. Now, if you were piloting that plane, you would have radioed that news back to your base immediately. Only a fool would have stuck around to wait for a destroyer to come a-running. Both us and the cow would be making top speed away in opposite directions as fast as we could. Nobody would expect us both to stick right here in the same spot."

Understanding finally crept into Kirchner's brain. "Oh. Now I see. Yeah. That was smart. Real smart. He's a wizard all right. I wonder if those boys in the milk cow are all right. She was a much bigger target to that plane than we were."

Knapp frowned. "We'd better hope to God they didn't

Tom Lewis

get hit. We didn't have time to transfer any of the food before that damned plane showed up. You wouldn't want to have to make soup out of old boots, would you? Not that you wouldn't try it. What if—"

"Stand by to surface," came Horst's order.

Fifteen minutes later, Horst's deck crew was cheering lustily when the milk cow broke clear a hundred meters off their starboard quarter. First Officer Heidt shouted, they made it, too. "Look, Captain!"

Horst didn't answer. Binoculars to his eyes, he was checking the huge submarine for any external damage. *Not a scratch, you lucky bastards.* A new thought came to him. "Grab that lamp! Signal her not to use her radio to talk to us. Quickly, man!"

Heidt had no sooner jumped to follow his Captain's order when Second Officer Schmidt poked his head through the hatch. He was holding a piece of paper in his hand. "Herr Kaleun, she radiod she was not hurt at all. Tells us to stand by for transfer of stores."

Horst cursed loudly. "Too late, Heidt. Those idiots have already been sending. Hand me that megaphone!"

The dressing down and insults Horst shouted over to the Commander of the milk cow might have been enough to provoke the man to leave without transferring their food and supplies, but he managed to get his point across about using the radios. And, Horst was at least satisfied that the humiliated Commander finally understood why he had wanted to do the fueling and transfer at night. In an aside to Oskar, he said, "I smell trouble coming, Chief. I'd be willing to bet my whole year's pay there is a British destroyer on her way out here as we speak, making thirty

Hitler's Judas

knots."

"What's your plan, Herr Kaleun?" Knapp asked, nodding sagely.

"If the plane's crew reported accurately, and if there is a destroyer coming, she'd naturally want to go after the tanker-sub. Well, we're going to help that destroyer out."

"I don't understand."

"We're going to follow the milk cow north, right on her fat tail. Our only chance is that the enemy vessel won't see us, and we can kill her before she realizes there are two of us."

"You young wizard, you. I get it. You're going to let the milk cow be our con as well as our decoy."

"Right. And we can fire a four shot spread from under the cow's belly. Even if the enemy ship sees the fish coming, she would not dare turn. That would be suicide."

Oskar raised his eyebrows. "A bow shot? That's risky, Herr Kaleun. Mighty risky."

"More risky to the boys in the cow, but that's the only way I see out of this mess."

Oskar looked over at the cow, now riding a lot higher in the water. "She'll be a sitting duck."

Horst clenched his jaw. "A lame sitting duck, that's true. The tanker probably will take some hits, but this is war, Oskar. Nothing polite or fair about it. Take those signal flags from Heidt and let's tell them what they will have to do."

"First message, sir?"

"Tell them to set a course of thirty-five degrees. That should put us directly on a path to Gibraltar. Next message: Tell them to move everything; men, torpedoes, crates of

Tom Lewis

food, everything not nailed down, to their starboard side. I want them to affect a list, and on my signal, they are to make smoke. Oh, and by the way, Oskar, tell them to pray."

The naval action that occurred the following day would be talked about over many a beer at the One-Eyed Whore. Horst's plan worked to perfection, aided by a choppy sea and an unexpected, fatal error of judgment on the part of the British Captain of the lend-lease destroyer. In his greed to sink the listing, smoking, and seemingly helpless milk cow, the English Commander had sped bow on toward his lame-duck target, firing his foredeck cannon. At very close range, his lookouts suddenly spotted torpedoes coming right at him, and he had panicked and ordered a hard turn to port. The old ship had speed, but not enough to get out of harm's way fast enough. Three of the four torpedoes from the U-119 slammed into her, one right after the other, blowing her half in two. She sank within minutes, and most of her crew died. A handful of survivors were fished out of the sea by the brave crew of the milk cow, who had sustained only one serious hit—at the base of their conning tower. She would have to limp home without submerging, but she would make it, and with no loss of life.

But Lieutenant Horst von Hellenbach and his men did not have time to celebrate their latest kill. No sooner had they surfaced than a radio message from Doenitz came. Second Officer Schmidt hurried to decode the message on the Enigma machine. He handed it to his Commander who read it, heaved a sigh of resignation, and picked up the intercom microphone. "All hands, this is the Captain. Congratulations on a fine piece of work. I am proud of you.

However, summer vacation has just been unfortunately cut short. I am afraid our lone wolf days are over. We have just been ordered to proceed to Grid 29 in the North Atlantic. It seems that wolfpack number two needs our help."

CHAPTER 9

He would never admit it to anyone, but Martin Bormann hated flying. He felt something close to helpless panic every time he climbed aboard an airplane. Logic told him that if he was on a sinking ship, at least he could swim, giving him a slim chance of survival. Likewise, a rail or automobile accident did not necessarily have to be fatal, but if something happened to a plane in flight... Well, he couldn't sprout wings and fly, that was a fact. He was glad he was sitting in the belly of the Heinkel carrying him and Otto Skorzeny to Rome. From there, he could not see out, or below, where hungry, razor-sharp spines of white Alps were patiently waiting for something to go wrong.

To take his mind off such thoughts, Bormann glanced at his travelling companion who was dozing, apparently completely unconcerned about the cold, the noise of the engines, or the fact that they were a mere flyspeck droning along, suspended between the stratosphere and an unforgiving earth. Bormann studied the sleeping man's features. Nondescript. Ordinary. Much like his own, but he knew Otto Skorzeny was no ordinary man. He was the quintessential commando leader. Physically tough, fearless, shrewd, of above average intelligence, and except for his adoration of Adolf Hitler, totally devoid of feelings or emotions. Not afraid to die, and not in the least squeamish about killing, he could break a man's neck with no more thought about it than stepping on a cockroach. The perfect, dependable man for the ultra-secret, nasty little jobs the Fuehrer needed done from time to time. Those which Hitler kept secret from Himmler or any of the other top Nazis. Moreover, since he always got his orders through Bormann, he would never even *think* of questioning Bormann about any kind of operation, large or small, that the Reichsleiter instructed him and his men to do — 'in the name of the Fuehrer'. If Hitler ordered him to, Skorzeny would fight Max Schmelling with bare knuckles, or strangle his own mother. That is, if he had a mother.

"How is your wife, Herr Bormann?"

Damn! The son of a bitch hadn't been sleeping at all!

"She's well, Otto, thank you for asking."

Skorzeny's eyes opened to slits. His mouth formed a half smile. "You know what the Fuehrer told me one time?"

"No, what?"

"He said that Frau Bormann was even a more devout Nazi than you!"

Bormann couldn't help but silently agree. What

Tom Lewis

Skorzeny had said was the truth. Gerda, bless her stupid heart, had been brainwashed from the beginning of National Socialism. That Adolf Hitler had been the best man at their wedding was, to her, the highest honor a woman of the Third Reich could hope to have. He chuckled to himself again at Edda's revelation of his sleep-talking. He knew for a fact that Gerda herself never knew about that, since from the very night of their wedding, after he'd screwed her brains out, she'd fallen asleep and snored like a sawmill, and from that night on, they had slept in separate bedrooms. Gerda's idea of the marriage bed was for making babies, and she had been damned good at it.

"And your children?"

Bormann realized Skorzeny was simply making polite conversation, like the way two professors riding in the same train compartment might. "They are all well. Active. Healthy. I don't see them as much as I'd like to." Bormann decided to change the subject back to the business at hand. "Are your men in place on the trains?"

"Yes, sir. They are all good men, too. Not even the whole Italian Army could dislodge them if it came to a fight."

Bormann grunted, good naturedly, "Shit, the last thing on earth the Italian Army wants to do is fight. I think everything in Rome will be all right. And if Ciano doesn't play ball, we'll simply turn those trains around and send them right back to Germany."

"Who's Ciano?"

"Count Galeazo Ciano. Mussolini's son-in-law. Very bright fellow, but a royal snob. His official office is that of Prime Minister, but in reality he has, more or less, the same job with Mussolini that I have with the Fuehrer. It would

Hitler's Judas

be better if their positions were reversed. *Il Duce,* in my humble opinion, isn't worth a pot full of his own piss. He's a strutting clown. A military eunuch. I don't understand why the Fuehrer puts up with him like he does."

"Well, that's none of our concern, is it?"

"No, Otto. We have our orders. God, it's cold up here. How long before we land?"

Skorzeny glanced at his watch. "In about two hours. Why don't you try to sleep some? We have a full day ahead of us."

"I'll try." But Bormann wouldn't have allowed himself to drift off even if he could have. Instead, he closed his eyes and went over the first moves of his plan for the ten thousandth time.

Three hours later, he was riding away from the small airport twenty kilometers north of Rome in the comfortable warmth of Ciano's car, the window between them and the chauffeur snugly closed. "I must say, Herr Reichsleiter, this visit and your rather cryptic telephone call beforehand are a monumental surprise. Does Hitler not know you are here?"

"No, nor I trust, does your father-in-law. It is important that I talk to you alone."

"Really! What could we possibly have to talk about?"

Bormann gave Ciano his most menacing look. "Plenty. And don't you look down your aristocratic nose at me, Ciano. I don't give a tinker's damn how you personally feel about Hitler or me. I'll make this short and to the point. At precisely two o'clock this afternoon, the two ammunition trains you and Mussolini have been begging for will be at

Tom Lewis

the border. If you want them to proceed on to Rome, you will be kind enough to do me a small favor. If you refuse, I'll have them both turn right around and your pathetic Army won't see one single bullet."

"No need to threaten me, Bormann. What is it you want?"

"I want to see the Pope. Tonight."

"You want— *what?* Are you *serious?* The Pope considers you and your mad master no less than the Antichrist!"

Bormann came right back at him, "There are many who think Pius himself is the Antichrist, but that is all neither here nor there. I want you to set up a private, and I do mean *private,* audience with him, and I know you can do it."

"This is insanity. Blackmail!"

"Correct, but no skin off your nose. As the two kids said after their first fuck, you don't tell nobody, I don't tell nobody."

"You're a crude peasant, Bormann, and crazier than Hitler is. What makes you think the Pope will see you, of all people?"

"Because, my dear *Count*, you and I both know that the operation of the Catholic Church doesn't depend on faith, it depends on money. Positive cash flow. And I have brought along a rather large personal gift. In addition, I have certain extremely critical information he will want to know immediately. I'm well aware you're bright enough to figure out that I want something in return, but that's my business. You just tell him that there are ten millions of good green American dollars I wish to dump in his personal

Hitler's Judas

collection plate tonight, with more to come. He'll see me."

"He will crucify me."

"He will bless you. Now. Do you want those trains or don't you?"

The audience was held in a small room that was part of Pius' private apartment, but Bormann couldn't have cared less whether it would be in the Sistine Chapel or in the smallest Vatican broom closet. Carrying the heavy suitcase, he followed Ciano and a Cardinal whose name he couldn't remember into the sparsely furnished chamber and found himself face to face with Pope Pius XII, who offered his ring to be kissed. Bormann bent over it willingly. For what he was after, he would have kissed the Holy Father's ecclesiastic behind!

"Sit, my son. We can spare you ten minutes."

Bormann did as he was bid, plopped the suitcase down between them, opened it, and watching the Pope's eyes for a reaction, said, "Then, at one million dollars per minute, I had better talk fast, Your Holiness, but what I have to say is for your ears only."

The face of the bespectacled Pontiff with the strong chin and receding hairline showed nothing. No frown, no smile. Nothing. He raised his hand ever so slightly and Ciano and the Cardinal instantly beat a quiet but hasty retreat. "We are alone, Herr Bormann. What is the meaning of this... This rather generous gift to Mother Church?"

Bormann knew the Holy Father, a known Germanophile, spoke perfect German, having lived there during the 1920's as nuncio. Before he was elected Pope in 1939, he had served as papal secretary of state, had worked

− 108 −

Tom Lewis

hard—and successfully—to fashion concordats with several authoritarian regimes, including Italy's Facist State and Stalin's Communism, in addition to those of Nazism (which Hitler had repeatedly violated) and though he had been slow to recognize the danger of Hitler's rise to power, he had been just as slow to publicly denounce the Nazi dictator to the world.

Bormann decided to waste no time in his opening gambit. "The Fuehrer is furious over your blatant and continuous assistance to refugees and escaping Jews. He is planning to bomb the Vatican."

Now Pius' face took on some expression, quickly passing from pale shock to red indignation. "You lie. He wouldn't *dare.*"

"Haven't you read *Mein Kampf*? I assure you that a man who is ready and willing to eradicate the entire Jewish race *would* dare. He wouldn't think twice at swatting a few priests who have irritated him like so many mosquitoes. He is irrational, and in my opinion, rapidly slipping over the edge of insanity."

"But what of his alliance with Mussolini? Italy?"

"What of it? He likes Mussolini for some unfathomable reason, that's true, but he has nothing but contempt for your native country or its people. He uses Italian soldiers as mere cannon fodder, and you know it. But I can stop him from dropping bombs on your church."

"How?"

"That, Holy Father, is my secret."

"You are bluffing."

"From your point of view, I certainly could be, but do you really want to take that chance? And be the last Pope of the Holy Roman Empire? Well, at least the Roman part of it."

"Assuming all this is true, why have you come to warn me?"

"Because I want something in return. To use the only Latin I remember from school, *quid pro quo*."

This brought, finally, a smile from Pius. "My son, before I was Pope, I was a priest, and all priests are taught to listen carefully. Go on."

Bormann leaned forward, sensing the right moment had come to play his trump card. He pointed to the suitcase, and looked Pius XII in the eye. "This is good American currency. Ten million symbolic tokens. I am sure this war will be over within two years, three at most, and our German currency will then be worthless because Hitler will surely lose this war and we Germans will lose our country. However, at the Rome train yards, there are trucks being loaded as we speak, with crates marked as 8mm ammunition, but several crates hold no bullets, Holy Father, they are full of German gold. Forty million dollars worth of it. As soon as I leave here, and make one telephone call, it will be delivered to your front gate! Yours to dispose of as you wish, on one condition."

"Which is?"

"I don't delude myself that I am the only one who can see doomsday ahead in Germany. I know there is a shadow movement afoot in the Fatherland; a secret cabal of highly placed military types, industrial leaders, men in high political position, who are scheming to get out before the end and save their Nazi necks. I also have reason to believe you are helping them. You and your priests. I'm cognizant

Tom Lewis

Germany is divided, north and south, by a high Protestant wall, but I also know there are little Catholic chinks and gaps in it here and there, all the way through Schleswig-Holstein to Denmark. Churches and monasteries that also serve as safe houses. Priests who walk around as ordinary citizens and vice versa. An intricate system of escape routes.

"I have been called an opportunist in my time, and maybe that is true. I certainly am a realist. I wish to know the code name for that group, how they operate, and who their leader is, and I know you can tell me."

"So you and Hitler can arrest and execute them?"

"No. So I can *join* and help finance them. The gold I have arranged to deliver to you tonight is, let's say, a down payment for tickets to Argentina. Tickets for myself and my family. Give me what I want, and I will also guarantee that not so much as a smoke bomb falls on your house."

Bormann leaned back in his chair like a smug defense lawyer who had rested his case brilliantly. By his mental calculations, he had about one minute left. Pius made him wait only half of it.

"The man you should seek out is Alois Manfred von Bittnerhof."

"The Hamburg shipbuilder? Bittnerhof! Of course. I should have guessed. He has a wallet fat enough to do it, too!"

"Not, I assume, as fat as yours."

Bormann laughed heartily. "True. True enough. And what is the code name for his organization?"

"They call it— Odessa."

"*Odessa*. Thank you, Holy Father. We have struck a good deal."

"Are you Catholic, Herr Bormann?"

"I am now, I suppose. Your latest convert."

"Is there anything else you would like to, ah, confess?"

Bormann shook his head. "You only gave me ten minutes. I have personally signed orders for deeds already done—and will be—that would make your past inquisitors seem like cherubs and archangels. Such a confession would take all night, and I still have much to do— on your behalf."

"Then go in peace, my son."

CHAPTER 10

Frau Irmgard von Hellenbach came downstairs and showed her son the bravest face she could. "She's finally asleep. I'm sure she will be all right after a few days rest. I've never seen such hysteria. It must have been terrifying for her."

"It's gone, Mother. All gone. Leveled to the ground. Must have been a direct hit. I found her wandering around in the rubble, babbling like an idiot child. Out of her mind."

"You did the right thing to bring her here, Harald. They didn't find her mother's body?"

Harald von Hellenbach took another swallow of the cognac before answering, noticing how badly his hands still shook. "No. Not even any body *parts*. *Verdammte Amerikaner*. I hope the Fuehrer kills every last one of them, down to the last man, woman, and child."

Hitler's Judas

Frau von Hellenbach walked to the frosted-over window and stared out over the frozen garden. *What can it possibly be like in Russia right now?* "She will be all right, son. Do you have to go back to Berlin right away?"

"Yes. Immediately. There's only the one train from Freiburg nowadays. Damn it, Mother, I warned them both to sell that ratty hotel and get out of Stuttgart. Elisabeth and her mother *knew* ball bearings and engines are manufactured there. English and American planes are bombing every industrial town in Germany, and Goering's so-called Air Force can't seem to stop one of them. Damn them *all!*"

"Elisabeth will be quite safe here, I should think. I doubt if the enemy would waste bombs on the pitiful toys and cuckoo clocks they make around here."

Harald hadn't heard her. He slammed the empty tumbler down on the table, stood, put on his overcoat, and headed for the door. His hand on the knob, he paused, looked at his mother with a grimace, and said, "I only had three days, and was going to ask her to marry me."

"Is that so? Your brother may have something to say about that."

"He's had his chances. Elisabeth belongs with me, Mutti. I'm the one who can best take care of her, especially now. Besides, I don't think Horst is the marrying kind anyway."

"That's what people said about your father until I came into the picture."

"That was another time altogether. How is the old soldier, by the way?"

"Getting still older, I hope. I haven't heard from him

– 114 –

Tom Lewis

in a while. You'd better go if you don't want to miss that train. Don't worry about Elisabeth. She'll be fine. She'll be good company for me as well. This is much too big a house to be alone in."

"Yes, well, I'm off then, take care, Mother. Heil Hitler."

Frau von Hellenbach watched him limp down the path. No hug, no kiss, no wave, nothing but yet another 'Heil Hitler'. *But that's all right, Harald. You are a good man. A faithful son, and a good Nazi. Oh, yes, you're a very good Nazi.*

Frau von Hellenbach sat down and picked up her knitting, unable to force back her tears. That's all the women of Hitler's Reich could do any more. Knit, cry, and wait for more bad news.

It took Elisabeth five days to get her emotions under control. Her future mother-in-law then put her to work altering a number of her own dresses and coats so the poor girl would have something decent to wear. In the afternoon of the seventh day, Elisabeth was surprised to hear her say, "Why don't we go into town and see if we can find you a pair of shoes. I also want to pay a visit to our lawyer."

"Lawyer? Why?"

"Elisabeth, you may know I come from Kiel. When my parents died, I inherited their remote beach cottage on the Baltic, just north of Travemunde. It isn't much, but if worse comes to worse, and we are invaded, you and Harald could live there in relative obscurity until Germany can recover from this disaster. I want to deed it over to you now. Consider it an early wedding present."

"Why, that's a wonderful gesture, but I don't

Hitler's Judas

understand, are you saying I should marry Harald?"

"I'm saying I know I will never see my husband again, and I don't believe we will see Horst alive again either. I want to hold at least one grandchild on my lap before I die."

Elisabeth hugged the older woman. "You are wrong about Horst, Mama Irmgard. He will come back to us. He told me he would, and I believed him. I wonder where he is right now?"

"I don't know, Elisabeth. I pray I'm wrong and you are right, but my intuition tells me he's at the bottom of some cold ocean. Come, put your coat on. Let's go shopping."

The U-119 had never been under this long. Or this deep. The depth charge explosions had stopped over two hours ago, but Horst had kept them down. The two destroyers could still be lurking up there, waiting them out. It was slow torture. Every new creak and straining bolt was a sign that the next sound would be the last one they would ever hear before the boat imploded; millions of tons of seawater crushing them all like squashed ants. Every leak, every new spout of water from this pipe join or that one was perhaps the satanic prelude to the total rupture of the steel hull around them. Death would be almost instantaneous. Through the blue-yellow haze, Horst looked at his watch. Only three more minutes before the life-giving oxygen in the cylinders each man wore would expire. There was nothing left to do but go up and fight it out. Horst removed his own mask long enough to shout, "Blow tanks. Surface!"

Tom Lewis

The U-119 shuddered, and then rose like a cork. Three of the men standing around him fainted from the inertia caused by the sudden, rapid rise, like that of an out-of-control elevator.

It seemed forever. An excruciating eternity. But at last, the bow of the U-Boat broke above the surface. Horst pushed the Battle-Stations button, climbed up the ladder, and with the last of his strength, undogged the hatch cover. Men below him tore their masks off as God's great gift of fresh, cold air flooded into the hull. Horst was only halfway into the tower before his starved brain registered their good luck. The U-119 had surfaced into the midst of a north Atlantic gale! Over the fury of the wind and crashing, twenty-foot waves that would have easily capsized a surface vessel, he heard Chief Oskar Knapp's voice, screaming, "Ain't this the most beautiful sight you ever saw? We made, it Herr Kaleun. Goddamn us all to hell, we fucking *made it!*"

Automatically, Horst gave fast orders to turn the boat's nose into the teeth of the wind. Then, "I want double lookouts. Now! Every man does one hour watches, and nobody so much as blinks!" He turned to his First Officer, "Go below, Rudiger, get some rest. You'll have to relieve me in an hour. Their planes may be gone, but you can bet those destroyers are still in the neighborhood."

The baby-faced officer didn't need to be told twice. As his head disappeared through the hatch, Horst looked at his Chief. "Damage report?"

"It's a miracle. Nothing we can't fix if we can stay up for a while."

"Casualties?"

"Torpedoman Fromisch is dead. Lost his hold and took a blow on the temple. One man has a broken leg, and several others have bumps and bruises."

"That's it?"

"Yes, sir."

"We were lucky this time. We'll stay up just long enough to charge the batteries, Oskar. Go below and have somebody sew Fromisch up. We'll bury him before we dive again."

"Aye, aye, sir"

Horst glanced at the men around him. Each was braced against the weather, glasses fastened to their eyes, though none could see more than fifty meters. Horst smiled into the spray lashing his face. This time, he didn't mind the vicious cold and wind that, with soaked clothing, could freeze a man where he stood in under two hours. The storm had been their deliverance, and from the looks of it, would last a while. Certainly long enough to charge the batteries. Then they could dive and turn west, putting distance between them and the east bound convoy they had attacked. That done, they could change to a southerly course, and hope they could make it home before they ran out of fuel. It would be close, but he was sure they could do it. *If* they were not spotted by enemy aircraft, bringing more destroyers that were faster than greyhounds. His only choice was to run submerged by day, and on the surface at night.

And pray.

Forty-eight hours later, Horst held a quiet conference in his cramped quarters. First Officer Rudiger Heidt and

Tom Lewis

Chief of the Boat Oskar Knapp raised their eyebrows when Horst said, "It has to be the radios. Their ASPIC is good and their planes are better, but the enemy knows where we are, where we have been, and where we are going. It *has* to be the radio signals. They have broken our codes. I'm sure of it."

"But Captain," Heidt protested, "Admiral Doenitz and the High Command say the Enigma machine code is unbreakable. It's so complex, no one could—"

"Nothing is unbreakable," Horst broke in. "Think about it. For a while, after the Good Time, it was just like now. Not only did they seem to know which convoy our wolf packs were going to attack, they even knew precisely where we would do it. Then, Uncle Karl had that fourth wheel added to the machine, and we had a spell of relative freedom of the sea, with good results. Now, it's the same thing all over again. I think they had broken the machine codes and it simply took them some extra time to break the fourth wheel."

"It makes sense to me," Oskar agreed. "The odds are they just can't be that lucky every time. We're like minnows in a tub. I'll bet we are losing half our boats on every patrol. That's a lot of good men. A lot of good friends."

"Too many," Horst whispered. "But we're not going to be next, not if I can help it."

"What do you plan to do, Captain?" Heidt wanted to know.

Horst looked up at both men, a smirk on his face. "Chief," he said with innocent eyes, "That last depth charge attack destroyed our aerials, didn't it? We can neither send nor receive, can we?"

Knapp grinned back, knowing exactly where this was

Hitler's Judas

going. "No, sir. Not a single word!"

"I thought not. Now, when we surface tonight, do another inspection and make sure your initial report was correct."

"Yes sir! I'll make damn sure."

"Right. You're excused, Knapp. I want to speak to Heidt alone for a moment." Oskar Knapp jumped up, saluted with another knowing smile, and hurried away.

Horst looked at his wide-eyed junior officer. "Rudiger, you have been through a lot since you've been with me. I'm sure you have noticed that the convoys have increased by leaps and bounds, which is why Doenitz ordered us back into wolf pack duty. It can only mean one thing. The Allies are beefing up for an invasion. I know you're a capable officer, but I also know you are a dedicated, dyed-in-the-wool Nazi. You want to know what my greatest accomplishment has been since I took over command of this boat?"

"I, well..."

"Yes, we have been successful. Yes, we have sunk a lot of tonnage. Yes, we have all earned medals, and yes, we all have a great deal to tell our grandchildren one day. But the most important thing is we have managed to stay alive! I know you silently question why I sometimes turn and run after firing torpedoes at ships. It's true that sometimes we don't know for sure whether or not we sank them, but we have stayed afloat long enough to fire time and time again, and tally enough confirmed kills to be considered one of Admiral Doenitz's best boats. Now, the way I see it, you have two choices: When we get back to base, you can tattle to Uncle Karl that I have defied his orders by refusing to use our radio, in which case I will face a court martial and

Tom Lewis

probably a firing squad, and you will be reassigned to another boat, one very likely commanded by a man who is even more a zealot than you are, and get yourself blown to bits on your very next patrol.

"Or, you can keep your mouth shut, take your chances with me again, and hope I can help you celebrate your twenty-third birthday. Think about it. Sleep on it. It's your choice."

"I don't have to sleep on it, Herr Kaleun. I shall be exactly like those three monkeys. Hear no evil, see no evil, speak no evil. Like you said, we will have a lot to tell grandchildren one day. I'd like to be around to do that."

"Good. I knew you were a smart sailor. Now go see if you can spot anything we can shoot our last torpedo at."

Heidt saluted stiffly and left. Horst watched him go, and frowned. Poor kid. This time, there would be no brass band playing. No pretty girls on the quay waving their flowers. No Admiral to come aboard and pin his medal on. But he would get his leave, and he would see his mother and sister— at least one more time.

When the U-119 finally made port, Horst was met at the pens, not by his Admiral, but by another man he had always called Uncle. Brigadier General Karl Heinz Eppinger took him by the elbow and gently told him his father had died a hero's death in Russia, that his girlfriend's mother was also dead, and the Stuttgart address where he'd planned to go no longer existed.

He soon discovered he would not have to make the long detour to Dresden, either, to see the parents of Torpedoman 2nd Class Emil Fromisch. They were also dead.

Killed in a fiery bombing raid worse than the one in Stuttgart.

Horst von Hellenbach was beginning to feel that the stink of his boat, his men, and he, himself, was a far better odor than the stench of death that was spreading over his country like an unstoppable plague, and he had no illusions, no doubts that it would get worse before it was all over. A lot worse.

CHAPTER II

Fraulein Kemper looked distraught. Harried. "Sir, my office is full! All of them are demanding to see our Fuehrer at once. Please, what shall I tell them?"

From behind his neat desk, Bormann frowned at her. "Stop wringing your hands, Fraulein. Relax, I'll take care of it." With the frantic woman at his heels, Bormann got up and walked into the outer office. The moment he opened the door, Himmler, von Ribbentrop, Goering, and Albert Speer all jumped to their feet in unison, each trying to outdo the other with their shouts of indignation at being kept waiting for so long.

Bormann calmly held up both hands, a manufactured look of sympathy on his face. "I'm very sorry, gentlemen, the Fuehrer is extremely busy, and not feeling at all well

Hitler's Judas

today. I suggest you all try again tomorrow. I'll see what I can do. But do call first to make your appointments. First come, first served."

As had happened so many times before, the shouting gradually subsided to putrid grumbles of anger and frustration. To a man, they glowered at the Fuehrer's personal secretary, not even trying to mask their hatred and jealousy, but knowing they had no other choice, they filed out of the office. Only Himmler held back. He turned to face Bormann and in a soft voice full of pure venom, said, "Sometimes you overstep the boundaries of your privilege, Bormann. One day you will have to pay the piper."

Bormann cocked his head at the diminutive creature who so looked like a small town schoolteacher. With mocking contempt, he answered, "And when might that be? When *you* become Fuehrer? Don't try to threaten me, Himmler. I know full well that's what your ultimate ambition is. But that will never happen so long as Adolf Hitler lives, or I do. Run along and find some more undesirables to shoot and another batch of Jews to deport. That's what you're good at. It's the *only* thing you're good at." With those words, Bormann turned on his heel, gave the white-faced receptionist a wicked wink, and went back inside his own office, leaving the former chicken farmer stewing in his own sick gravy.

He sat back down at his desk and reopened the file his brother had passed to him, studied it for yet another half hour, then placed it in his briefcase, highly satisfied. He glanced at his watch. All right. *Time to start phase two*. He knocked twice, and entered Hitler's gigantic office, carrying a dozen or more papers that needed the Fuehrer's signature.

Tom Lewis

Hitler signed them all without question, then looked up and said, "Will you have a cup of tea with me, Martin? I need a short break from all this. Those cowardly Generals are making me crazy with their ineptitude."

"Certainly, my Fuehrer. I'd love a cup. Shall I pour?" This was a calculated gesture on Bormann's part, knowing Hitler's already severe nervous condition had worsened considerably in recent weeks and months. He now exhibited more twitches and facial tics than ever before, and though he tried his best to hide it, his hands were hardly able to hold a cup, let alone pour from a teapot.

"Yes, thanks," Hitler said. "I'm tired, Martin. I think I will take the short rest at Berchtesgaden you suggested yesterday. Only for a day or two, mind you."

"I have already made the arrangements, Fuehrer. A couple days with Eva and your dogs will have you back in fine fettle within hours. I can take care of things here, so long as Himmler behaves."

"Himmler?"

"Oh, you know Himmler. He will never be satisfied until he has a Reich of his own to rule. Goering, too. Don't trust those men, my Fuehrer. Goering's excesses have ruined what once was a splendid body and a fine mind. Himmler is, well, Himmler. Capable of a lot of things, and none of them good, but you know that, too. I think the man was born without blood. His heart pumps snake poison. In any case, a little rest will do you no harm at all."

"That's a fact, sure enough. What about you?"

"Me, Fuehrer?"

"Yes, you. How long has it been since you took some leave?"

Hitler's Judas

"I don't need time off, especially while you're away, but now that you mention it, there is one tiny little favor I might ask of you."

"Ask. I can't remember your ever asking for one."

"I have an elderly uncle. He's too feeble to do his rough farm work now. I've been thinking of bringing him here next month, with your permission of course, to look after my apartment. Clean up, keep my clothes and uniforms up to snuff. You know, like a personal valet. Having him with me would save me a lot of time I could put to better use, while giving him some useful work."

"By all means, bring the old boy to town. He won't—embarrass you will he? In public, I mean."

"Not at all, Fuehrer. He's as close-mouthed as all of us Bormanns, and I doubt if he would ever venture further away from my place than to the nearest pub for his evening beer and schnapps."

"That wouldn't be all that bad a life, would it? Well, you have my permission, and do take a day or two off yourself, Martin. I gather you have things in order, as usual. Say, did you ever get that business with the Treasury worked out? Last time I talked to Schackt, he told me you were driving him insane with all that movement of money."

Bormann admitted, "It's true I have been shifting much of it here and there, to different banks here and in Switzerland, but I know where every penny is, and if any one bank suffered an unlucky bomb blast, it would not be enough to cause the slightest hitch in the country's financial transactions. As far as that fool Schackt is concerned, any movement farther than to his kitchen or his toilet would confuse him hopelessly."

– 126 –

Tom Lewis

"So, so right. Will you pour another cup, please? You know, I think I might take the rest of today off as well. Do you suppose you could push my schedule up a bit?"

"Your chauffeur is standing by already, and your plane is fueled and ready to fly this very afternoon if you wish."

"Martin, you are a wonder. What would I do without you?"

"I live only to serve you and the Reich, my Fuehrer, as best I can. I'll go call the staff at the Obersalzburg right now. Shall I call Eva as well?"

"No. Let me surprise her. Poor girl, she waits for me just as patiently as Blondi does. She deserves a better life than one with me, but she's made her choice hasn't she? Mind the store, Martin, and when I get back, you are ordered to take a week off yourself."

"Thank you, Fuehrer. Gerda will be happy to hear that!"

Back at his desk, Bormann made the official calls then dialed Skorzeny's number. "Otto, the Fuehrer is leaving Berlin this afternoon for a short rest at home. He wants that second little operation we discussed done tonight. Can you manage it?"

"With pleasure, Herr Bormann. Will you meet us at the church?"

"Count on it. I wouldn't miss it for the world."

At midnight, one of Skorzeny's men, a lock-picking specialist, took no more than twenty seconds to let Bormann into Dr. Blashke's office. Bormann instructed the man to wait outside the door, turned his flashlight on, and made straight for the filing cabinets, making a mental note to

Hitler's Judas

give his brother a small bonus. What an extraordinary piece of luck that Helmut had thought to include in his thorough report that he and Klaus Berger shared the same dentist! He deftly exchanged his and Berger's dental records, and was back in his car in ten minutes. Taking his time, he drove to the Wansee area, easily found the dirt street he had carefully scouted weeks beforehand, parked the car and turned off the lights, glad the heater was working.

Klaus Berger wrapped the quilt around him tighter, wondering if he would ever be warm again. It was impossible to even go to sleep nowadays on this hard living room sofa that had been his bed for almost two years, while Trina, naturally, enjoyed the relative warm comfort—and soft bed—of the only bedroom of the small apartment they shared in the rundown building in the *Prinz Eugin Strasse*. Shit. This rat hole was anything but Princely.

Klaus, teeth chattering, cursed himself yet again for the decision he had made to marry Trina Linz. Though it had not saved their careers, the trick, the phony marriage, had probably saved both their lives. But what life? One bad decision always leads to another. He and Trina, a flaming lesbian, had both had to also forgo any kind of companionship, and lack of sex made both of them irritable when they were forced to be together, which was at least part of every night. The worst? Sharing the tubless bathroom! The added fact that both were living off their theatrical friends didn't make life any better, either. If it wasn't for the occasional bits he did at The Hole, he would have gone round the bend long ago. When would this goddamn war ever be over? When would he ever see—

– 128 –

Tom Lewis

The crash of the front door being bashed in was not louder than Trina's scream. Only *different*. His eyes were really not seeing her ugly naked body running towards him, yelling for help at the top of her ugly voice. In total denial, his mind was too numb to realize what was happening even as he saw her being clubbed senseless by the brutes in the black uniforms, all shouting at the same time.

Coarse hands reached for him. Yanked him off the sofa.

Bad Breath number one said, "Klaus Berger, you are under arrest."

Bad Breath number two added, "For crimes against nature and the State."

Bad Breath number three pinned his arms behind him and growled, "March, you fucking queer. Next thing up your ass will be a bullet!"

No! It was not real. None of this was *real*. It was only a dream. A nightmare. A grainy scene from a surreal movie. None of the pain or bruises he felt from being kicked down three flights of uncarpeted wooden stairs was real. This wasn't happening, was it? The freezing outside air was not colder than his bed, was it? He was not being thrown like a sack of grain into the back of a truck, was he? Trina, coming back to consciousness from the cold on her naked body, was not grasping, holding on to him like a lover and begging to know what was going on, was she?

What? Was somebody else screaming?

"Klaus? My God, they got you, too?"

"Hans? Hansl, is that you?" Klaus' eyes, adjusting to the darkness of the canvas-covered truck bed, recognized his former lover. "God in Heaven, Hans. What in God's name is *happening?*"

— 129 —

Hitler's Judas

The three of them had no idea how long it took to get to where they were going. They didn't feel the cold, or the bumpy ride. Klaus didn't recognize the smell of urine when Trina—or was it Hans—pissed on his bare feet. Probably on all their feet, since they had huddled so close together out of common terror. But then the truck lurched to a halt. Its back cover thrown back. The tailgate dropped down.

"Get out, you homo swine." A voice ordered.

Klaus and Hans clambered out first. Neither man had on a jacket or coat they could offer poor Trina to cover her nakedness when they helped her down. Klaus looked around. Took it all in at once: Churchyard. Churchyard and *graveyard*. Three open holes— on top of already existing graves. Expressionless, helmeted storm troopers, standing around with shovels in their hands, their faces, hands, and glint of the dreaded *Waffen-SS* insignia lit up by the lights of the truck and a car, which also lit the windowless rear wall of the church itself. *We are going to die!*

Other soldiers grabbed the three of them by the arms as their leader, a stocky Major, walked into the light, holding a piece of paper. He pretended to read from it. "You, Johannes Christian Trindle, have been found guilty by a Court of the People of crimes against nature and crimes against the Reich. Your sentence is death."

They pushed Hans up against the wall and moved out of the way. Klaus noticed the shovels had been replaced by submachine guns and the men holding them had moved back about five meters. The Major yelled, "Fire!" and the frigid night air was instantly filled with a barking noise. The smell of cordite assaulted Klaus' nose as he watched

– 130 –

Tom Lewis

Hans slip sideways down the wall like a passed-out drunk falling off his chair. Four soldiers picked him up and carried him over to one of the open graves. His body made a muffled thump as it dropped in on top of an uncovered coffin.

Klaus barely heard the terrible words repeated as they pushed Trina up against the pocked gray plaster. Klaus watched her squint against the light from the vehicles, take a step forward, and begin to plead, screaming, "I have done nothing! Nothing at all, do you *hear?* I—"

The chattering guns silenced her. Bullets flung her body backwards against the wall, and she fell to the hard ground like a dropped and broken doll, arms and legs all-akimbo. Her hair covered most of her face, but Klaus could distinctly see, almost *count*, dozens of small, black holes in her white skin, now oozing—

"Klaus Gerhart Berger, you have been found guilty by a Court of the People of crimes against nature . . ."

Klaus didn't hear the rest. He didn't hear the plop of Trina's body being dumped into the second open grave. He didn't feel the pressure of hands forcing him into the glare of the headlights. He didn't smell his own fear or taste his own bile. He was not aware he had closed his eyes, his nose, his mouth. But his brain was finally working, telling the rest of him that this was no dream. No surrealistic scene from a horror movie. In the next instant, he was going to find out if there was a God after all. Was there time enough to pray there was one?

"Ready..."

No, there wasn't.

"Aim..."

Klaus' bowels let go.

Hitler's Judas

"HALT! Hold your fire!"

Klaus fell to his knees, not conscious that he had. Had the voice he'd heard come from God? Must have, since it stopped the bullets. He opened his eyes, but saw nothing but light. He blinked.

"I may have a use for this man," the voice of his unseen savior said. "Clean him up and give him a blanket or a coat. Then tidy up here and leave. I'll take him with me,"

It was then that Klaus Berger fainted.

He came to, warm— and alive, but found that he was still shaking uncontrollably from his ordeal. It took him several minutes to discern he was in an automobile driving at speed through a dark countryside. He glanced at the driver. "I know you, don't I?" he croaked.

"We've met."

"You saved my life. I don't know how to thank you." It was all Klaus could think to say.

"I do. But first, allow me to tell you what I know about you. You were born at Wiesbaden in 1901, a year after I was born. Your mother still lives there. You have no other relatives. Until the war, you enjoyed a very successful career, and have the reputation of being one of Germany's best actors, if not the best. I have seen several of your movies, and have been very impressed with your many talents, especially your diversity. You are quite convincing in all your character roles, whether the dashing millionaire playboy, or the old, snooty butler. You are a master at makeup, disguises and language dialects. My file also tells me you have a photographic memory in addition to a formidable intellect. In short, you are able to truly *become* the characters you play, whether on stage or on the screen.

"I have saved your miserable, homosexual hide because I have a job for you. A role. Actually, two roles. Your life depends on how well you play them.

"If you do them perfectly, as I expect, you will become rich, and one day famous beyond your wildest dreams. If you fail, you will assuredly join your unfortunate friends in that church cemetery. Have I made myself clear?"

Klaus shuddered again. "Crystal clear. What... Who am I supposed to play?"

"Not just play. Become."

"I understand. Who, then?"

"First an intermediate test. I am taking you to a farm near Halberstadt. You will have one week to become my elderly uncle. You will have to look like him, act like him, walk and talk like him, convince me you *are* him. If you do, then you will train for the largest, most important role of your life. You will become me. Martin Bormann."

CHAPTER 12

Manfred von Bittnerhof hoisted his elephantine bulk part way out of his chair and offered Bormann the seat opposite his desk in the makeshift office bunker. "Please sit down, Herr Reichsleiter. I apologize for having to receive you here in such shabby surroundings, but my former office overlooking the yards has been destroyed. Hamburg is being bombed almost daily, you know. May I offer you something to drink? A glass of wine, perhaps? Whiskey? I have some good Scotch."

Bormann sat down and eyed the man with the porcine features, who, after Krupp and one or two others, was the richest man in all of Germany. *I'm sure you do.* "No. Not just yet, thank you. I take it you have been expecting me?" Bormann patted the suitcase he had brought in with him.

Tom Lewis

"And this modest birthday present?" He watched for a gleam in the little pig eyes.

It was there, all right. "Yes, I have. A certain Latin cleric has informed me you have had a change of heart regarding your politics and wish to join our ah, travel club."

"Change of heart? Let me tell you something, Bittnerhof, I haven't 'changed' my politics. I never had any— except those of survival. To me, politics equals convenience. If I were Italian, I'd be a better fascist than Ciano. If Russian, I'd be Stalin's most ruthless communist. Here, I am—"

"Hitler's best and most faithful Nazi. I'm sure they don't call you 'the Brown Eminence' for nothing."

"Exactly. And when I get to America, I'll probably become a first rate Republican capitalist, expert in silent partnerships."

Bittnerhof laughed lustily at Bormann's play on words, then leaned forward. "America? I thought you wanted to join us in Argentina."

"I do, but only for a while."

"I see. Hell, if I were a few years younger, I might join you there, but I imagine I shall be content to live like a baron in our fictitious Odessa Fourth Reich. In any case, getting out of Germany cleanly will not be a cakewalk for any of us. Timing will be critical. We must wait until nearly the last minute, when there is total confusion in both the government and the country."

Bormann didn't comment on that pearl of wisdom. He had no intention whatsoever of waiting for Hitler's *Valhalla* to come crashing down on his head, courtesy of the onrushing Russians, or the English and Americans

Hitler's Judas

when they came pouring in from the west, or both. That would be much too risky. Too many things could go wrong. But Bittnerhof didn't have to know that, did he? "Do you have the escape routes and contacts already set up?"

"Yes, and I am prepared to share them with you, provided you show me the same kind of good faith you have with our devout friend in the south."

Bormann patted the suitcase again. "Ten million in here, and as soon as I can arrange it, fifty million in gold bullion, to be sent in two installments, by submarine. All you have to do is tell me the precise spot to drop it off."

"Fifty million! How the devil have you managed it?"

Bormann affected a yawn. "Creative bookkeeping and constant, secret shifting of funds. It's hard to hit a moving target, and Walter Schackt couldn't hit the floor if he fell out of bed. Hitler doesn't know it, but on paper, his Treasury is worth about a hundred and fifty million more than Schackt can show him. Only I know where the excess is. That, by the way, is something you'd best keep in mind, Bittnerhof. Your mind alone."

"Don't worry," the fat man assured him, "Our organization hasn't eluded the Gestapo thus far by being stupid or indiscreet." He reached into a desk drawer and removed a bound multi-file envelope which he handed over. "It's all in here. I suppose I don't need to tell you to burn it after you have committed it to memory. We operate our network on a highly controlled need-to-know-only basis. Mr. A doesn't know what route Mr. B will take, or even who Mr. B is. Odessa's internal security is tighter than the hulls I build."

"Code system?"

— 136 —

Tom Lewis

"Of course. Based on biblical references. Your code name will be passed to you in two weeks time by a total stranger whom you will never see again. He will tell you his name is Noah. So. Are we in business?"

Bormann nodded, offering his hand to seal the deal. "Noah, eh? Interesting symbolism. I'll take that glass of Scotch now. And, I want to see the plans for the new U-Boats you're building. I promised the Fuehrer I'd give him a report— my 'official reason' for this short visit."

"I understand," Bittnerhof said, reaching into a second drawer for a bottle. He gave Bormann a conspiratorial wink. "Just between you and me, Herr Reichsleiter, if I wanted to get to America myself, I'd bypass Argentina altogether."

"Is that so?"

"Sure. Why waste time and money in the Argentine? I'd simply take one of those U-Boats in close to Mexico or the east coast of the United States, take my money with me, and sneak ashore. From what I hear, their coastal surveillance is atrocious, especially in the southeastern part."

Bormann took the offered glass and snidely answered, "That's the most ridiculous joke I've ever heard. For your information, we've landed a few spies in America that way, with disastrous results. No, thanks, I'll take my chances being an Argentine gaucho for a while. Besides, I don't speak English very well. Where are those plans?"

Bittnerhof pushed a button. "Send Kellermann in, please." He clinked glasses with Bormann. "A toast?" he suggested.

"Why not?"

"*Ein prosit*, Herr Bormann. To all the rancheros in

Hitler's Judas

Argentina."

They had no more than set their glasses down when two raps came on the door. With a loud grunt, von Bittnerhof came out of his chair and admitted a thin, sallow faced man whose skin looked as though it had never seen a single ray of sunlight. He peered at Bormann through wire-framed spectacles, pushing back long hair that kept falling down over them as he very formally bowed. He was carrying an armful of blueprints.

"This is Ludwig Kellermann, Herr Riechsleiter," von Bittnerhof said by way of introduction. "He's our chief naval architect, and will be glad to answer any questions you may have. He knows everything there is to know about U-Boats."

Bormann acknowledged the man with a slight nod. "Kellermann."

"*Ja!* Now, then," von Bittnerhof added, and with surprising nimbleness for such a large man, hurried around his desk and picked up the suitcase Bormann had brought in. With his free hand, he pointed across the room. "Feel free to use my drafting table. I'll just hop down the hall and deposit these papers in a safe place. Call me on the intercom if you need me, and Herr Bormann, do help yourself to more Scotch if you please."

Bormann, however, was not interested in another drink. He got up, walked over to the drafting table and said, "All right, Kellermann. Let's see what you're working on."

"Reichsleiter, the best way is to first show you what we have been using." He spread scaled U-Boat blueprints out, pinning the corners. "What you see here is the Type VIIC. We have built hundreds of this model, and her design

– 138 –

Tom Lewis

hasn't changed appreciably since the last war, which was part of our problem..."

Bormann listened patiently as the man explained how the thing worked, how it could fight, and what its limitations were. Kellermann then pinned over it the plans of a longer, fatter version. "This one is the Type XIV, the tanker/tender the *Kriegsmariner* affectionately call the 'milk cow.' As you can see, she has a much broader beam. She can carry 700 tons of fuel and about 45 tons of munitions and other supplies. We have a number of them, which extends the range of the fighting boats considerably. But, as I said, the biggest problem with both these models is that they must surface to charge the batteries, which last but just so long when boats are submerged. They are terribly vulnerable on the surface. If they are spotted, fast destroyers and especially airplanes can kill them before they can dive deep enough—"

On top of the 'milk cow' plans, Kellermann pinned up cutaway drawings of something entirely different. "—Until now!" he said with professional pride. "We have invented a device which will make all the difference in the world. This is called a snorkel. In lay language, what it does is allow a boat to remain under for an indefinite time, with air to breathe *and* charge batteries."

"Impressive," Bormann said. "When will this— snorkel go into service?"

"Early next month. Mid-January at the latest, but now let me show you our pride and joy."

Bormann smiled indulgently as Kellermann lovingly revealed a third set of blueprints. The thin designer tapped the table with his forefinger. "This beauty, Herr Bormann, is the new Type XXI electroboat. You can plainly see she is twice as big as the old Type VIIC, and much more streamlined. She can carry many, many more torpedoes, can dive deep as 650 feet, has hydrophones capable of picking up an enemy vessel at a distance of fifty miles, and submerged, can do twice the speed of the older boats, some 16.5 knots, in fact."

"Herr Bormann," Kellermann said, his eyes practically misting, "This is the answer to Admiral Doenitz's and the Fuehrer's prayers: The total U-Boat. Utterly lethal, and practically invulnerable. The enemy has nothing close to it."

"How long before it goes into production?"

"In less than a year, by my best estimate."

"Say, by Christmas of 1944?"

"Yes, sir. By then, we should be able to build nearly a hundred, in spite of the bombings."

"I see." *Too late, my talented friend. Far too late for Hitler and the Third Reich, but maybe not too late for me.* "Tell me something, Herr Kellermann. Suppose... Just suppose it was you instead of von Bittnerhof running the show here. What would you do?"

"Well, sir, we both know that could never happen, but if it *was* up to me, and I had *carte blanche*, I would move at least some of them, prefabricated, of course, to bases in Bergen and Trondheim and secretly build them there where bombs aren't falling. At least not yet."

Bormann crossed his arms in front of him. Squinted at the skinny architect. "Could that really be done?"

"Certainly. We couldn't accomplish mass production up there, naturally, but we could build enough of them to perhaps turn the tide."

"One other hypothetical question. If you and von Bittnerhof got direct orders from the Fuehrer to do just that, how long would it take to get the first new model U-Boat operational?"

Kellermann pursed his thin lips. "I could have the prototype ready and tested inside three months. Four maximum." He sighed. "You know, she even has a deep freezer for storing food plus a water maker! This boat could stay under forever." He looked at Bormann wistfully. "Trondheim is a lovely pipe dream, sir, but I doubt if the powers that be would be farsighted enough to move any U-Boat operations up there. It just won't happen."

"No, probably not." *But don't bet on it, little man. Some dreams have a way of coming true. Adolf Hitler — or his signature at the bottom of an order — can make anything possible.* "Thank you, Kellermann. This has been most enlightening. The Fuehrer will be pleased, and you and your staff are to be commended. Don't be surprised if you hear from me again."

CHAPTER 13

Exhausted from driving, Bormann quietly let himself into Edda's apartment and headed for the bathroom, not bothering to check the bedroom. At three in the morning, Edda would no doubt be fast asleep. For once, he decided not to awaken her, since he was too tired for anything but a hot bath and some sleep. He turned the taps on, peeled off his clothes and while the tub was filling, walked into the kitchen to make himself a drink. Edda was sitting there at the table, bent over, her head cradled in her arms which rested on an open, tearstained newspaper. She heard him come in, and raised her head. Bormann immediately noticed her puffy eyes. "What's the matter? Why are you up so late?"

Tom Lewis

Fresh tears ran down Edda's cheeks. "It's terrible, Martin. There was a fire. An old apartment house in the Prinz Eugin Strasse. Burned to the ground."

"So?" Bormann kept his face neutral. "What of it?"

"Several people died. Burned beyond recognition. Klaus was one of them."

"Klaus?"

"Klaus Berger. You know, the actor you saw at The Hole. He lived there with another friend of mine, Trina Linz. It was horrible. Horrible."

"I'm sure." Bormann walked over to the cabinet and reached for the bottle and a glass, smiling. He'd have to commend Skorzeny next time he saw or talked to him. The man was certainly thorough in his work. He poured himself a drink and patted Edda on the head. "I'm sorry to hear about that. Listen, I'm very tired. I'm going to take a bath and get some sleep— on the sofa. How's work on the new film coming?"

"All right, I suppose. My heart just isn't in it."

"Get some rest. You'll feel better tomorrow. Where's the alarm clock? I can't afford to sleep more than three hours."

"On the nightstand where it always is. Why do you have to get up so early?"

"Unfinished business requiring still more driving. I have to be back in Berlin tomorrow night. Hitler will be here by then, and I'll have to be in my office first thing the morning after. Go on to bed. It's too bad about your friends. I'm really very sorry, Edda."

Bormann left her and walked back into the sauna-like bathroom. He adjusted the water temperature, got in, took

– 143 –

one swallow of his drink, and promptly dozed off.

The usual standing water in the two-rut lane to the old farmhouse was frozen solid, making steering a straight line impossible. To keep from having to stand at the door in the cold for more than a few minutes, Bormann blew the horn several times. The heavy oak door cracked open and a white-haired head poked through it momentarily, then, having recognized the visitor, withdrew, out of the wind. Bormann cursed under his breath. No way his Uncle Friedrich would have come out to the car to greet him.

Old Friedrich had hated him since he'd been a child, mainly because young Martin had showed no interest in farming, or anything remotely connected to farm life; animals, the soil, the seasonal changes which dictated what work had to be done. Work that was hard, and never ceased or even let up enough to do more than eat and fall asleep every night, with nothing to look forward to the next day but more of the same. Not the kind of life Bormann had aspired to, though he was strong of back, and quite capable, and had done the summer chores his father had forced him—and Helmut—to do, under his older brother's peasant-rough tutelage. This was an important part of the personal discipline most Prussians considered prerequisite training for adulthood.

Bormann sat there another minute, mulling over his latest lie to Hitler. In spite of his uncle's age, which had taken its gravitational toll on his body, the old horse was still tough. Gnarly as a tree root. His mind, always eccentric, had now reached that no man's land of senility, and inevitably, his life long solitary existence, never once

Tom Lewis

usurped by any woman or even a pet dog, had, like the stone boundaries of his tiny farm, fenced out the rest of the human world to such a degree he never had any visitors, and when he died, he would never be missed.

Bormann got out of the car and walked into the house. Everything was exactly the same as it had been thirty years ago. Every piece of rough furniture. Every unpainted wall. Every ragged rug. But standing by the door to the kitchen was not one but *two* uncles! He stared at first one, then the other, his mouth open.

One of them spoke. "Look at him. Fancy pants Martin. Hitler's little errand boy. Damned if I don't think we fooled him. What do you think, Friedrich?"

"Hee, hee, hee," the other old man cackled. "You're right, Friedrich. He don't know which is which. Hey, boy, lucky thing you had that truck bring his makeup case and wig box out here. Hee, hee. Whatsamatter, Martin, don't you recognize me? I used to make you tote pig shit all day long."

Bormann stood speechless, squinting from one to the other, then laughing with them. "All right. You've had your fun, both of you. Now take those hands out of your pockets and let me see them."

Grudgingly, both men showed their hands. Bormann knew in a second which belonged to his uncle and which were those of the talented actor. He spoke to the man on the left. "Nothing in your makeup kit could hide those swollen, arthritic joints and filthy, broken fingernails, Berger, but otherwise, yes, you fooled me completely. Congratulations. The disguise is remarkable, and your accent perfect. You sounded just like the old fart."

"Damn!" His uncle said. "Never thought about my

Hitler's Judas

hands." He walked into kitchen, sat down heavily on one of the two chairs. He looked up at his nephew, smirking. "But we've had a hell of a lot of fun these last couple of days." Pointing to his imposter, he added, "This guy's good. Hee, hee. Oughta be in the pictures."

Bormann walked past them into the kitchen, making a beeline to a cigar box resting on top of the antique cabinet, which held his uncle's few dishes. He started to open the box.

"Hey, you nosy little turd. That's my personal stuff. You stay outa there!"

Bormann ignored his uncle's outburst, satisfying himself that all the old man's identification papers were just where they had always been, nestled between banknotes, some of which dated back to the time of the Kaiser. He put the box back on the shelf, turned and said. "Get your coats on, both of you."

"What for?" his uncle wanted to know.

"We're going for a walk. There's a chore to do."

He led the two bewildered men through the door that connected the farmhouse to the barn, both structures heated by a huge coal-burning furnace. He made straight for the stalls where his uncle's two oxen stood, chewing cuds. Bormann looked at Klaus with a scowl. "These stinking beasts are Uncle Friedrich's only companions in life. When I was a boy, he had two named Albert and Victoria. Meanest creatures on the face of the earth. Now, lets see if I can remember how to do this."

Klaus and his uncle watched as Bormann expertly led the two monsters from their stalls and hitched them up. He looked around and grunted with satisfaction when he

– 146 –

Tom Lewis

spotted what he wanted; a large hook which he attached to the end of the traces. "Open the door, Berger."

"What are you up to, Martin?" his uncle said, a hint of suspicion in his voice. "It's freezing outside, and snowing to boot."

Berger opened the barn door. It was indeed snowing. Bormann said, "All the better. Pick up that hook, Uncle. Let's go."

Grasping the long switch used as a whip, he drove the reluctant team out, got his bearings, then headed for a spot no more than fifty meters from the house. When they reached it, Bormann looked at the actor and said. "This is where the old well was. I remember how hard my brother and I worked putting in a modern pump and tearing the walls of this one down." He reached down, and with his gloved hand, brushed the snow off a concrete slab which had a large iron ring imbedded in its center. "This must weigh a ton."

At last his uncle understood what Bormann was doing. Without being told to, he lifted the ring and inserted the hook. "Why in hell you want to uncover this old well? Ain't even no water down there any more."

Bormann didn't answer. He switched the team on their rumps, and in a moment, they effortlessly pulled the slab away from the opening. A foul odor gushed upward and caused all three men to cover their noses. The wind soon took it away, however, and Borman handed the reins to Berger. "Hold these."

The actor took them without commenting, and watched in absolute horror as Bormann removed the glove from his right hand, drew a pistol from his coat pocket and

Hitler's Judas

shot his kinsman twice through the heart!

"Good God, man! Your own *uncle?*"

"Shut your mouth," Bormann growled. "He's not the first man I ever killed and probably won't be the last. He served a purpose and after today, he was a liability. You had better serve your purpose, too, Berger. Here, give me a hand."

Still in shock, Berger seemed not to have heard. He stood rooted in his tracks. Bormann shrugged, picked up his uncle's body and dumped it into the well. It took a little maneuvering with the team, but he soon had the cover back over its opening. "The snow will cover it all in a matter of minutes, and no one is likely to find him for years, if ever. Come on, it's cold out here."

Obediently, the shaken actor followed him back to the barn where he unhitched the team, put them back in their stalls, and, with Berger on his heels, went back into the warmth of the house. He once more took the cigar box from the shelf, extracted his uncle's papers, and handed them over "You're my Uncle Friedrich now. Gather up some of his clothes. He keeps a suitcase in the bedroom under the bed." He stared at the still shivering man. "Well? Move, damn you. I'm going out to warm up the car."

Berger jumped to it. In less than five minutes, and with shaking hands, he had the beat-up cardboard suitcase crammed with the old man's washed-out clothing, including a pair or two of long underwear and an ancient cap. He straightened, resisted the sudden urge to run out the back door and keep on running, and carried it out to the waiting car. He threw the suitcase and his makeup and wig cases into the back seat of the Mercedes sedan, climbed into the

– 148 –

cozy front seat and asked, "Where are we going now?"

"To Berlin for one night. Then south. I have a week's leave coming to me. Your performance back there was impressive. Did your homework, too, didn't you? We'll see how well that photographic memory of yours really works."

He put the car in gear and started down the path to the highway. "Might as well begin now, Berger. In heavy increments, I will give you my oral history, down to the most intimate detail. How quickly and how thoroughly you memorize this first installment will possibly determine whether you live long enough to hear the second one. I was born on June 17, 1900, at Halberstadt. My father was a regimental sergeant-major..."

CHAPTER 14

When Bormann got to his office at seven, Hitler was already at work in his. Fraulein Kemper quietly informed him there was one person waiting in hers as well.

"Who?" Without waiting for an answer, he opened the outer door. Seated primly on the sofa, uniform and boots immaculate, the ever bulging briefcase on his lap, was Joseph Goebbels. Bormann decided to be friendly in spite of the fact that the little shit didn't get up.

"Joseph!" Bormann said, in the warmest sarcastic tone he could conjure up. "Did you have an appointment?"

The thin Minister of Propaganda oozed condescension from every pore. His cologne could be smelled from twenty feet away. He arched an eyebrow and replied, "I didn't need to make one, Bormann. The Fuehrer asked me to come

Tom Lewis

first thing this morning. He didn't tell you?"

Bormann let that pass. "Well, why don't we go right in, then." He turned and led Goebbels through his own office to Hitler's door. To teach the smug little bastard a lesson, he inclined his head politely and said, "Wait right here, please." He waved a casual hand at the two SS sentries on either side of the door, knocked twice softly and walked right in, closing the door behind him.

Hitler looked up. His face seemed fresher, the eyes more alert. *Old bovine Eva must have done a number or two on him.* "Good morning, my Fuehrer. You look rested. Did you enjoy your time at home?"

Hitler smiled back at him. "Oh, yes. As always."

"Goebbels is just outside. Would you like to see him now?"

"Yes, bring him in."

Bormann turned and reached for the doorknob. It hadn't escaped his ears that Hitler had said to *bring*, not *send* Goebbels in. He was going to enjoy this. Whatever business he had with the Fuehrer, Goebbels would be inwardly furious. Incensed as hell because Bormann would also be present. They all were, every time. He gave Goebbels his most saccharine smile. "Do come in, Joseph."

Goebbels gave him an answering glance that could have petrified pure water, then marched stiffly past him half way to Hitler's desk and flung up his best Nazi salute. With a loud click of polished heels, he barked, "Heil Hitler! You wished to see me, Fuehrer?"

"Yes. Have a seat, both of you."

Both men took chairs facing the desk, and Hitler wasted no time. "Since the Allies landed in Sicily, I have sensed our

Hitler's Judas

people becoming uneasy. We need to create a diversion for them. Something to boost their Nationalistic spirit, and inspire the men in the armed forces at the same time. In short, they need another hero."

"I shall begin a study of the problem at once, Fuehrer," Goebbels said, a little too fast.

Hitler's cheeks showed two spots of color. His voice rose half an octave. "I have *already* studied the damned problem, Goebbels, and what to do about it. What you're here for is to organize the propaganda for my solution."

Bormann could hardly repress his laughter.

"At first," Hitler went on, "I thought of having a filmed medal ceremony for one or two outstanding and courageous individuals each from the Army, the Navy, and the Air forces, but then decided that wouldn't work. Too many of them. Besides, I want to punish the Army and Goering's bunch, too.

"Talk about carrots and sticks! I've done my best, but every time I promote another General, thinking it would lead to some backbone in him and his men, it backfires on me. Soon I will have more Generals than troops! And the Navy can't do much of anything either, it seems. Only the U-Boat arm is really fighting this war with proper enthusiasm and, I might add, with credible results. I've decided to promote Doenitz to Grand Admiral, and what I want you to do, Joseph, is go see him and find another one of those splendid men like Gunther Prien. I'm sure there must be one out there. You remember how the public took to Prien after that marvelous piece of work at Scapa Flow? He was better known and admired than any movie star in the Fatherland."

"Yes, Fuehrer, I do indeed."

— 152 —

Tom Lewis

"Then go find me one, and use all the parts of your machine to get his photograph and exploits plastered all over the Reich. When you do find him, we'll throw a big party for him in the great hall and go from there. Now get out of here and do your job. Oh, by the way, can't you make a couple of U-Boat movies, too? Make them... well, you know how to do that quite well. If not, Leni surely does. Any questions?"

"No, my Fuehrer. I shall go and see Doenitz immediately!"

"Good. Dismissed, then."

After saluting again, Bormann followed the mortified Minister of Propaganda to his own office door. "You see, Joseph?" he said, his voice full of honey, "What *confidence* the Fuehrer has in you! I envy you."

Goebbels pretended he hadn't heard, and stormed out of the office, slamming the door.

"What was all that about?" Fraulein Kemper asked.

"Mind over matter, that's all. Is everything in order for my absence?"

"Yes, sir. All the shopping, too. You can always depend on me, sir."

Bormann placed a gentle hand on her shoulder. "Oh, I do, Fraulein. I do." *And if you weren't so damned homely, I'd screw you on top of your own desk!*

He walked back into his office and made the phone calls he'd planned to, then, carrying a few final papers for Hitler to sign, went back to the Fuehrer's door. He knocked again, moved to Hitler's desk and said, "I can't get over it, Fuehrer."

"What?"

"How you always think of the right thing to do just at

— 153 —

Hitler's Judas

the right time. Your intuition is astonishing."

"Isn't it, though."

"And you do it over and over! Are you sure you can allow me to be gone for a week?"

Hitler said, "Don't worry. Nobody around here will bother me. I'll be visiting the front again. No, go on home, and please give my warmest regards to Gerda and the children."

"I shall, and thank you again, Fuehrer."

Bormann loved first class train compartments. Best way in the world to travel. One could unwind and nap, or read a newspaper, or talk, in complete comfort, warmth, and privacy. After two days at home, he had been glad to board the Munich-Freiburg express, if for nothing else, a little peace and quiet. He loosened his jacket and tie, pulled off his shoes and stretched out, allowing his heart rate to settle into a pleasant counterpoint to the rhythmic clicking of the wheels. He felt in a really good mood. Fraulein Kemper had shopped well. The children all had fine presents, Gerda had been delighted with her new fur coat, and best of all, Klaus Berger had performed brilliantly, managing to make a boorish pest of himself with Gerda, and terrifying the kids. None of them were sorry to see 'Uncle Freddy' leave, though the older ones and his wife had been politely sympathetic when Bormann told them his elderly uncle was a very sick man, and that he had to take him to a specialist in Basle, but would for sure be back in time for Christmas. He wondered if Berger would also fool Helmut, who had met them at the station, and was now closeted with the actor in the next compartment. Bormann sniffed. He wouldn't bet on it, either way. Berger

– 154 –

Tom Lewis

was good, but Helmut was a perceptive man. Very perceptive. After all, he was a Bormann.

As if by some strange kind of telepathy, Helmut Bormann, after knocking, eased into his compartment. "Can we talk a little, big brother?"

"Sure. What's on your mind? Is Uncle Freddy sleeping?"

"Uncle Freddy my ass! Who is this guy, Martin? Uncle Friedrich's hands and teeth were never that clean, not from the day he was born. And another thing. How the deuce did you fix it to get me transferred to your service for two whole weeks? You should have seen Mueller's and Himmler's faces. I thought they were both going to have a stroke. Why are we in civilian clothes and what are we going to Freiburg for anyway?"

"Whoa. One question at a time, please. First, the man's an actor, and you'll have to admit he's an exceptionally good one, too. I have a specific use for him, which is none of your business. Second, you're going farther than Freiburg. I have need of your talented nose for a couple of days, and if you're as efficient as usual, then you can have the rest of the time free plus the extra expense account money to spend as you wish. Call it a paid Christmas vacation. I'm going to meet a third party at Freiburg, but I'm sending you on directly to Zurich. Never mind how I managed to get you transferred. Now answer my question. Is Uncle Freddy asleep?"

"Yes. He's dead tired."

"Good. And from now on, he actually *is* our Uncle Freddy. Understand?"

"*Bestimmt.*"

"Anything else you want to know?"

Hitler's Judas

"I'd like to know what I'm supposed to do in Zurich."

"Easy. I want you to quietly contact a man at our Embassy there, and set up a private meeting with me."

"Who?"

"His name is Drucker. Anton Drucker. Before the war, he served in our Embassy in Washington."

"Ought not to be too hard to do. Where will you be?"

"One hotel or another. I'll let you know. Now please let me get some sleep."

The drafty train station at Freiburg was not nearly as crowded with military people as the one at Munich—or many of the other major cities within the Third Reich—where nowadays, outbound troops could not help but notice the weary, defeated faces of those coming home. Whether they were walking wounded or stretcher cases, they all had the vacant look of zombies. Still, in spite of the war, there were surprising numbers of ordinary civilian travelers milling about, and Bormann was certain that more than a few of them were Gestapo types. From Himmler's point of view, (he saw a spy under every hat) this Black Forest town so close to the Swiss border was surely a place to be watched, no doubt with good reason, and he was equally sure that every train going south or coming in from Basle would be closely scrutinized.

None of this bothered him. 'Uncle Freddy's' papers were quite in order, and there would be no questioning of them, nor certainly his own. No, there would be no trouble here. Or coming back. He relaxed, ordered two beers, lit a cigarette and told Berger to do the same. Bormann had always enjoyed the atmosphere of Germany's gothic train

Tom Lewis

stations. Solid as any cathedral, (and just as drafty) at any time of the year, they were always perfumed with the pleasant smell of roasting chickens and bratwurst, fresh, hard bread, and good beer that could be bought cheap from the outside perimeter vendors or inside the usual *Bahnhofscafe* where the noise level was much reduced. But Bormann had chosen the former area for the rendezvous for just that reason. No one was likely to hear what was being said.

He glanced up at the huge clock, which could be seen from every gate. Skorzeny would be coming along any minute now. The man had never been known to be so much as a half-second late. Bormann looked across the table at the actor, who seemed relaxed and confident in his role. "I'm expecting someone. He will sit at the table next to us. Pay him no attention at all, understand?"

"Sure, I do. Where the hell we going anyway?"

Bormann chuckled good-naturedly, pleased that Berger's voice and accent remained totally in character. "I'm not sure just yet. Be patient. Enjoy your beer."

He had to smile yet again when the big clock struck four, and Otto Skorzeny, freshly promoted to Colonel after his daring mountaintop rescue of the deposed Mussolini, with beer in hand, nonchalantly sat down in a chair no more than elbow distance away. From his pocket, Skorzeny removed a newspaper, pretended to read it for a few minutes, and having finished his short beer, got up and walked away, leaving the newspaper on the table. Bormann reached for it, spread it out, and read (stuck between two of its pages) the short, hand printed note:

4:18 train to Basle. Compartments 6 and 8. Have

located right party and booked same.

Bormann slipped the note and the two first class tickets clipped to it into his pocket, dropped the newspaper back on the abandoned table, and stood. "Finish up. We have a train to catch."

"Where to this time, fancy pants?"

"Basle. To see a famous physician. Listen to me carefully, Uncle Freddy, you didn't fool my brother Helmut at all, but after this Swiss Jew is done with you, you'll be able to deceive your own mother. Let's go."

CHAPTER 15

As Bormann had anticipated, there was no problem at either border. Two minutes after crossing into Switzerland, he said, "Wait here, Uncle. I'll be back in a few minutes." He got up and walked to the next compartment, knocked once and let himself in. Arms and legs crossed, Otto Skorzeny was sitting across from a short, well dressed, goateed man of around sixty, whose face and eyes plainly showed his amusement at so clandestine a meeting. Skorzeny laconically made the introductions, "Dr. Jules Feinstein, meet Mr. Brown."

Bormann shook the hand that was soft, yet surprisingly strong. "What's so funny?"

"Your name," Dr. Feinstein said. "You would be surprised at how many Mr. or Mrs. Browns I have met in

Hitler's Judas

my line of work. Browns, Whites, Smiths, Joneses. At one time or another, I think I have met more than a hundred very uncommon individuals who had the most common names imaginable. But that is rather beside the point, isn't it? It is of no matter. Your associate here has paid me an uncommon amount of money to make this ridiculous train trip; Geneva to Basle to Freiburg, and back again. So then, here I am. What can I do for you, Mr. Brown?"

Bormann gave Skorzeny a glance that said, 'Take a walk, Otto.' Skorzeny promptly got up and left without a word.

Bormann sat down. "It isn't far to Basle, *Herr Doktor*. Let me be brief. I'm aware there are not more than a handful of men in the world who do what you do, and I also know you're the best of the lot. A real pioneer in your field. You have a unique private clinic at your mansion on the lake at Geneva, which itself is a testament to your success. Whatever your fee is, I am prepared to pay you triple for a discreet operation you probably do several times a month."

"Ah. I can tell you're a thorough man as well as the curious type."

"I'm the careful type."

"Just so."

"Tell me something, Doctor. Why do you call it 'plastic' surgery?"

Bemused still, Dr. Feinstein eyed Bormann like he would have a lowly undergraduate medical student. "In a nutshell, the word 'plastic' derives from the Greek. It means 'to mold' or 'to reshape.' There are two types of physical deformities; those that are congenital, such as a hare lip, and those that result from injury or disease. In the early part of my career, I

Tom Lewis

worked almost exclusively on the latter. Cases of reconstruction, but in recent years, I have concentrated on cosmetic surgery. To be blunt, I found it to be exceedingly lucrative. How is it you know about me? I don't generally advertise."

Bormann was not about to tell this pompous Jew he had first read about him in an article in one of Edda's insipid magazines, and knew that he was the darling of the wealthy ugly, and incognito Hollywood stars who needed both his skills and his doctor-patient discretion. "Your work is not unknown in the Reich, Dr. Feinstein, in certain informed circles, that is."

"I'm flattered. Are you to be the patient?"

Bormann shook his head. "Not exactly. I'm the model. Your job will be to make a carbon copy."

"An intriguing idea. I'm listening..."

The suite of connecting rooms Skorzeny had booked in Basle's exclusive Hotel Excelsior served Bormann's needs well. He considered its heavy opulence not an extravagance, but a necessary expense. It was important to impress the good Doctor, then let the man draw his own natural conclusions; hopefully that 'Herr Brown' was most likely one of the eccentric, rich German industrialists who desired, eventually, a secret way out of Hitler's hell— which wasn't far from the truth.

After an elegantly served room service dinner for just the two of them, cigars lit and brandy glasses in hand, Bormann rose and walked to the door to the first bedroom, cracked it open, and told Klaus Berger, who had eaten alone, to join them. Klaus had, on Bormann's earlier instructions,

— 161 —

removed his white wig and makeup, and still clad in 'Uncle Freddy's' shoddy clothes, followed Bormann into the sitting room.

The effect was instantaneous. Seeing the two of them standing side by side, Feinstein's eyebrows shot up. "Remarkable. Absolutely remarkable! You could be twins."

Nonplussed, Bormann replied, "Perhaps, but not identical twins. That's your job, isn't it? Judging from your reaction just now, I assume your task should not be a difficult one. Do we have a deal?"

Feinstein pulled on his goatee, unwilling to answer immediately. He stood, walked over to the two men, and lightly ran his fingertips over each one's face, probing gently, pinching skin, feeling texture. "Good. Approximately the same age. No disease. Very similar bone structure." He looked at Bormann. "For the figure you mentioned? Oh, yes. We certainly do have a deal. This will be quite enjoyable! Now. First thing is, we need the services of a fine professional photographer. There is a man here in Basle who has done work for me before. I can arrange to bring him here tomorrow morning."

Guessing the logical reason for the photographer, Bormann said, "Why wait until then?" He pointed to the telephone. "Call him now. Offer him four times what he would normally charge. Tell him to take a taxi. No, wait. He will have to bring equipment, won't he? Get his address and tell him my man will pick him up."

While Dr. Feinstein was making the call, Bormann slipped into the other adjoining bedroom. Skorzeny was just finishing up his own dinner. "Otto, don't drink too much. I have a little errand for you. Where is the car you hired?"

— 162 —

Tom Lewis

"Parked across the street from the hotel."

"Good. Wait here. I'll be right back."

In a little over an hour, Skorzeny delivered a thin, balding—and loudly grumbling—man named Slichter to the main door of the suite, both men carrying camera cases and double armloads of lights and ancillary equipment. After it was all inside, Bormann sent Skorzeny back to his room, then turned to his guest. "Who first?"

The surgeon smiled. "You, please. Undress to the waist if you don't mind. Do you have some paper I can make some notes on?"

"Use the hotel stationery."

The photographer set up his lights and reflectors, mounted his camera on a tripod, placed a chair where he wanted it, and pronounced himself ready to shoot. Stripped to the waist, Bormann sat, following Slichter's instructions without a word of protest while the man took dozens of shots, from every possible angle, including from overhead. All the while, Dr. Feinstein nursed another glass of brandy, made notes, but refrained from smoking, which he knew the photographer would frown at. Finally, Feinstein said, "I think that should do it, Mr. Brown. Have your brother come in now, please."

Bormann went into Berger's room, gave the frightened actor his orders, along with a caution not to open his mouth, and while the photographer was busy with him, got dressed, and went back into Skorzeny's room. "Otto, listen carefully. When everything here is finished, take the photographer back to his place, but don't let him out of your sight, even for a second. He will be instructed to make one print of

– 163 –

Hitler's Judas

each picture he has taken. I want you to bring them, along with the negatives, back here to me."

"As you wish, Herr Reichsleiter."

"One thing more. As you doubtlessly know, the chemicals used to develop film are highly flammable. Herr Slichter's shop is to suffer an unfortunate fire, and poor Slichter, well, you know."

Skorzeny understood. "Don't worry. His is a small shop, with his private apartment upstairs. He lives alone. It will be a fast and fatal fire, Reichsleiter."

Bormann returned to the sitting room, told Klaus to go to his own room and get some sleep, and after the photographer had packed up all his gear and left with Skorzeny, he sat down again with Dr. Feinstein. "Well?"

"It will not be difficult. Your brother is nearly bald, and there is, of course, nothing I can do about that, but a carefully constructed hairpiece should suffice. You are heavier, and a little more puffy around the eyes, lips, and cheeks, but that is not much of a problem for me. I will have to do a bit of bone work on the bridge of his nose and the chin, but again, that is not a major worry. As you said, I am indeed the best there is, and when I'm finished, no one will be able to tell you apart, at least from the neck up."

Dr. Feinstein stroked his goatee again. "Your most serious problem will be the weight difference. Although you both have basically the same frame, you are thicker in the arms and waist. I daresay a cunning tailor could pad his clothing enough to disguise it. That done, and unless you both stood side by side stark naked, I don't believe anyone could tell you're not surgically separated Siamsese twins."

"You're sure? Absolutely positive?"

"I'd stake my reputation and my life on it."

Tom Lewis

Bormann didn't say what he was thinking behind his unblinking eyes. "How long before he can leave your clinic?"

"Two weeks, provided he has adequate nursing when the final bandages come off."

"I have a very good nurse for him."

"Excellent. Then we can leave first thing tomorrow for Geneva?"

"Yes, but I will not be joining you. My associate will accompany you, stay until the other Mr. Brown is well enough to leave, and pay you in full. Is that arrangement satisfactory?"

"Quite satisfactory."

"Good. I do have a few more questions. About your staff. How many assistants, nurses, orderlies and such do you employ? Do you have a housekeeping staff there? Cooks? Servants?"

"Of course. Several. Why?"

"Send all of them home for a long holiday except for one assistant and one nurse. In other words, close up shop for a while. Mr. Brown is to be your only patient. My man can perform any necessary household chores."

Feinstein started to protest, then thought better of it. "All shall be done as you ask."

Bormann stood. "Then our business is finished for the night. I have taken the liberty of booking you a room just down the hall. Your luggage is already there. You should be comfortable enough. Do bring a few of those cigars with you."

Bormann led the astounded doctor down the corridor to his door, said goodnight, then came back to the suite and made straight for the telephone. He called the switchboard and requested a Zurich number. It rang only once. "Helmut?

– 165 –

Hitler's Judas

It's me. Where and when?"

"He will meet you here in Zurich. At the Boar's Head, tomorrow night at ten o'clock. Table fourteen, downstairs. Will you recognize him?"

"I remember him from earlier conferences with von Ribbentrop and others. I'll know him. Good work, little brother. Enjoy your Christmas bonus."

"Thanks. You, too."

Bormann hung up, lit another cigar, and let himself into Klaus's room. "Already in bed? Sorry. Listen, one last thing. Tomorrow, you will be traveling to Geneva disguised again as my uncle. You are to say nothing to anyone. Do you understand what is to happen?"

"Completely."

"No second thoughts?"

"No."

"Good man. Sleep well, then, and try not to think too much of that churchyard in Berlin."

He returned to the sitting room, poured himself a glass of brandy, and waited for Skorzeny to return. So far, so good.

Lighting his pipe to buy a little time, seventy year-old Anton Drucker looked across the chessboard into the predatory eyes of the man who was closest to Hitler. The Brown Eminence. Except for a weak professional smile, all the rest of his life's training and experience in diplomacy was forgotten in sudden panic. "What can I do for you, Herr Reichsleiter?"

Bormann held up both palms in a gesture of good will. "Relax, old boy, I'm not here officially. You're not in any trouble at all. I merely want to pick your brains about

– 166 –

Tom Lewis

something."

"Yes?"

"In your opinion, why did our scheme to land spies by submarine in America fail?"

Drucker puffed a few times, his brain racing. This booth in the basement of the Boar's Head was maybe the most private spot in town to hold a quiet, unobserved conversation. It was really not a restaurant, but a rather exclusive men's club, catering to elderly types whose only passions in life left to them were the weekly sampling of Europe's best wines and casual games of chess.

"Two primary reasons. The men chosen did not speak American English well enough, and, they were landed in the wrong places."

"Explain."

"The English you and I learned at school was just that— pure Oxford. Americans speak practically a different language altogether, with more regional accents and dialects than we Germans do. The poor men we sent over there were doomed the moment they opened their mouths."

"I can see that. And we sent them to the wrong places, too?"

"Absolutely. Our people thought to land them close to where they would actually try to do their jobs. It was a stupid move. The basic problem was population. Too many people around. I warned them about that but they wouldn't listen, though I had spent all those years in both Washington and New York, and had studied the country and its people all my life."

"Where would you have landed them?"

"Well, I would never have sent them over there in the first place, but if it had been left up to me to decide, I would

Hitler's Judas

have landed them much further south, perhaps on the coast of the State of North Carolina. I suggested that in fact, but they paid me no more attention than they did my assassination plan."

Bormann leaned forward. "What assassination plan?"

Warming to his subject, Drucker re-lit his pipe and continued. "I'm surprised you don't know about it. Three years ago, I submitted a highly detailed, very feasible plan to the espionage people for sending a team ashore to kill Roosevelt."

"Really?"

"It might well have worked, too, but, as instructed, I turned it over to that one-armed General in the Abwehr and—"

"You're talking about General Eppinger?"

"That's the one. Anyway, I never heard a word from him or anybody else. Instead, I was posted here and told to keep my mouth shut."

"Very interesting. What do you suppose happened to it?"

"No idea. I suppose it's locked up in somebody's safe gathering dust."

Bormann leaned back and lit a cigarette. Something von Bittnerhof had said about sneaking ashore in Mexico or on the southeastern American coast kept rattling around in his mind. Had been for weeks. What if this old fart was right? Was there an alternative route of escape? Still more fucking headwork to do?

"Anything else, Herr Reichsleiter?"

"What? Oh. No, nothing else. May I buy you a glass of wine?"

"Surely." The old man's face brightened. He pointed

– 168 –

to the chessboard. "Would you care to play a game?"

Bormann laughed. "No, no. Chess, as I understand it, is a game that requires a great number of pre-planned moves. I'm not very good at that sort of thing. Too simple a brain, I guess."

Three days later, after spending a boring Christmas at home with Gerda and the children, Bormann was back in Berlin, a small, gift-wrapped package in his pocket. "Edda," he said, "I brought you a belated Christmas present."

Squealing with genuine delight, Edda tore open the box and held up the expensive Swiss diamond watch to the light. "It's lovely, Martin. Thank you a million times, only..."

"Only what?"

"I don't know what on earth I could give you that would match it."

"I do, little sparrow. Two things. I want you to give me a crash course in improving my English. Specifically, *American* English— with a southern accent."

"I think I can manage that without being too curious. Wonderful! I can play Scarlett O'Hara and you can be Ashley, the love of her life."

"Who?"

"Ashley Wilkes. Didn't you ever see *Gone With the Wind?* The best film ever made in America? Never mind, it'll be fun. What's the second thing you want?"

"Can't you guess?"

Hitler's Judas

CHAPTER 16

Abwehr Headquarters, Berlin, 10 January, 1944

General Karl Heinz Eppinger held his nose and swallowed the last few drops of the awful brew that could no longer be called coffee. The only reason he drank it anyway was for its temporary internal warmth. He lit a cigarette and opened the file on his desk, reminding himself that if the investigation he was currently running proved successful, he would probably receive a promotion, possibly to Major General. If so, he would surely have more freedom of movement outside the Abwehr, making his secret liaison work with Colonel Stauffenberg and the other conspirators considerably easier to manage. He, like the other courageous men who were willing to risk all in their

Tom Lewis

commitment to kill Hitler, knew for certain that in order to keep from falling under suspicion, each man would have to perform his official duty to the very best of his ability.

But this latest assignment Admiral Canaris had given him—with a humorous wink—was an impossible task, and asinine to boot. He read through the most recent meager additions to the file and emitted a long sigh of frustration. All he knew with certainty was the code word: Odessa. The only actual person he had to go on was a shadowy Bishop named Hudal, and some sketchy theories of an underground railroad Hudal allegedly was running. What irony! Canaris's instructions (clearly full of innuendo that meant he was to drag his feet regarding this investigation) were to find out who among prominent Nazis were planning to desert the sinking ship. If he could discover who they were, he might be able to enlist the braver ones in the plot to exterminate the mad dog. But which ones? Who could be trusted? Though he couldn't prove it, he was fairly sure that many of them were officers of the Abwehr itself! Possibly even Canaris, too. What a mess.

Not like it was in '42 when he had tracked down and closed in on the *Rote Kapelle*. Eppinger hated Nazism with every fiber of his being, but he had no less abhorrence for Communism. Stalin was as bad as Hitler. Maybe worse. As he saw it, his Abwehr duty back then was not a necessary evil at all. The well-organized 'Red Orchestra' had been broadcasting its filth every day and every night completely unaware they would all soon be rounded up. The terrible bloodbath that had followed his *coup* had helped him gain more access to Hitler's inner circle and therefore—

"Excuse me, General," his white-faced aide had not

Hitler's Judas

even bothered to knock. "You... You have a visitor."

"Who?"

"It's...Reichsleiter *Bormann*, sir! What shall I do?"

Eppinger controlled the shock he suddenly felt. *Bormann? What in hell could he want with me?* He rose from his chair. "Well don't just stand there, Major. Send him in."

Bormann marched in and gave Eppinger little chance to offer an exchange of pleasantries. "I want to see that plan Drucker gave you."

"What plan, Reichsleiter?"

"Don't play games with me, General. Drucker's plan to assassinate Roosevelt."

Eppinger had not come this far in the mad world of the Third Reich to be intimidated by a mere secretary, even Hitler's. He sat back down, closed the file on top of his desk, calmly extinguished his cigarette, and said, "If there was such a, plan, as you put it, it would be classified as top secret. You would have to get Admiral Canaris' permission to look at it, or an order from the Fuehrer himself. The Abwehr is a secure—"

"Horseshit. Security be damned. You and I both know Canaris has never laid eyes on it." With a sneer, Bormann extracted a folded paper from his pocket and dropped in on the desk. "Maybe this will move you off your ass."

Eppinger read the order:

General Eppinger:

You are herewith ordered to turn over to Reichsleiter Bormann any and all files, records, and transcripts in your possession pertaining to the solution to the Roosevelt problem proposed by Anton Drucker.

Adolf Hitler

Tom Lewis

Eppinger recognized the signature, having seen it countess times before. "Very well. Give me a moment, please." He got up, went to his safe and dialed the combination, hoping his hand didn't shake. *How could Hitler know about it? That old idiot Drucker must have shot off his mouth to the wrong person.* He removed the dusty folder and took it to his desk, pushed it over to Bormann and to cover his back, said, "You know, this might have a fair chance of working now."

"Why now?"

"Because we now know where a lot of their Prisoner of War camps are."

Bormann stared at him with a look that could not be deciphered. Then he smiled broadly. "Do excuse me, General. I apologize for being so abrupt. I've had a bad morning. Tell you what, let me take you to lunch." He held up the file. "I want to hear your professional opinion on this, and more about the prison camp thing."

General Eppinger did some rapid mental calculations. If he refused the offer of lunch, he might very well escalate an unexpected, nasty situation into a disaster. If he went, he might figure out a way to wiggle out of the corner Bormann had him neatly boxed into. His decision wasn't long in coming. He stood. "It's early for lunch, but why not? I'll get my coat and cap."

Bormann's chauffeur, who had apparently been given his directions beforehand, stopped the car at the entrance to an apartment building in an upper middle-class neighborhood. He ran around and opened the door for Eppinger. Bormann got out right behind him. "Thank you,

Hitler's Judas

Jacob," he said to the blank-faced chauffeur. Come back in one hour, please."

The chauffeur saluted, ran back around to the driver's door, got in and drove away. Bormann said, "General, you were right, of course. It's a bit early for lunch, but I feel more comfortable talking here." He extended his arm. "This is where my girlfriend lives. Come on up, she's not at home right now."

Bormann unlocked the door and ushered Eppinger into a small but beautifully furnished apartment, explaining, "She's an actress. A good one, and a fantastic lover, but she's a terrible cook. Therefore, her kitchen is hardly ever used. We'll go in there. Here, let me help you with your coat."

Eppinger knew Bormann had a mistress, and also knew that Hitler never seemed to mind his married thugs having girls on the side. Hell, Goebbels had several! But that was the least of his concerns at the moment. He took the chair Bormann offered and watched as the Reichsleiter removed the contents of the file and spread them out on the kitchen table.

The first document was a rather small-scale map of the eastern United States, from New York to Florida, a few cities marked in red circles. The second item was a large, detailed map of a section Bormann didn't recognize. "What's this?" he said.

"The easternmost part of the State of North Carolina," Eppinger said, pointing. What they call the Outer Banks. See? Here is Cape Lookout. Up here is Cape Hatteras. These are barrier islands, sparsely populated."

Bormann sat down. "Why don't you save us both some

—174—

Tom Lewis

time and explain briefly what Drucker's plan was."

Eppinger took a deep breath. "To begin with, Roosevelt is a cripple."

This was stunning news to Bormann. "Cripple? Really?"

"Yes. He contracted Polio years ago and totally lost the use of his legs. With a lot of hard work, therapy, and clever manipulation of his public appearances, he has managed to hide his condition rather effectively. We think not more than a few Americans actually know of it. Anyway, some years ago, he founded a kind of hot springs type spa for treatment of cases like his." Eppinger pointed to a spot on the smaller map. "Here, in the southern State of Georgia. This little town called Warm Springs. He goes back there for a sort of therapeutic vacation every year. Drucker thought he might be assassinated there on one of his visits, rather than in Washington or at his New York home."

"Doesn't he have a wall of security around this spa as well?"

"No. Hardly any at all, if you can believe it. Drucker figured it would not be difficult for a well-trained team of two men to land at an isolated spot on one of these barrier islands, take a rubber raft inland, then separately and leisurely make their way to Georgia by bus. Many southerners travel that way. No one checks their comings and goings the way we do. It would have been relatively easy."

"What about weapons?"

"They are easily obtained there, at practically any hardware store. They could be bought or stolen. Ammunition, too."

— 175 —

Hitler's Judas

"So why didn't you try it?"

"We had no way of getting the team out again. With the job done, the place would be immediately crawling with police and security people. Our men would never make it back to the coast to be picked up. They certainly couldn't swim home. Everybody in America would be looking for them."

"Then why do you think the plan might work now? What do the Prisoner of War camps have to do with it?"

Eppinger spread the large-scale North Carolina map out again. "Look here. Only a few miles inland from these barrier islands are several towns that have P.O.W. camps full of German and Italian prisoners. He pointed: "New Bern, Willamston, Rocky Mount, Durham. There are others we know of in other southern states as well. A team could very possibly infiltrate one of them and meld into the prison population until the war is over. Williamston and New Bern might be the best choices. They are both small, sleepy little towns, and both rather close to the coast, easily accessible by water."

"Are you serious?"

"Quite serious. With bribe money, it would be a good deal easier to get into a camp than to escape out of one. Especially these camps. Security is minimal. Prisoners, we hear, are even allowed to work on farms and in warehouses!"

"Why don't they try to escape? Our American and British war prisoners are forever trying. Some manage to succeed, too."

"I hate to say this, Reichsleiter, but I don't think any of our soldiers *want* to escape. Their treatment is the Ritz compared to what we do with our prisoners. Besides, where would they go? The United States is a big country. From

$-176-$

where we are talking about, it's a long way to Mexico or Canada, and as I said, the Atlantic is a long swim."

Bormann leaned back in his chair, his brow knit. Eppinger could tell the man was weighing what he'd heard. Calculating. After a few minutes, he said, "All right, General. Now tell me the details. The fine points. And please don't leave anything out."

General Karl Heinz Eppinger missed his promised lunch that day, but upon swearing on the Fuehrer's name he would never say anything to anyone about the morning's business, he was eventually delivered back to his office, and not to 'Gestapo Mueller' (as Himmler's sadistic assistant was called) minus one arm, one forgotten file, and, as far as his boss was concerned, a believable alibi.

CHAPTER 17

The Mediterranean, 20 March, 1944

"We have to get out of here, Herr Kaleun. We're in a big bottle with a small neck, and the neck's already in the English Navy's mouth."

Horst listened, as he always did, to his Chief's quaint wisdom. As usual, Oskar was right. The enemy knew they were there, and also knew they would soon be out of fuel, ammunition, and supplies, and the only way they could reach safety—or a milk cow if there was still one left—was through the narrow Strait of Gibraltar, which was as crowded with their warships as the *Kurfuerstendamm* used to be on a Saturday afternoon. "How much fuel do we have left, Oskar?"

Tom Lewis

"Barely enough to get home with, if we get out now. By now, I mean today or tonight."

"Well," Horst replied, in good humor, "The boat is a lot lighter. That should help."

Oskar had to agree. It was true. They had spent every torpedo on board, as well as all but a few of their shells, and had made every one of them count. It was no wonder the Allies wanted their scalps so badly. The U-119 had knocked quite a few holes in the chain of British and American shipping in this inland ocean they felt they now owned. Then, just as quickly, a frown replaced Oskar's smile. Their situation really was desperate. While the new snorkel worked very well for the most part, they'd still have to run the gauntlet of the Bay of Biscay and sneak into Brest by night, like a cheating husband with his shoes in his hands. Nowadays, air protection was nil, no thanks to Goering's failures and they certainly didn't have the fuel to sail the long way home, around England to try to reach Kiel or even Bremerhaven. Anyway, they'd have to somehow get through the Gibraltar bottleneck first. "Any ideas, Herr Kaleun?"

"One." Horst turned to his faithful Chief, with yet another impish grin splitting his beard. "What's the first thing you do when you get caught in the rain, Oskar?"

"Me? If I had one, I'd raise my umbrella."

"Right. We need to find us a fat, slow umbrella, going west."

Slowly, understanding crept into Oskar Knapp's brain. "I'll be damned. I get it. We swim underneath a wide tanker or freighter like a whale calf under his Mama's tits and let her take us through. Brilliant. Fucking brilliant! I swear

Hitler's Judas

to God, I thought you had already tried every trick in the book. I was wrong. The men don't call you 'The Wizard' for nothing. You going to wait till dark?"

"No. By now, they're on to my tricks, Oskar. That's when they'll be looking for us to attack. We're close to the mouth now. They won't be expecting us to be crazy enough to show ourselves in broad daylight. We have to spot a ship trying to hurry out *before* dark, and if we're lucky, we can wait just under the surface for her to close, dive under, then fall in behind and under her just as the sun sets."

"I understand. If they are sailing west, their lookouts will be hard put to spot our scope with the sun in their eyes. Seems our best chance."

"And even if another ship picks us up on radar, they wouldn't dare try to kill us as long as we're directly underneath a sister. Once out, we can dive deep and change course. It's not only our best chance, Oskar, it's our only chance. Now, go pass the word to rig for silent running. If any man drops so much as a spoon or a pair of calipers, or even sneezes, I'll shoot him through one of the bow torpedo tubes."

"Aye, sir. This boat will be quiet as a tomb."

Horst wagged his head. "You do have a way with words, Chief."

At Brest, eight days later, Commander Adalbert Schnee hung up the phone and cursed softly. Admiral Godt heard him and asked, "Who was it?"

"Goebbels again. Told me he and the Fuehrer were both running out of patience. He's like a broken phonograph record. 'When is this von Hellenbach fellow coming back

Tom Lewis

in?' It's the fifth time he's called in three days. Maybe we should pick another man for his propaganda scheme. Maybe this time old Horst isn't coming back."

Godt shook his head. "Don't you ever believe it. No, Admiral Doenitz has his mind made up. No one deserves the honor more than Lieutenant von Hellenbach, and the Admiral has faith that he'll make it back again. So do I. He always has. It bothers me, though, that we never hear from him. The patrol he's on now marks the third time he's had radio trouble. I'm beginning to think he's doing it on purpose. What do you think, Schnee?"

"May I speak plainly, Admiral? Off the record?"

"You may."

"Sir, von Hellenbach is not the only one of our commanders who believes the enemy has broken our Triton codes. I'm sure he's not communicating on purpose. If by some miracle the English and the Americans have broken the Enigma machine, they can't pinpoint his whereabouts if he doesn't send. I think he can hear us all right, but dares not transmit. Frankly, I think he's right, but for God's sake, please don't tell Admiral Doenitz I said that."

"I won't, mainly because I agree with you."

Schnee got up and paced the floor. "Where has the Admiral gone, anyway?"

"To Berlin to get some answers. There's some strange activity going on up in Norway, at both Bergen and Trondheim. We've gotten rumors of extra construction at both places that have nothing whatever to do with our plans for the backup pens we're building there. Another thing. As you know, last time he and I went to Hamburg to see how things are coming along there, neither von Bittnerhof

– 181 –

nor Kellermann were to be found. Admiral Doenitz thinks they are at Trondheim, overseeing that mystery construction. We also found out Reichsleiter Bormann had been up there, too."

"Bormann? What the devil could he be up to?"

"No idea. But the Fuehrer must be behind it. If he says jump, Bormann only asks 'how high'? Hitler must have some plan up his sleeve he hasn't seen fit to tell us about. Admiral Doenitz thinks they are getting ready to build some of the new model U-Boats up there."

"Well, if that's true, it would be a great blessing. Heaven knows we need them. Before it's too late. When is the Admiral due back?"

"Any minute now. You know how punctual he is."

Both men lapsed into a lethargic, finger-tapping silence, watching the big clock. Schnee wondered if Admiral Godt was thinking the same thing he was. Things were pretty damned grim right now. A far cry from just one year ago. It had been exactly twelve months since the U-Boat Command had its finest hour. On 5 March, 1943, *B-Dienst* had gotten wind of an enormous trio of convoys leaving New York. Doenitz had sent three groups of boats, thirty-eight in all, to intercept the east-bound armada. Horst von Hellenbach had been right in the thick of it, too, and was responsible for six out of the twenty-two ships sunk, though he'd had another of his narrow escapes. Now, the days of the wolfpack were over, yet Lieutenant von Hellenbach kept chalking up kill after kill on his lone wolf patrols. Schnee admitted to himself he was more than a little jealous. He'd like nothing better than to have another crack himself. If only—

Tom Lewis

He and Godt both jumped to attention as the door opened. Grand Admiral Doenitz stomped in and threw his cap down on his desk, his face black as a squall. "Good news and bad, gentlemen. Oh, stand at ease, both of you. Godt, we have to begin clearing house. We're moving our headquarters back to Germany within the month."

"To where, Admiral?"

"A landlocked base in the woods just east of Berlin. I argued, but lost. Anyway, we—"

The knock on the door interrupted him before he could relay the good news. Chief Petty Officer Werner Knorr rushed in and saluted. "Admiral! He's on his way in!"

"Who is?"

"The Wiz— Lieutenant von Hellenbach, sir. The U-119 radioed. They'll be coming in tonight."

"He *radioed?*" Godt said.

"Yes, sir. About five minutes ago. He's only a couple of miles out." He should be in the pen within half an hour."

The beginning of a smile crept up on Doenitz's face. He turned to Schnee. "Call Goebbels. Tell him his wait is over." He grabbed his coat and cap again. "Godt, come with me." While Admiral Godt moved to the coat rack for his own coat, Schnee, the telephone already in his hand, asked, "Sir, what was the good news in Berlin? Did you see the Fuehrer?"

"No. Couldn't get past Bormann, but he told me Hitler had ordered production of the Type XXI to begin immediately at the yards in Hamburg, and that the prototype is already being built at Trondheim. Go ahead, make that call. Are you ready, Godt?"

"Ready, sir."

— 183 —

Hitler's Judas

"Good. Let's go to the pens and greet our prodigal son."

Horst, like the rest of his crew, was dog-tired when they eased into the safety of the impregnable slip and under its sixteen foot-thick roof. Oskar and *Unterleutnant* Heidt were standing in the tower with him. Oskar pointed, "*Ach, Herr Kaleun*. Is that who I think it is?"

Horst had already seen the two men. "Sure is. Uncle Karl himself, and Admiral Godt. I think I'm in for it, boys."

Silent salutes were exchanged while lines were made fast by the docking crew, who then disappeared. Except for the two admirals, the U-119 and her crew were alone in the concrete slip. Doenitz waited until the engines were shut down before lifting the megaphone, pointing it up, at the tower. "Lieutenant von Hellenbach, assemble your crew on deck."

Horst saluted again, then gave the order. From both hatches, the filthy, bearded crew materialized, lined up, and came to attention. Doenitz raised the megaphone once more. "Attention. Congratulations on your safe return. You will be given your proper leave in a few days, but for now, you are quarantined. Confined to your boat. You will all be given hot food and hot showers, but only two at the time, under guard. Then you will proceed to clean this boat up, inside and out, stem to stern. After that, you will repaint her. I want this vessel to look like she did the day she was commissioned. After that, you will each give yourselves the same kind of scouring. You will be issued complete new uniforms, down to your 'whore's undies.' Further orders will be forthcoming. Lieutenant von Hellenbach, I'm glad to see you have repaired your aerials. You will come with

– 184 –

Tom Lewis

me now. Dis*missed!*"

Horst had no choice but to climb down and disembark. Facing his Commander in Chief, he saluted again and started to open his mouth to say something, but Doenitz didn't give him the chance. "Not a word, Lieutenant. Come along."

The Grand Admiral led Horst to his own private quarters. Once inside, he gestured toward the open bedroom door. "You will find all you need in there. Take a bath and shave. Then we can talk."

Bewildered, Horst walked into the warm bedroom. Lying on the neatly made up bed was a fresh new uniform, shoes, and even a new white cap. Shaking his head, he stripped and went into the bathroom where he found an extra shaving kit, washing cloths, and towels. He turned taps on, adjusted the temperature as hot as he thought he could stand it, and got in. As he lathered down in scented luxury, he thought, Well, if I'm to be court-martialed, I might as well be clean and well-dressed.

Not willing to take too much advantage of the Admiral's hospitality and patience, he got out before he really wanted to, shaved carefully, and got dressed, not surprised that the new uniform fit perfectly. He walked back into the living room and got a second surprise. Doenitz, in his shirtsleeves, his tie loosened, was sitting at a low coffee table, smoking. Two glasses of Cognac waited on the table.

"Thank God for soap. You look and smell a lot better. Sit down, son, and have a drink with me. You'll need one for what I'm about to tell you..."

Hitler's Judas

Five nights later, under a fingernail moon, Horst took his now almost unrecognizable U-119 out of the blacked-out harbor to a spot only two miles offshore. There, he hove to and waited for daylight. At ten, he gave dress-ship orders to his still mystified, grousing crew. Oskar Knapp climbed up beside him. "I ain't felt so clean since my sainted mother gave me her last scrubbing. This old bucket, too. Smells like a church below-decks. What's going on, Herr Kaleun? The men are all just as confused as I am."

Horst looked at his watch. Squinted up at the already high sun. "You're all about to find out, Oskar. It's almost eleven." He glanced at Rudiger Heidt. "All right, First Officer. All ahead slow. Let's take her back in. Chief, bring the rest of the crew on deck."

Her most recent kill pennants flying, her clean-shaven crew (sporting brand new uniforms) standing at attention on her deck, the U-119 blew her horn to announce she was coming home. Soon, her unbelieving crew heard the strains of martial music coming from a brass band, then the noise of shouts and cheers from the gaggle of pretty girls lining the makeshift quay, waving handkerchiefs and flowers. Standing like spars of tall ships were the figures of Grand Admiral Karl Doenitz and his staff. Crews of two outbound boats waved them in as well, shouting their envy and congratulations.

Not one of them noticed the dozens of strategically placed movie cameras, their operators cranking away, taking advantage of the sun's position. But the U-119 didn't stop at the hastily constructed quay. She went on past, and back into her pen. Just in time, too. Looking behind them,

– 186 –

Tom Lewis

Horst and his men watched the entire crowd scatter like chickens when the siren sounded and the first of the six British planes came screaming over. This particular day, they dropped only a dozen bombs.

Hitler's Judas

CHAPTER 18

Fascinated, Edda watched Klaus attach yet another hair to his masterpiece. He had set up shop in her kitchen, his make-up kit and wig box open on the kitchen table, along with a strong light over the area where he was working, using a magnifying glass. "One hair at the time? Is that how you do it? No wonder it's taken you three weeks."

Klaus looked up from his work, waving the tweezers. "It's the only way to do it so no one can tell it's fake, and this one has to be perfect. It's easy to make a hairpiece of bushy hair. His is thin, which makes the job much more difficult. Every follicle has to also hide the edge of the skullcap. At least he doesn't part it. The way he combs it straight back helps. It should be done in a few more days."

Tom Lewis

"It looks fine to me now. Try it on. Let's see how it looks."

Klaus smiled at her. "All right. Close your eyes."

Edda complied while Klaus carefully set the hairpiece in place, using the mirror. He made a couple of minute adjustments, turned his head both ways, then said, "Well, what do you think?"

Edda opened her eyes. "My God! You...You're *him!* Even this close to you, I wouldn't be able to tell you apart."

"Let's hope no one else can either." Klaus carefully removed the piece and placed it again on the dummy head he had painstakingly molded from clay. "My life depends on it. Edda, my hands are becoming cramped. I'd better take a break. Is there some more coffee?"

Edda poured two cups. Since the night Martin had brought him to her apartment, all bandaged up, she'd had a series of shocks. That Klaus hadn't been killed in that fire had been a terrific surprise, but when those bandages came off, and the thin red scars and purple swelling faded, the face that had gradually emerged had jolted her to her very core. But like any sensible woman given her unique circumstances, she had adjusted, had asked no questions, and had nursed Klaus as best she could. This was something made easier since she was at home all the time now, having had to stop work on her film. Goebbels had ordered every current project thrown aside in order to hurriedly start, with Leni Riefenstahl's help, making two new U-Boat films.

She bent forward, lowering her voice. "It's been a hell for you, too, hasn't it?"

"Edda, not in a million years could you imagine things I have seen, but he did spare my life. No matter what I look

– 189 –

Hitler's Judas

like now, I'm alive. A lot of others aren't. That doctor who worked on me... Never mind. Besides, in order for me to *stay* alive and keep what little sanity I have left, I have to think of this as accepting a great acting challenge. Biggest one of my career, and I'm determined to do it well."

"Do you really think you can pull it off?"

"Yes. Every night, he quizzes me, and not only about himself, either. You could show me a photo of anybody who has even a minor position in the Third Reich, and I can tell you who he is, what he's like, what his job is, what his strengths and weaknesses are, where he works, who his family is. You name him, I know him. From Goering to Erich Kempa and back again."

"Who's Erich Kempa?"

"Hitler's chauffeur. I've learned all Bormann's personal mannerisms, too. His speech patterns and inflection. During the day, when he's gone, I'm his housekeeping uncle. At night, he brings me here to work on this hairpiece. He told me the other day he's planning to bring a master tailor in to alter some of those clothes and uniforms hanging in your closet. I'm sure it won't be long before he will give me the acid test."

"Acid test?"

"Yes. Sort of like a dress rehearsal. I will have to impersonate him somewhere. Probably in some scene with his brother, Helmut. If I can fool him, I can fool anybody. Even Hitler. From what Bormann said, the Fuehrer is really deteriorating physically. His quack of a doctor gives him injections practically every day."

Edda poured more coffee. She had no idea how much Martin had told Klaus of his escape plans, if anything. And,

Tom Lewis

she had no doubt that if Klaus did know something, he would have been instructed on pain of horrible death not to open his mouth to her either. She and Klaus both had to play the guessing game. But it didn't take a genius to figure out that when Bormann made his move, poor old Klaus would take his place. The time couldn't be far off either, she thought. Of late, Martin had not made many demands on her. He was more and more preoccupied. Moody. Hadn't slept with her in weeks.

"Where is he?" Klaus said, as if reading her thoughts.

"Sitting in the living room with a glass of whiskey in his hand. Tearing another clock apart."

"What?"

Edda snickered. "It's his expression for 'Don't bother me, I'm thinking.' He's doing a lot of that these days. Anyway, I hope to God you can do this role he's given you."

"Oh, I'll be able to do it, all right. I must. The consequences of failing are unthinkable. You also have to—"

Both Edda and Klaus were frozen into instant fear when the knock came on the door. They looked at each other in near panic. "Who can that be?" Edda whispered.

Before Klaus could answer, Bormann's voice sang out from the living room. "Relax, you two. I'll get it."

Bormann got up, glancing at his watch.

Good old Otto. Right on time as always. He opened the door and admitted the SS Colonel and a skeleton of a man wrapped in a filthy, smelly blanket.

"Reichsleiter," Skorzeny said, "May I present Herr Abrahim Liebewicz, formerly of Warsaw, now the finest resident tailor in Dachau..."

Admiral Doenitz looked up from the sheaf of papers

Hitler's Judas

lying on his desk. He tried his best not to glance at Schnee or Admiral Godt who were standing on either side of his office door, both not even trying to hide their malicious grins. Doenitz coughed once, then turned a fish eye to his visitor, who was occupying the chair opposite the desk, his legs crossed as daintily as any woman's. "Herr Goebbels, all this looks satisfactory to me. If any men in the Kriegsmarine deserve such treatment, it is surely the officers and crew of the U-119. I am quite happy for you to report back to the Fuehrer that my staff and I will be in attendance. And, with great pleasure."

Goebbels arched an eyebrow. "I should think so, Admiral. My office has gone to a great deal of trouble to organize this event. To be blunt, it has taken me away from more pressing duties, and has taken up a lot of my precious time. As a matter of fact, I—"

"I doubt if you have lost much sleep over it, Minister. Now, as you can see, I have a very hot war to fight, and your visit here has come right in the middle of our packing up for the new headquarters. Is there anything else?"

With a sneer, Goebbels stood, reaching into his tunic pocket for his trump card. "Just one other item, Admiral." Aware that Doenitz's two assistants were standing behind him, Goebbels theatrically handed the letter across the desk, and in his most condescending voice, added, "The Fuehrer asked me to give you this personally. Your eyes only. No one else is to see or read it."

Admiral Doenitz suppressed his laughter. "Oh, I do understand what 'Your Eyes Only' means, Herr Goebbels." He stood to his full height, dwarfing his guest, and leaned across his desk, signifying the interview was over. "And, I

– 192 –

Tom Lewis

do thank you for bringing all this yourself, and not trusting one of your subordinates to do it. We will see you in Berlin next week."

Goebbels threw his arm up in his best Nazi salute. "Heil Hitler!"

"Yes, yes, Heil Hitler," Doenitz mumbled, retaking his seat.

Seething, Goebbels turned on his polished heel and stalked between Godt and Schnee out the door.

As soon as he was out of sight, all three men roared with laughter. First to recover his sense of normalcy, Doenitz ordered. "Open a window, Schnee. My God, there cannot be an ounce of *Eau de Cologne* left in Paris. He's wearing it all!"

Schnee did as he was told, then both he and Admiral Godt took chairs offered by their boss. "Now, let's see," he said, eyeing them with one eye closed, "what our illustrious leader has to say." He opened the letter and read, aloud.

Admiral:
Following the ceremony in Berlin Dr. Goebbels will have outlined, I am ordering you to attach young von Hellenbach to the Office of Propaganda for a period of one month. After that, and until further notice from me directly, assign him to some sort of job that will keep him out of combat.
Keep up the good work.
Adolf Hitler

Schnee whistled. Godt said, diplomatically, "Well, those are certainly kind words."

Doenitz sighed. "As kind as we will ever get from him." He straightened. "All right, that's enough frivolity for one

Hitler's Judas

day." He picked up a single sheet from the stack Goebbels had brought. "Admiral Godt, will you please take care of this matter for me? If I don't get cracking, we'll never get out of here."

Aboard the U-119, in the freshly painted galley, Chief Oskar Knapp angrily raked the pieces from the board. "Damn you, Kirchner, how is it such a stupid man like you always wins? You some kind of mind reader or something?"

His long-time regular chess partner giggled and poured them both a mug of fresh coffee. "No, Chief. Just because I'm a cook doesn't mean I'm dumb. You telegraph every move you make. You're so damn anxious to attack, you get careless. Thank God you ain't that way with this boat. We'd all be dead by now."

"Shut your fat mouth. If the Allies don't kill us, your cooking will. Tell me something, how did you get to be a Navy cook anyway? Big as you are, and from all the fights I've seen you in, you might have made a pretty good soldier."

"Money."

"What?"

"Money, old friend. Way I see it, Army duty is just as hazardous as what we do, but we get paid more for doing it. Simple as that. Besides, with my luck, if I was cooking for some land-based outfit, they'd probably give me a gun between meals and stick me in a hole on the front line at the Eastern Front, and with these eyes of mine, I couldn't hit a Russian tank if it rolled right over me."

"Come to think of it," Oskar said, "I ain't never seen a cook besides you who wore specs. Look, Kirchner, you may be a butter-belly, but I know you ain't soft, and I know

Tom Lewis

that's why you get in fights all the time when we're in port."

"I can't help it, Chief. I sit down with some guys for a couple drinks, it ain't five minutes before one of them starts in on me. Listen, you want another game? We got time before—"

The klaxon went off, interrupting him.

"Attention, all hands. Men, this is the Captain speaking. All of you are to shave, put on your dress uniforms, and assemble on deck at exactly four o'clock. Admiral Doenitz has a little surprise for you. That is all."

"Fuck!" Kirchner said in disgust, flinging the rest of his coffee in the sink. "I don't like surprises. Good or bad, and Uncle Karl dishes up more bad ones than good ones, that's for damn sure."

Horst watched as his crew spilled out of both hatches onto the deck. The inside of the pen was lit up by dozens of powerful lights, each casting a surreal shadow on the dark water. As soon as the last man had lined up, from stem to stern, Horst glanced at his watch. At precisely four o'clock, Admiral Godt, Commander Schnee, and several others of Grand Admiral's staff appeared from the shadows. "*Achtung!*" Horst shouted. Every man on deck stopped muttering and stood ramrod straight, all eyes on Admiral Godt.

Godt wasted no time. Though a small man, he had a powerful voice; one that needed no megaphone. From a paper he brandished, he read, in solemn tones, "Stand easy. Men of the U-119, by order of the Fuehrer, and the Commander in Chief of the Kriegsmarine, and in recognition of your bravery and outstanding record on every

Hitler's Judas

patrol you have undertaken for the Fatherland, every one of you except Lieutenant von Hellenbach is hereby promoted one rank. In addition, I am hereby authorized to present each of you with the Iron Cross, First Class."

An instant loud cheer echoed in the cavernous concrete walls of the pen. Chief Knapp, who was standing beside his friend Kirchner, jabbed him in the ribs. "You see, I told you The Wizard would get you the Iron Cross."

Kirchner frowned. "Yeah, but what about *him?* I know he's already got his Iron Cross, but ain't he going to get a promotion too?"

As if Admiral Godt had heard this exchange, he coughed once and spoke up again, "Boys, don't be concerned about your Commander. There is to be a big party in Berlin next Friday; a very special ceremony to be given in his honor, and all of you are invited. Your time in Berlin will not be charged against your leave time, either. I trust all of you will behave like the professional sailors you are."

Another cheer, this one louder than the first, thundered through the pen. Horst, standing in the conning tower alongside his officers who were pounding him on the back, blushed crimson.

But Admiral Godt wasn't yet finished with his speech. When the men quieted down some, he added, "One other thing. Lieutenant Heidt, as of this moment, you are in command of this vessel. Lieutenant von Hellenbach, would you please assist me with these medals? Then you will accompany me back to headquarters, you and Chief Knapp. You are both to be reassigned."

Horst saluted and climbed down, glad to shake every

– 196 –

Tom Lewis

hand when the Admiral hung the prized medals around every clean neck. He didn't give a thought to what his reassignment would be, nor did he realize that this would be the last time he would ever lay eyes on the U-119—and most of her crew.

CHAPTER 19

Edda leaned sideways in her chair and nudged Bormann. "Impressive as hell! I'll say one thing for old Casanova Goebbels, he really knows how to throw a party. Look around. Except for those sailor boys, it's a veritable who's who of Nazism. I'm surprised you brought me here."

"Don't worry," Bormann replied. "Where we're sitting and with everything that's going on, nobody's going to pay us the slightest bit of attention." He leaned back and surveyed the scene. Edda was right. The Great Hall was, by any standards, decked out magnificently. Walls were draped with huge Swastika flags and banners. Tables were overloaded with food. Champagne was flowing freely. At the far end of the hall, thirty or so members of the Berlin Philharmonic string section were playing muted

Tom Lewis

Unterhaltungsmusik. Beneath the noble chandeliers (boosted by extra spotlights for the benefit of Goebbels' cleverly hidden movie cameras) the crowd was equally impressive. Light reflected off hundreds of glittering medals and jewels that festooned the formally clad throng who were, as Edda had said, the cream of Nazi society, including attractive widows of dozens of fallen officers who had been invited and instructed to 'make themselves available for conversation and dancing' with both officers and crew of the U-119. Bormann snorted. Those poor *Kriegsmariner* had truly been fish out of water for the first half hour, but were feeling no pain of embarrassment now! They weren't likely to get too drunk, though, not with the steely eyes of Grand Admiral Doenitz watching them.

"He's a fine looking man, isn't he?" Edda was saying.

Bormann shifted his gaze to the table where the guest of honor was sitting with his family. "Lieutenant von Hellenbach? Yes, I suppose he is, but right now he looks about as comfortable as a whore in a convent."

Edda laughed. "From what you've told me, I take it Goebbels has really done his job well. For the last month, that man's face and deeds are all you see in newsreels, on posters, kiosks, and in the papers. Did he really sink all those ships?"

"Yes. For once, Goebbels didn't have to lie through his crooked teeth. The man's a legitimate hero, all right. Deserves this fleeting moment of fame. Would you like to see what he's getting tonight?"

"The award? Sure I would."

Bormann reached into his pocket for a velvet covered case, which he opened. The highest order ever given within

Hitler's Judas

the Third Reich was this medal. Suspended from a black-bordered red and white ribbon, the onyx and gold Knight's Cross with Oak Leaves, Crossed Swords and Diamonds rivaled the famous "Blue Max" of the last war in beauty, and was even more coveted.

"It's gorgeous," Edda whispered. "Looks like something that could have been designed by Faberge."

"It might have been, for all I know," Bormann said, closing the box. "It's amazing what men will do for a little piece of ribbon and tin."

Edda sipped her champagne. "Where's the Fuehrer?"

Bormann shifted in his chair. "Oh, he'll show up after a while." He cocked his head to the right. "He will come through that door. That's why we're sitting here next to it."

"I don't understand."

"He's in bad shape, Edda. He doesn't want to walk more than two or three steps into the room and let everyone here get a close look at the kind of physical condition he's in now." Bormann pointed to spot on the floor that had been taped off. "He'll simply stop right here, and von Hellenbach will march across to him. I'll give Hitler the medal, and he'll make the award, stay just long enough for the cameras, then probably leave. It's all been rehearsed."

"Naturally. Would you like some more champagne, darling?"

Across the room, Irmgard von Hellenbach agreed with Admiral Doenitz's kind statement. "Yes, it certainly is a big night for Horst. For my family, too. It was very kind of you to make all our travel and lodging arrangements. A

– 200 –

special train from Freiburg to Berlin! My, my."

"The Fuehrer insisted on it, Frau von Hellenbach. He can be exceedingly kind when he wants to."

"My only regret is that Horst's father could not be here to see it."

"Your husband was a splendid man, Frau von Hellenbach. A fine and dedicated soldier. It's a truism that war robs us of our best."

Irmgard knew, from Horst, that Doenitz had lost both his sons to the war. It was said that when he heard the news, he didn't even flinch. She touched the taciturn senior officer lightly on his arm. "I pray it ends soon."

"So do I, Madame. So do I."

Doenitz was sitting at her right, Horst (trying hard to keep his nervousness at bay) on her left. Across the immense table, between Horst's young First Officer, Lieutenant Rudiger Heidt and Harald, Elisabeth Kroll was in her element. Dressed to the nines and wearing some of Irmgard's jewelry, her face was alight with joy, not only from the occasion, but because it was the first time in many years she had seen both twins at the same time. She was trying her best to make the most of it, too, but poor Horst was so distracted, he was paying her scant attention. Harald was not much company for her either. He was drinking too much, and wasn't making much of an effort to disguise his envy.

Irmgard sighed. Hadn't it been like that all their lives? Harald was the classic overachiever, but because of his physique and his handicap, seemed to always come out second best no matter how hard he tried! Everything had always seemed to come so easily and naturally to his older

Hitler's Judas

brother. And now this. Also, she knew there was one other reason Harald was so down in the mouth. Irmgard knew he had proposed to Elisabeth, but the girl had stalled, and he knew exactly why. Now, with Horst about to receive a most high honor from the Fuehrer himself, Elisabeth was really betwixt and between.

Irmgard's thoughts were interrupted by the sudden hush that had fallen over the crowd. A door across the hall had opened, and Adolf Hitler entered the room. Everyone instantly stood. The orchestra stopped playing. Three hundred arms flew up and a resounding 'Heil Hitler' thundered forth. Hitler jerked his right arm part way up in answer. A short, stocky man moved to Hitler's side and handed him something. In a surprisingly strong voice, Hitler said. "I am happy to see everyone having such a good time. As you know, we are gathered here tonight to honor one who represents all that is good and brave in our fighting men. A true hero of the Third Reich. Lieutenant Horst von Hellenbach, will you please come forward?"

Jaw firmly set, Horst stood, bowed curtly to his mother and the others at the table, and with a back straight as a ruler, marched to the spot where the Fuehrer stood. He gave Hitler a military salute which was acknowledged by another rapid arm jerk, then stood at attention while Hitler spoke, his voice carrying to every corner of the room.

"Lieutenant Horst von Hellenbach, you are herewith promoted to the rank of *Korvettenkapitan*, and on behalf of a grateful country, I now have the honor of presenting you the Knight's Cross with Oak Leaves and Diamonds." Horst bent his head, the Fuehrer hung the medal around his neck, offered his hand and said, "Congratulations. You are a credit

Tom Lewis

to your service, your country, and your Fuehrer. It is I who salute you."

Wild and continuous cheering broke out and was sustained through the several minutes it took for all the flashbulbs to pop, with Hitler beaming and holding the young officer's hand in a most informal pose. No one was happier than Dr. Joseph Goebbels, who was certain his job was secure again.

When the noise finally subsided, Hitler released his hand, and in a quieter voice, said, "Relax now, young man. Go and dance with that pretty girl sitting at your table." With those words, he turned and was through the door before anyone could react. The orchestra, right on cue, began playing dance music, and the newly decorated honoree turned and made his way back through the applause to the table. "Would you care to dance, Lizzle?"

"I would love to, Herr Korvettenkapitan."

Irmgard von Hellenbach, tears in her proud eyes, watched them move out onto the dance floor, soon surrounded by others who were clapping him on the back and offering their own congratulations.

She glanced sideways at the Grand Admiral, who seemed to read her thoughts. "Don't worry, Frau von Hellenbach, his fighting days are over."

"Really? No more patrols?"

"No, Madame. He's now a celebrity. The Fuehrer has planned a tour of the country for him. Then he is to report back to me and begin his new job, of training other young officers. Hopefully, they will all learn from him. He was my best."

— 203 —

On the dance floor, Horst held Elisabeth close. "Are you happy?"

"Oh my darling, I can't tell you how much. You're a famous hero. Everyone in Germany knows about you, and here I am, in your arms at last."

She kissed Horst behind his ear, whispering, "My love, my Horst, your mother wants a grandchild soon, but don't you think we should marry first?"

Horst stopped in his tracks. He looked into those blue eyes for a long moment. "Are you telling me you have finally made your decision?"

"Oh, yes, my fine hero. I think I always knew it would be you. Yes. *Yes!* I want to be your good wife and raise your fine children. Lots of them!"

Horst forced his feet to start moving again. After a while, he said, "We must wait a little longer, Lizzle."

"But why?"

"I must do a silly promotional tour. After that, I'm to be assigned to a training unit, but with the way the war is going, I wouldn't doubt that Doenitz sends me back to active combat again, and if he does, I... Maybe he won't. I pray to God he won't, but we must wait a little longer. Do you understand?"

Elisabeth fought back her tears. "Yes. I understand. But can we at least live together?"

"Oh Lizzle, please don't tempt me like that. A widow is a widow, whether she's married or not. I don't want to do that to you."

Elisabeth turned her face up. "Don't you think that should be my choice? Besides, nothing's going to happen to you, Horst.

Tom Lewis

"Nothing, do you hear me? You're going to live forever, and I can wait a little longer if you can. Just tell me you love me."

"I love you, Lizzle." *But I will not marry you until after this war is over.*

At that moment, Bormann nudged Edda under the table with his knee. "Sh:t. Here comes trouble."

Resplendent in a beautifully tailored, powder-blue uniform, Hermann Goering, pomaded and perfumed, approached their table, his beady eyes fastened on Edda. He gave Bormann a sideways glance. "My dear Bormann, where have you been hiding this wondrous flower? She makes the other women here look sickly."

Bormann smoothly made the introductions. "Fraulein Edda Winter, may I present Field Marshall Hermann Goering."

Edda the actress didn't miss a beat. "I am so pleased to meet you, Herr Field Marshall. And honored. Your fame is only matched by your charm."

"And I am a superb dancer as well. May *I* have the honor?"

"*Ach,* how could I refuse such gallantry?"

Bormann could hardly contain his mirth as he watched them move out into the crowd on the dance floor who politely made way for them. He sat back and sipped his champagne. The evening had been a nice one, indeed. There wouldn't be many more like it, that was certain. But he didn't care. He thought of the small, nondescript man who had brushed by him on the street outside Edda's apartment several weeks ago, had quickly said his name was Noah,

— 205 —

Hitler's Judas

and told him his own code name was Moses.

Moses! Bormann laughed behind his hand. At the time he had said nothing at all, but had wanted to remind the Odessa messenger that Moses had brought his born again—and now doomed again—people out of Egypt but had never reached the Promised Land himself. That sad and ironic fate was not going to befall Herr Martin Moses Bormann, little messenger man. No way! All the clocks but one had been torn apart and put neatly back together, and it was time to start on the last one. Phase three. All he needed was for the right moment to come along.

CHAPTER 20

Bormann didn't have to wait very long to begin phase three of his plan; the first part of which was to methodically poison the Fuehrer's fragile mind against Roosevelt. The long anticipated Allied invasion commenced on the sixth of June, throwing Hitler into a paroxysm of rage— leveled mostly at his Generals, but also at anyone else who happened to be near him when the news came in and was sorted out. "Damn them all, I *told* them to watch Normandy. Idiots! None of them agreed with me, Martin. When will they learn that my intuition is unerring? Normandy *had* to be the *Schwerpunkt!*"

"So true, Fuehrer. Of course you warned them. I heard you myself, but children never listen to their elders. It's as if some of them are serving that Jew Roosevelt instead of

Hitler's Judas

you."

"Roosevelt isn't a Jew."

"He might as well be. He's surrounded by them. Half his cabinet. His main advisor. His best friends. I wouldn't doubt that he's also circumcised."

Hitler laughed in spite of himself. Then his face clouded up again. "They were all wrong. All of them. Even Rommel. He also thought the landing would be further north, where the Channel is narrowest. *My Generals!* I should have a dozen of them shot to teach them all a lesson."

"Well, Rommel will give a good account of himself, Fuehrer. If anybody can stop them, it's him. Our soldiers would follow him into hell itself. And when your new secret weapons are ready, the Allies will rue the day they invaded your domain."

This gave Hitler just the opening he needed. For an hour, Bormann sat, patiently listening to the man rave on and on, frothing at the mouth, about how his new weapons would soon wipe them all off the face of the earth. Roosevelt, Churchill, Stalin. All of them— and their children, too! "You know what, Bormann? The only thing I can do now is to take complete command of the Army myself. *Then*, by God, they'll listen. Go ahead and make the necessary arrangements for me to go out there."

"I already have, Fuehrer. We can leave tomorrow, but there are one or two necessary things I need to take care of here first. May I be excused to do them?"

"Yes, yes. By all means, but hurry."

Bormann left Hitler muttering to himself, in far more senile a state than Uncle Freddy had ever been. He hurried out, pausing in his own office only long enough to pick up

Tom Lewis

his briefcase and order Fraulein Kemper to have Jacob Glas bring his car around. Downstairs, he instructed his chauffeur to drive to Himmler's headquarters.

Obergruppenfuehrer Gottlob Berger (no relation to the actor) was the rather simpleminded Chief of the SS Head Office, and also the man who headed Himmler's Prisoner-of-War Administration. A man of unswerving devotion to National Socialism, Himmler, and Hitler, but otherwise one of limited mental capacities, Berger was just as surprised to see Reichsleiter Bormann come, unannounced, through his door as he had been the last time.

"Do you have the information the Fuehrer requested?" Bormann said.

"*Jawohl*, Herr Reichsleiter." He stood, walked to his file cabinet and extracted a red-tagged, sealed file. Three weeks before, after reading the signature at the bottom of the order Bormann had handed him, he had known better than to ask why Hitler had made such an unusual request— an order which Bormann had told him was absolute top secret, and had then snatched it up and stuck it back into his uniform pocket. Nor was Berger about to ask about it now. He handed the file over.

"And no one knows about this?" Bormann said. A statement, not a question.

"No, sir. Not Mueller, not even Himmler, no one but myself."

Bormann stuck the file in his briefcase. "Good. Make sure you keep it that way. Have all the subjects been transferred?"

"Yes. All six have been taken to *Stalag* 14, near

-209-

Hitler's Judas

Regensberg."

"Excellent. The Fuehrer will be highly pleased. You may have even contributed to stopping some prisoner escapes."

Without further explanation, Bormann turned abruptly and left, leaving the career bureaucrat more confused than ever. Berger sat back down. So. if the Fuehrer wanted to transfer a handful of American prisoners—all draftees, non trouble makers, all from southern coastal States, and all unmarried—to a common camp, that was his business. The Fuehrer's mind was so superior to anyone else's, who was he to ask questions? It was certainly none of *his* business, and likely none of Bormann's either. The Reichsleiter was, after all, merely an errand boy, following orders like everybody else in the Third Reich. He reopened the file he had been working on, already putting the interruption out of his mind.

Bormann opened the file in the car on the way back to his own office.

He read through it once, and closed it with a smile. There were six names to choose from. Not bad odds. He leaned forward. "Jacob, I've changed my mind. Take me to Edda's place."

"Yes, sir. Shall I wait for you?"

"No. Take the rest of the day off, and pick me up there about midnight."

At half past eleven, shaking his head, Bormann watched Klaus dress. He still couldn't quite get over how perfect his clone was. He chuckled to himself. It really was too bad Dr. Feinstein couldn't see the remarkable results

Tom Lewis

of his last and most successful operation. The Polish tailor had indeed been an expert, too. Had performed his two week's task admirably, had been rewarded with the last of many good meals, three final glasses of good wine, and was now resting in peace in a certain churchyard, courtesy of one of Skorzeny's bullets in the back of his head. A merciful blessing, actually. A bullet in the brain was much quicker than the slow gassing which would have been his eventual fate anyway.

"I'm ready," Klaus said, mimicking Bormann's voice perfectly. "Now, let's see. I'm to stay more or less in the background. Only speak when spoken to, which would be completely in character. Not that it will matter much, since many of those Generals have never even seen you—I mean, me, and Hitler will be too busy to give me the time of day anyway, except to maybe say, 'Isn't that right, Bormann?' I'm to make sure Dr. Morell is always nearby, ready to give the Fuehrer his useless pills or another injection if necessary, and to take notes only if told to."

"Correct," Bormann confirmed. "You're as ready as you'll ever be, and after fooling Helmut twice and Fraulein Kemper and Glas three times, I'm sure you will manage fine. What do you think, Edda?"

Edda's answer was in a low, awestruck voice. "It's truly unimaginable. I never thought it would work, but now that I see both of you like this, hear both of you talking... Oh, yes. Bormann The Second will pass muster just fine, no matter where he goes. I swear, Klaus, I believe you're really enjoying this!"

"I am, Edda," the actor replied. "It's better even than playing Faust." He turned back to Bormann. "And when I

Hitler's Judas

return, I'm to have Glas drive me home after a routine stop at the office."

"Correct again," Bormann said. "All right. Here is your briefcase. Everything you're likely to need is in there. Good luck."

In a perfect parody of his master, Klaus turned, an arrogant half smirk on his face. "It's not a matter of luck, is it? It's a matter of skill and talent. You needn't worry. You and Edda have yourselves a nice three day holiday."

"Oh, we will, 'Herr Reichsleiter.' We will."

A few minutes later, holding hands, Bormann and Edda watched through the window as Klaus got into the waiting car. Bormann hoped Klaus would sweat a little after boarding the plane. Now, that would really be in character. He turned, kissed Edda on the tip of her nose and said, "I could use a drink and a hot bath, little sparrow. Then we'd best get some sleep. Helmut doesn't know I was supposed to go to the front with Hitler. He's picking us up first thing tomorrow morning."

"*We're* going somewhere?"

"Yes. To Regensberg."

Camp Commandant Colonel Heinz Jurgen Trappe glanced at the list of new prisoners he had recently acquired. It was a short list, but puzzling nonetheless. These men had not been troublemakers at their previous camps. None were officers, none of them very bright, and none had ever attempted an escape, according to his information. So, why had they been sent here? To a maximum security camp that held only officers? Officers who had escaped and had been recaptured. What was even more disturbing was that

$-212-$

Tom Lewis

they had been sent to him on direct orders from Obergruppenfuehrer Berger (who had in no uncertain terms told Trappe that *his* orders had come from no less than 'The very top!') That meant Hitler himself. Well, the way things were going in the Third Reich these days, nothing was surprising any more. He almost wished he was back at the eastern front, where with luck, he might lose his other foot and be out of it altogether.

Sighing heavily, he put his glasses on and looked back down at the list. All were American airmen who had been captured after being shot down:

Williams, Richard T. Sgt. Nashville, Tennessee
Colby, Robert M. Sgt. Richmond, Virginia
Kingman, Gerald S. Cpl. Charleston, South Carolina
Reams, Bobby J. Cpl. Morehead City, North Carolina
Chambliss, Murray F. Pvt. Savannah, Georgia
Pinner, Norwood J. Pvt. Baltimore, Maryland

Another thing. Why did his orders include instructions to keep these men in isolation, completely away from the general camp population? Trappe was poring over the list for the fourth time when his adjutant knocked and came in, his face showing deep concern.

"What is it, Captain?"

"Sir, we have *visitors*. They just drove through the main gate."

Colonel Trappe got up and went to the window. The Mercedes sedan had stopped in front of his walkway, and three people had gotten out; a beautiful woman and two men. Trappe growled a curse under his breath. One of the men was wearing the black uniform no Camp Commandant ever

Hitler's Judas

wanted to see. *Gestapo*. Worse, though the other man was dressed in civilian clothes, Trappe, having seen him once or twice before, recognized him. *What in hell could Reichsleiter Martin Bormann want here?* He looked at his nervous second in command. "Could be trouble. Bring them right in, and for God's sake, don't forget to say 'Heil Hitler.' "

Bormann told Helmut to stay by the car, and following the straight-necked *Wehrmacht* Captain, led Edda up the wooden steps, past the stiff sentries, and into the Headquarters building. They were promptly ushered into the main office where they were offered seats by a polite but wary Commandant, who said, firmly, "Colonel Heinz Trappe, Herr Reichsleiter. At your service."

Bormann lifted an eyebrow. "You recognize me? Good. Then you will have surmised I am here at the request of the Fuehrer. Allow me to present my secretary, Fraulein Winter."

Trappe bowed formally. "Fraulein." His suspicious eyes went back to Bormann. "How may I serve you and our Fuehrer, Reichsleiter?"

Bormann got right to it. "The six prisoners you were sent. Are they all well?"

"Yes, sir."

Trappe was a smart man, Bormann thought. Not about to say more than necessary, and not about to ask questions either.

"Tell me, Colonel, do you have a good cook in this camp?"

"Yes, sir. We have a very good cook."

"I'm happy to hear it. I want you to have him prepare

— 214 —

Tom Lewis

a fine meal for those six men tonight. By fine meal, I mean just that, not bowls of weak cabbage soup and moldy bread. A dinner such as you yourself eat on Sundays and holidays, but with beer, not wine. Fraulein Winter and I will share it with them, and in a private room, please. A separate tray is to be served to our driver. Do you think you can arrange that on such short notice?"

Trappe didn't bat an eye. "Yes, sir. What time?"

The Colonel was as good as his word. At seven sharp, a gigantic meal was placed on a table in the abandoned Officer's Mess. Roast beef, boats of gravy, mountains of potatoes, beans, hot bread, and steins of beer awaited the six Americans. One by one, they filed in past Edda and Bormann, who were wearing Red Cross armbands, and as directed, took their places. Confused and frightened, not a single word was spoken by any one of them, but their hunger rapidly overcame their initial fear, and all six dived into the food like greedy pigs. Throughout the meal, Edda, in one of the best performances of her life, chatted with them in her Scarlett O'Hara English. "...And before the war, my Daddy had a sugah bizness down in New Orleans, but we had to come on back home... Where y'all from?"

Only one man, Sergeant Williams, failed to gradually relax. Suspicious from the beginning, he refused to talk at all, though he ate and drank with the same gusto the others did. The rest, however, quickly succumbed to Edda's beauty and charm, especially after she passed out packages of Lucky Strikes and Zippo lighters to each man. Bormann himself said very little, but by turn kept a broad grin or an understanding frown on his face while watching and

Hitler's Judas

listening closely to each man rattle on and on about missing loved ones, and home, and how they had been treated in their other camps, all thinking they were talking to *bona fide*, sympathetic Red Cross personnel.

The strong beer loosened tongues all around the table. One man was far more talkative than the rest. Corporal Bobby Joe Reams, a wiry little fellow shorter even than Bormann, seemed to enjoy telling them how the Army had almost been ready to turn him down until they found out how well he could shoot, then had assigned him to the Air Corps where— "...They shipped me over to Limey-land, stuck me in the ass end of a B-17 Flyin' Fortress and told me to shoot the shit out of anything smaller than our plane. Oh, 'scuse me, Ma'am. I forget. Anyways, I didn't get no chance to. My first trip over, we got blown up and I was the only one got out. Landed in a tater field and here I am. 'Cept for testing my gun, I ain't pulled a trigger yet in this friggin' war."

Bormann noted that Reams was the one from Morehead City, North Carolina. He waited until the best moment came, and gave Edda a prearranged signal that he had chosen his man. Edda stood, saying. "Well, it sure has been nice talking to you sweet boys. May I walk you back to your barracks? No, take the cigarettes and lighters with you. Courtesy of the Red Cross. I do hope y'all enjoyed your meal. Maybe we can all do this again sometime. No, Corporal Reams. You stay a while longer. Mr. Brown wants to ask you a few questions about Morehead City."

Edda led the others out, and Bormann faced the suddenly apprehensive tail gunner. Both palms up, he said, "Relax, son. Let's just talk some more. Would you like a cigar?"

— 216 —

Tom Lewis

"A real cigar? You bet I would!"

Bormann handed him one, waited until Reams had it going, and continued, "Bobby Joe, if you had one wish, what would it be?"

"Man, I'd get my ass back home and get my job on the shrimp boat back."

Bormann pursed his lips, then reached into his pocket. He handed over a hundred dollar bill. "I'll bet you could buy a few camp cigarettes with that."

"Jesus H. Christ and Kilroy, too. I ain't never seen but one of these in my whole life!"

"It's yours."

"Mine? For what?"

"Just for talking to me. How would you like it if I arranged for you to go home?"

"Home? You kiddin' me?"

Bormann then reached into his briefcase and removed a money belt. He showed the wide-eyed Corporal that each pocket of it was packed with hundred-dollar bills. "There's fifty thousand dollars in here. Try it on— under your shirt."

Bobby Joe Reams stared at him with narrowed eyes. "What you gettin' at, Mister?"

Bormann took time lighting his own cigar. "I know a way to get you back home, and if you cooperate with me, there's another belt just like that one waiting for you. I imagine with that much money, you could buy your own shrimp boat."

"Hell, I could buy half a dozen of 'em. What would I have to do?"

"Help *me*. You see, I wish to go to America, too."

This statement left Corporal Bobby Joe Reams speechless.

– 217 –

Hitler's Judas

Bormann reached back into his briefcase for a map, which he spread out on the table, pointing to a small town with a red circle around it. "If a submarine landed us somewhere on one of these North Carolina beaches, could you take me there without anyone knowing about it?"

"To Williamston? Sure I could. Small boat. Piece of cake at night, but why Williamston?"

"There's a Prisoner of War camp there, with a lot of Germans in it."

"I know. I seen a bunch of 'em myself down at New Bern one time, workin' on farms."

"Right. And for one hundred thousand dollars, you'd be willing to take me there?"

"Mister, I don't know who you really are, or what in hell you're up to, but for that kinda dough, I'd take old Rudolf Hitler there. You just got yourself a guide. When do we go?"

Bormann stood. "Right now, first stage by automobile. So, take your shirt off and put that belt on. It's all yours, but a word of caution. Once we are out of this room, you are not to move a muscle or open your mouth again until I tell you to. You will do precisely what I tell you to from now on. If you don't, I will make sure that money belt is taken from your waist and replaced by a rope around your neck. Do you understand me completely?"

It was barely dark when Colonel Trappe and his adjutant watched the Mercedes drive back through the gate. "Sir, what do you suppose Hitler wants with an American draftee?"

"No idea, and I'm not going to ask. Neither are you."

"What are we supposed to do with the other five?"

Trappe turned to his second in command, his mouth a tight, thin line. "Bormann told me those poor boys really enjoyed their last supper. He ordered me to take them out into the woods at midnight and shoot them."

CHAPTER 21

There were many things that caused Horst to soon hate the tour he was required to make. Erich Dremmel, Goebbels' young adjutant, who was in charge of bookings, travel arrangements, lodging and other details, was a pleasant enough fellow. He was decent company for Horst and Elisabeth, but in spite of his enthusiasm and good will, Dremmel could not avoid showing Horst off in places that produced just the opposite effect that was intended. To be sure, still-living residents of Berlin, Hamburg, Stuttgart, Frankfurt, Leipzig, and every other major city in Hitler's crumbling Reich were delighted to shake hands and have their pictures taken with an authentic, good-looking war hero and his very pretty companion. Just as many of them, however, were afraid to venture out in the open, any time of

Tom Lewis

day or night, leaving a safe cellar or similar shelter they might have found, having taken refuge from the incessant bombings. Every town they traveled to, large or small, showed the naked, depressing, and massive destruction that was now Germany's outer skin.

No, Horst was hard pressed to lie; to keep a false smile on his face and assure those brave, hungry souls who came out to see him that yes, the Fatherland was having a few setbacks, but would ultimately defeat the enemy that was closing in from both east and west. Whatever small boost in morale he gave these doubting citizens was subtracted in equal measure from his own. He was uncomfortable standing in front of the ever present, ubiquitous movie camera. Embarrased to see his likeness plastered across the front pages of local newspapers. Mortified that the youthful director had to keep reminding him to fling his arm up and shout "Heil Hitler!"

He missed his boat and crew. He missed the constant jolts of adrenaline that action brought. He longed for the sea itself.

And then, there was Elisabeth. All the things he felt negative about—the awkward limelight of publicity, the adoration of crowds, the unaccustomed luxury of first-class accommodations, food and wines, being waited on hand and foot—Elisabeth loved! She absolutely adored being on center stage. Her by-proxy status.

She saw nothing of the suffering all around her. She did not notice how many of the good folk were dressed in rags. She paid no attention to those who were missing an arm here, a leg there, or the children begging in the streets. Wearing Mama Irmgard's dresses and most of her jewelry, Elisabeth was a tireless, willing shill and alter ego, never

Hitler's Judas

straying more than inches from Horst's side, and never ceasing to prattle on and on about how famous her sweetheart was, how handsome he looked in his new, tailored uniform, how impressive his new medal was.

By day, she wore a permanent smile and affected the mannerisms and bearing of a Countess—or at least a film star, even leaning out of train windows, waving her handkerchief and blowing kisses to crowds gathered in various train stations. Finally alone in their hotel suite after supper, she painstakingly clipped articles and photographs from every publication, adding to an already stuffed scrapbook. And, she had sexual energy enough left over every night in bed to drive Horst to utter exhaustion. Horst gradually realized that Elisabeth was at long last, solidly in her element, living out all her shallow fantasies.

But he was not. He found himself counting days, hours even, until he would report back to Doenitz's Headquarters— more drained, physically and emotionally, than from any harrowing patrol.

The high, or rather the low point came in Cologne. On a dreary Tuesday, in a steady rain, they made their way through a filthy, stinking city that, except for its magnificent cathedral, had been totally leveled. The cathedral had miraculously taken only one bomb through the roof, which had not exploded. Inside, a makeshift hospital had been set up, which Dr. Harald von Hellenbach was in charge of. Harald, looking twice his age, his smock splattered with blood, accompanied Horst and Elisabeth through the first rows of cots and pallets where the wounded were practically stacked like cordwood.

Horst turned to Dremmel. "Please, Erich, no cameras in

— 222 —

Tom Lewis

here." With a serious glance at Elisabeth, he added, "Wait outside, Lizzle."

"But Horst—" she started to protest.

"No. Not his time." He then sincerely did what he thought was his real duty, stopping by most of the bedsides with a kind or encouraging word, a handshake, and a whispered promise that he would do his best to help bring the war to an end. Not one of the bleeding, maimed soldiers cared a damn any more about which side won. To a man, they just wanted it to be over.

Afterwards, Horst begged Harald to join them for lunch.

"Impossible, Horst You see what I must deal with here. I can't afford to be gone five more minutes."

"You are doing a splendid job, Harald," Elisabeth cooed. "We are so proud of you."

Harald gave her a twisted frown. "One does one's duty, whether or not medals are the reward. If I can save one life, or at least patch up one man enough to go back into battle against those American gangsters and Russian *untermenschen*, I will have done my bit for the Fuehrer. Oh, I almost forgot. I have a present for you. For you both."

Harald dug into the pocket of his stained smock, extracting a small box. "Actually, I bought these some time ago. I'd like for you to have them." He handed the box to his twin.

Horst opened it, already guessing what was inside. The plain gold bands glittered on their tiny velvet cushion. Harald grabbed Horst's hand. "The hero won fair lady, brother. Do me at least the honor of wearing those rings."

"Oh, Harald," Elisabeth gushed. "How beautifully

– 223 –

Hitler's Judas

romantic! Of course we will wear them. Forever. We shall have our engagement party this very night. Thank you." With those words, she reached up and kissed Harald on a cheek that had not seen a razor in a week, not trusting herself to say more.

Harald didn't wait for Horst to say anything. He mumbled, "I must go back in. Be well, you two." He turned on his elevated heel and marched back into the church with as much dignified gait as he could muster.

Elisabeth embraced her lover. "Tonight's the last one of the tour, my darling. Erich is driving us to Bonn, and we'll all have champagne and a fine dinner. Afterwards, we'll put our rings on, and, well, you'll see."

Horst shrugged. "If you wish, Lizzle. Let's hope the Americans don't rain bombs on our parade."

The following Monday, Horst eyed the gray brute resting inside the largest pen he had ever seen. Oskar Knapp nudged him at the elbow. "Ain't she the most gorgeous thing you ever laid eyes on, Herr Kaleun? I gotta hand it to our designers and engineers. What a boat! Of course, she's just Kellerman's old prototype, stripped-down for training, but still..."

Chief Knapp was talking as if Horst had never seen her design specs or studied her capabilities. "...Jesus, Herr Kaleun, she's *twice* as big as the old boats, and can go twice as fast. Just imagine, if you want to, you can shoot eighteen torpedoes inside of twenty minutes. All I'd have to do to reload is simply push a few little buttons. Amazing!"

Horst silently acknowledged what his old chief had said, and added, "True, Chief. The two new advanced

Tom Lewis

models built at Trondheim are total weapons. It's too bad we can't take one out to the real war. How is the crew?"

"Every rating is an experienced man, sir. And every man aboard is damn glad to be here."

"I'm sure of that. You and I should be, too. We have been very lucky, Chief."

"Don't I know it! I just wish we could have at least shanghaied Kirchner. Wonder how our old boat is doing?"

Horst shook his head. "No idea, but Lieutenant Heidt learned a lot with us. I believe he will give a good account of himself." He straightened to his full military stance. "Well, let's go and see what kind of babies we have to train."

Oskar frowned. "Babies is the right word, Herr Kaleun. I doubt if any of them shaves yet. Still…"

"What?"

"Oh, I hear rumors, you know. Hitler is drafting old men and children now. Can you believe it?"

"Yes. I wish I could say no, but I can believe it. I can believe anything now. Let's go."

Half an hour later, Horst was facing a classroom filled with recent cadet graduates. It seemed to him that it had been a million years since he had been one of them, and no doubt these boys would age even faster, no matter how well he trained them.

"*Achtung!*" Knapp yelled, and one hundred young men jumped to their feet in unison.

"Rest easy," Horst said, gesturing for them to sit. "This will be my only speech to you, and that first command marks the last time you will ever hear me speak those two words. From this moment on, you will *not* rest easy. You will work harder than you ever thought possible. Sleep and the dreams that go with it are not on your agenda any more. You no longer have a family at home. Your family is here. It's called a crew, and to a man, they all know more than you do.

"I am your new father, and you will be the most obedient of sons. This person here," he said, indicating Chief Knapp, "Will be your new mother. My advice is to always listen to your mother. Whatever she tells you, take dead seriously. If you don't, you will soon be seriously dead. You will now begin by standing and telling me your names."

Each man, trying his best to out-shout the previous one, jumped again to his feet and yelled his name, loud and clear. Horst repeated it softly, and when the last youth shouted, "Sir, Franz Michael Allerman, *sir!*" Horst nodded once, then said, "Good. You have been divided into two watches. First watch report to the boat in ten minutes. Dismissed."

Two hundred heels clicked, and a resounding "Heil Hitler" thundered forth. When the echoes died down, Franz Allerman glanced to the boy on his left. "He must be one tough nut. He didn't say Heil Hitler."

"One of the members of the crew told me he never does."

The following Tuesday, Horst von Hellenbach and Elisabeth Kroll posted their bans.

CHAPTER 22

Bormann barely had time to get Helmut transferred once again to his own office ('For a period of service time to be determined by the Fuehrer') and Corporal Bobby Joe Reams moved into his apartment (with his flabbergasted brother acting as host/guard) when the Third Reich's next calamity occurred. On the sweltering early afternoon of 20 July, barely a month after the invasion, a bomb exploded in the midst of Hitler's war conference at his 'Wolf's Lair' complex near Rastenburg, in East Prussia. Miraculously, Hitler survived with only a few cuts, bruises, and singed hair, but several others were killed and a number severely wounded. Bormann, like many others in Berlin, heard the incredible news on the radio and only believed it when Hitler came on the air to personally report it, to reassure his minions

Hitler's Judas

that he was indeed alive and well, and that the dastardly cowards who had attempted to remove him from his sacred duty would be severely punished. Bormann later found out that Hitler had met Mussolini that very afternoon, boasted about his immunity from a fatal fate, had showed him around the still smoking ruins, then had calmly taken *Il Duce* to tea!

And Hitler would keep his word. Before his thirst for revenge and retribution was slaked, nearly two thousand men and women—some guilty, many totally innocent—would be executed, often in horrible fashion, including General Eppinger and some time later, Admiral Canaris himself.

The weeks and months immediately following the attempted *coup* were busy but happy ones for Martin Bormann. He lost no opportunity to continue planting poisonous anti-Roosevelt seeds in Hitler's feverish mind. While Klaus took his place, Bormann made two secret trips to Norway, and arranged for fifty million in gold to be trucked from Essen to a hiding place beneath a barn near Flensburg. In September, during a rare free night in Edda's apartment, he sat drinking with Edda and Klaus. "The time is drawing close now, and I need to talk to both of you about what is to be done next. First, Edda, I want you to pack tonight. I'm sending you home to Munich tomorrow. You and Jutta. You will both be safe there."

Edda was not in the least displeased to hear that, since Berlin was being bombed nightly. She was also happy to hear that Martin was including her mother in his generosity. "That's very kind of you. What do you want me to do there?"

"Wait for word from me. I'm moving in here with

– 228 –

Tom Lewis

Klaus." He started to say something else, then thought better of it. "Come on, Uncle Freddy, let's take a little night air. It's nice outside."

The two of them left Edda's place and walked down the practically deserted street, taking advantage of a lull in the bombing. "Listen carefully, Berger. At first, I had decided on an overland escape route, through Austria and Italy. When you came into the picture, I decided to use my backup plan, which you needn't know anything about. Since you have done such a good job, I have decided to give you some money and my original plan. You probably won't need the money, since everything has been arranged for me, and well paid for in advance. If you're careful, you should be able to get to South America without any major difficulties, although it will certainly take time.

"Also, when the time comes, I'm going to give you a coded password for an organization that will assist you every step of the way, plus account numbers in two Swiss banks which will make you a very rich man."

"When are you planning to leave?"

Bormann didn't answer right away. He thought of something von Bittnerhof had said. The obese shipbuilder had been oh, so right. The time would be best when the country and the government were in a state of total chaos and disarray. "Soon. Possibly sometime right after the first of the year. France is already lost. The Russians are already pounding at the door in East Prussia, and Hitler is shooting more German deserters than enemy soldiers. I'll let you know when the right moment comes. For the present, you and I both still have important work ahead. Haven't you learned my patience yet?"

– 229 –

Hitler's Judas

Ever in character, Klaus snickered. "Sure I have, fancy pants. I can wait till doomsday if need be, and from the looks of this town, it won't be long."

The next afternoon, Edda and her astonished mother were on a packed train to Munich. Jutta glanced across the spacious compartment at her daughter. "First class, yet! I take back everything I said about him. Only..."

"Only what?"

"How the devil are we supposed to live? Neither of us has a job."

Edda patted the hat box in her lap. "There's enough in here for us to live on in good style for two years or more. Look." She opened the box, revealing well over a hundred thousand in dollars and Francs, all in small bills. "Martin told me that it will most likely be the Americans who will capture Bavaria. Possibly a few French. We should get along just fine if we're careful."

Jutta whistled softly, shaking her head in both surprise and reluctant admiration. "I guess he really does care for you. Do you ever expect to see him again?"

Edda looked sharply at her mother. "What are you saying? Of course I do. He more than 'cares for me,' Mother. He loves me, and I know he will come for me someday soon, or at least send for me."

"What about his wife and family?"

"What about them? They're safe enough at that place he sent them last year, and I imagine he left them pretty well fixed, too."

"When do you think he will send for you?"

"Who knows? Soon, I believe. I hope it's before I have

— 230 —

Tom Lewis

his baby."

"Good God! You're *pregnant?* Does he know?"

"No. Not yet. I'll find the right time to tell him. Trust me."

It was in early September that Hitler had a brainstorm. When Eisenhower's rapidly advancing armies finally outran their supplies, and had come to a muddy standstill, the Fuehrer hastily laid plans for a massive counterattack. Borrowing from Peter to pay Paul, he robbed his commanders in the east of troops and material needed to hold back the Russians, and by December, had slapped together a force large and deadly enough to cause the serious setback for the Allies that would become known as the Battle of the Bulge.

Shortly before Christmas, in Hitler's headquarters at Ziegenberg, Bormann found the chance he had been waiting for to start the final phase of his plan. On the twenty-second, the very day the German Commander, General von Luettwitz was drafting a note to the beleaguered Americans under the command of stubborn General McCauliff and demanding the surrender of Bastogne, Bormann poured a cup of tea and remarked to the jubilant Hitler, "My Fuehrer, you have done it again! The morale of your people and your troops will once more be sky high. Eisenhower may very well not recover from this, but you know what else you could do?"

"What?"

"One further brilliant move. Something that would absolutely crush the morale of the enemy and throw their war into reverse."

– 231 –

Hitler's Judas

"Go on."

"Stalin will probably be murdered someday by his own criminals, and Churchill is nothing more now than an impotent old bag of fart-wind. You could add a final, humiliating and unrecoverable blow to the Americans by killing the man who matters most to them. Roosevelt himself."

Hitler didn't reply, but narrowed his eyes and waited for Bormann to continue.

"I have thought about it for a long, long time, Fuehrer, and have formulated a plan I am convinced would work, and I also know just the man who can pull it off."

"Who?" Hitler finally said.

"Colonel Otto Skorzeny. Consider how he rescued Mussolini. Look, for instance, at the job he has done in this present action; infiltrating the American lines, his men dressed in American uniforms, using their own jeeps, raising hell with their supplies, misdirecting traffic. A brilliant operator, and dependable as bad weather. He's the man for the job, all right, and I'd like to go over the plan with you now, if you will permit me."

"Pour more tea, Martin. I'm listening."

At that same moment, at Kiel, Chief Oskar Knapp was asking his Captain about Christmas leave. "Do you think Uncle Karl will give us a day off?"

"I don't know, Oskar. I hope so, but I wouldn't bet on it. There's so much to do. This training business can't stop for holidays."

Oskar spat with disgust. "Training? A fat lot of training we're doing. Out to sea, what, maybe one day a

– 232 –

Tom Lewis

week? And when we do get out, we have nothing but dummy ammunition. We're safe enough in this pen, but the Allies are bombing our training areas just as often as they blast the yards at Hamburg. They can shoot at us but we can't shoot back. Besides, what's the use of training men when there are no U-Boats to put them in? We build ten and the *Amis* bomb nine of them. Doenitz sends ten boats out and only four come back. Practically suicide missions. What's the fucking use?"

Horst didn't answer. He *had* no answer. One of the last boats to go out and not return had been their beloved U-119, with Rudi Heidt in command. He had not told Oskar about that, mainly since his buddy, their former cook, Kirchner, had also been aboard, along with almost all their old crew. He wondered if he should tell Oskar what he'd heard the day before from Admiral Godt; that two of the new electroboats built in Norway were being launched any day now, and he would probably be given command of one of them, but for training purposes only, not combat. At least that boat would be the sophisticated finished product, not the stripped down prototype they had been using. No. Better to let Oskar be as surprised as he was at the news. He decided to wait.

After a few minutes of brooding silence, Oskar growled. "Hell, who wants to go out now, anyway? Real shit-weather out there. I wish I had a glass of grog. At least a beer. A woman would be better still, if one— Say, Herr Kaleun, did your girl get that place you told me about fixed up?"

"She's my fiancee now, Oskar. And yes, she's made that cottage up there quite livable. Not the Metropole, mind you, but livable. Really cozy."

– 233 –

Hitler's Judas

Oskar chuckled. "I can just imagine. When are you two getting married?"

"If Uncle Karl doesn't send me back into combat, and if Germany is still Germany, we plan to marry next spring."

"Don't wait, son. I wouldn't make bets on either one of those 'ifs.'"

Horst stared at his Chief. It was the first time he realized how old Knapp actually was, and the man had called him 'son.' Oskar had never married. Never had children. Horst blushed, pleased that the man thought so much of him, he'd call him son, forgetting rank and circumstances. He turned away, thinking wistfully of his bleak future, and Elisabeth.

Wonder what it would be like to have a son?

Not that many miles north, on the frozen edge of the Baltic, Elisabeth stoked the fire again. One thing about this little cottage, maybe the only *good* thing about it, was its fireplace. Central to all four rooms, it heated the entire place enough so that one could walk around without clothes on. She giggled. If Horst managed to get even half a day free at Christmas, that was one of the presents she'd planned to give him. She had a few others for him, naturally, but she knew that would please him the most. He had been so cool lately. So remote. Was he having second thoughts about their engagement? Their coming marriage? He wouldn't be the first sailor to leave a girl at the altar. But even if he did, well, there was one foolproof way to guarantee her future in prominent celebrity circles. Horst might run out on her one day, but he would never abandon a child. Especially a son...

CHAPTER 23

<u>Berlin, 20 March, 1945</u>

Grand Admiral Doenitz looked up from the papers on his desk when his assistant knocked and came in. "You wished to see me, sir?" Godt said.

"Yes. Have a seat. It appears as though we will be moving again."

Godt sat down heavily. "Where to now, Flensburg?"

"Yes. Fuehrer's orders. This time I didn't argue. It will be easier to manage our Trondheim and Bergen operations from there."

"True. Are we making a difference, Admiral? I mean, things are looking really bad. It's a sad state of affairs when whole armies are commanded by the likes of Himmler and

Goebbels!"

Doenitz didn't instantly respond. He didn't know quite how to give Godt a proper answer anyway. The noose was closing fast around the neck of the Third Reich. Eisenhower had bashed in Hitler's front door and Zhukov his back door. Russian troops were less than fifty miles from Berlin and the Allies had already crossed the Rhine. It was obviously only a matter of time, and any fool could see it. "The Fuehrer told me he is planning to move his own headquarters to the Obersalzburg and direct the rest of the war from there, Godt. He holds out hopes that his new weapons will turn the tide."

Godt sniffed. "New weapons! They might have made a difference two years ago. The new jet airplane is a wonder, but the Allies are destroying them on the ground before they can take off. The flying bomb bases have been overrun, and are useless. His only hope, as I see it, is for us to pull his chestnuts out of the fire with our new boats. Over a hundred have been commissioned at Hamburg in spite of the bombing."

"They won't do us any good now, unfortunately. We have no crews to man them, and no way to get them out of Germany to battle areas. Training has become almost impossible. Only the two new boats built in Norway are able to get to the open sea, the U-2511 and U-2512. Anyway, we will do our duty as best we can. All-out warfare. No quarter asked or given. No matter how it all turns out, we shall have done our jobs the best we could. Is von Hellenbach here?"

"Yes, sir. Right outside."

"Good. Bring him in, please."

Godt nodded, rose and went to the door.

– 236 –

Tom Lewis

"Korvettenkapitan, the Admiral will see you now."

Horst came in, saluted, and said, "You sent for me, sir?"

"Yes. Sit down. Make yourself comfortable."

Horst took the chair next to Godt and waited for the Admiral to speak.

"How was your trip from Kiel?" Doentiz asked.

"Fine, sir. Those little Storchs are wonderful airplanes. Like a boy's kite with an engine. We hugged the water and the ground all the way."

"Son," Doenitz said, clearing his throat. "How do you feel about your current assignment?"

"The training mission sir? Well, truth be known, not being out there somewhere shooting at real ships, I feel a bit like a square peg in a round hole, but I have seen some talented men come through the course."

Doenitz frowned. "Too bad none of them have any combat experience. I'm sure you have also heard the scuttlebutt about the two new boats. I have decided to give one of them, the U-2511, to Schnee, who has pestered me for two years to get back into action. The other will go to Mohr. Today is Saturday. By Monday morning, we will be in new headquarters at Flensburg. I am transferring you there to take Schnee's place on my staff, effective immediately." He watched the young officer's eyes for any sign of disappointment, but saw none. Instead, von Hellenbach's eyes lit up "That's wonderful news, sir. I will do my best for you."

"I know you will, but before you assume your new duties, you have a little leave time coming, and I insist you take it."

– 237 –

Hitler's Judas

"Thank you Admiral. That I will."

"Will you travel home to see your charming mother?"

"Uh, no sir. I— I think I'll try to bring her up to Kiel or to Flensburg."

"What on earth for?"

"My wedding, Admiral. And, I would be honored if you and Admiral Godt could be there, too. That is, if it's at all possible."

"We'll see. At any rate, congratulations. You may go now. Your leave starts immediately."

After Horst had saluted and left, Godt laughed and commented, "Happens to the best of us."

"The luckiest of us. I'm glad I didn't have to tell him I have been ordered by the Fuehrer to remove him from any kind of dangerous duty, combat *or* training missions. Hitler doesn't want his hero hurt. Frankly, I wish I could have given the U-2512 to him, and I would had Hitler not instructed me otherwise. Between von Hellenbach and Schnee, they could have done some real damage to the enemy, and both those men know how to do the job and come back. Around headquarters, he will still be a square peg in a round hole."

"One of us at least should plan to go to his wedding."

"As I said, we'll see." Doenitz pinched his nose. "But it would be nice to attend some sort of happy occasion, wouldn't it?"

Except for a day spent at Flensburg making wedding arrangements and where Admiral Godt, pulling a lot of strings, helped him contact his brother and arrange transportation for his mother, Horst spent his entire leave

— 238 —

Tom Lewis

time with Elisabeth at the cottage on the edge of the Baltic.

Their romantic vacation from war in their hideaway cottage on the Baltic lasted exactly four days and nights, the happiest (and longest) time alone together of their lives. They were still in bed the morning of the fourth day when they heard loud knocking at the door. Having not had that much sleep, Horst, cursing under his breath, grabbed a robe, slipped it on and went to the door, ready to throttle whoever it was who had interrupted their idyll.

He opened the heavy oak door and was struck dumb when he saw the stern face of the Grand Admiral himself, accompanied by a black-uniformed, unknown Colonel of the SS. He finally found his voice. "Admiral?"

"I'm very sorry, von Hellenbach, but you are to get dressed immediately and come with us."

"Right *now*, sir? But where?"

"First back to Flensburg, then Colonel Skorzeny here will fly you to Berlin. The Fuehrer wants to see you tonight. We'll wait out here for you. Please extend my profound apologies to your Elisabeth."

In nearly a catatonic state, Horst trudged back into the bedroom and headed for the wardrobe.

"Who was it, Horst?"

"Would you believe Grand Admiral Doenitz? I've been ordered to Berlin."

"Berlin? But why? You have three more days of your leave left."

"Why, Lizzle? Hitler wants to see me, they said, that's why. Don't worry, I'll probably be back by Friday."

"*Hitler?*" Elisabeth was more shocked than disappointed, so she didn't cry. Not right away. Watching

Hitler's Judas

her fiancée dress, all she could think of was that maybe, just maybe, these last few days in bed had been enough to start a baby. She hoped so. Prayed so. And when she tilted her head up to receive his good-bye kiss, she had no thought whatsoever that it would be the last one she would ever share with him.

Thus Horst made his second flight in a tiny Storch back to Berlin within a week! When Colonel Skorzeny ushered him into Hitler's office, there were only two other men there. Horst recognized Reichsleiter Bormann easily enough, but could hardly believe the wreck of man sitting behind the desk was the same Adolf Hitler who had hung the medal around his neck. With effort, the Fuehrer managed to rise and come around from behind the desk as Horst came to attention. The reason he didn't return Horst's salute was because he was holding his right arm with his left, in a feeble attempt to hide its trembling. He dragged his right leg like a cripple, his pasty face twitched, and his eyes were like those of a man in high fever. Yet, his voice was amazingly calm. Soft.

"Korvettenkapitan von Hellenbach. How good it is to see you again. Please be at ease. Take a chair." Hitler leaned back against his desk as Horst complied. "You must remember my personal secretary, Martin Bormann. Would you care for some refreshment? Some tea perhaps?"

"No, thank you, Fuehrer. I'm fine."

Hitler's eyes bore into his. "I have brought you here because Germany needs your expertise. *I* need your expertise. Tell me, hypothetically speaking, do you think it possible to make a secret round trip voyage by U-Boat from

Tom Lewis

Trondheim to South America without being discovered?"

Horst didn't hesitate. "Yes, my Fuehrer, if it was in one of the new model electroboats, carrying extra fuel instead of so many torpedoes, and provided the South American destination was on its eastern coast."

"Bravo! Just what I thought. And I am also convinced there is only one Captain capable of commanding such a voyage. So. Would you be prepared to undertake this mission? For your country? For me?"

Again, the habit of duty caused Horst to answer, "If you command me, I will take a boat anywhere, Fuehrer."

"Excellent! I knew I could count on you. Now, you must please excuse me. I have a lot on my plate just now. Reichsleiter Bormann will give you all your further instructions. From this moment on, bear in mind that his orders are my orders. His word is my word. Just remember that this mission is vital to the Reich, and no one outside this room must ever know about it. No one, do you understand?"

"Yes, Fuehrer. I understand perfectly."

"Then accept my personal thanks. Good-bye and good luck."

Bormann crooked a finger at Horst. "Come with me, please."

Bormann led the U-Boat Captain into his own office. "Please have a seat. I'll be right with you. Glancing at his watch, he then went through the door to his outer office where Skorzeny was waiting. "Is everything set?"

"All is in order, Reichsleiter. The 'merchandise' has been transferred to the boat at Trondheim as you ordered,

Hitler's Judas

stashed away inside the torpedoes marked with red numbers. The ones holding the demolition explosives are marked with blue numbers."

"What about the timing device?"

"Stowed in the place we chose. You can set it to go off any time up to one hour."

"And the, ah, special items?"

"Also in place."

"Good. What about the crew?"

"Already there, in separate quarters and under guard. My men have the entire complex under total security. Not even Doenitz himself could get inside that compound without your permission."

Bormann chortled. "If he could see inside it, he'd faint, wouldn't he?"

Skorzeny said, "I daresay. What about von Hellenbach? Will he be a problem?"

"No. He will be kept totally in the dark. As a matter of fact, two weeks from now, his mother and fiancé will get 'official' letters saying he was lost at sea, in yet another brave battle against the enemy. How's the weather?"

"Not bad. We should have no problems flying."

Bormann hid his sudden apprehension at hearing that word. "All right then. Go bring the car around. I have to make a phone call, then we can leave. And, Otto, once you get back from Norway, I wouldn't waste a minute of time disappearing. There won't be much time left, and the Fuehrer would not want you captured, especially by our Russian friends. Are you sure you won't change your mind and come with us?"

"No thanks, Reichsleiter. I'm just as scared of those

— 242 —

Tom Lewis

U-Boats as you are flying. Maybe more. No, I'll take my chances on land. Don't worry, I know how to take care of myself."

"Fine, then. I'll meet you downstairs in about ten minutes."

Bormann showed Skorzeny out, and picked up the telephone. Dialed. "Uncle Freddy, this is it. Glas will pick you up tomorrow morning. Are you ready?"

"Yes."

"Everything I told you committed to memory?"

"Yes."

"Good man. The extra money is in Edda's top dresser drawer."

"Thank you. Any last-minute instructions?"

"No, just as I predicted, the Fuehrer has decided not to leave Berlin after all. He will move everything and everybody he needs down into the bunker I showed you last month. Eva is joining him there, too. Do you have the whole bunker layout memorized as well?"

"Of course."

"One note of caution. He will be calling on you to do just about everything from wiping Eva's nose, to feeding his dog, to emptying his chamber pot, so be on your toes. You will have to use your own best judgment when to make your break."

"I understand. And, the first leg is to make my way to the south gate of the Zoo."

"Right. You'll meet your contact there. Try not to get yourself blown up. I've got too much invested in you."

"I'll be careful."

"Well, then, so long, and good luck."

"*Auf Wiedersehen.*"

Bormann hung up, took a deep breath, and went back into his office.

Korvettenkapitan von Hellenbach was pacing the floor.

"Having second thoughts, Captain?"

"I'm concerned about my family."

"I think about mine, too, all the time. But don't worry, you should see them again in a month, maybe less."

"I'm worried about two other things as well, Reichsleiter."

"Which are?"

"First, there are only two of those new boats able to make such a trip, and both of them are already at sea. What kind of vessel—"

"There is a third boat, just like the other two. Constructed in secret and highly modified by Kellermann himself. No one knows about it, not even Doenitz. What else?"

"My crew."

"We have managed to round up a few experienced men, those that are not dead, including your old Chief, along with some special forces volunteers, all of whom are already in place. Now, if you are ready, there is a plane waiting to fly us to Trondheim."

"Us?"

"Yes. Ah, one other thing, von Hellenbach. You are to have supercargo on this voyage. A young Wermacht Captain and myself."

CHAPTER 24

Bormann was pleased to find everything at Trondheim exactly as he had ordered. Once Korvettenkapitan von Hellenbach was ushered by one of Skorzeny's SS Sergeants to his quarters, Bormann, taking no chances on anything going wrong, decided to make a final inspection tour. He and Skorzeny, with Bobby Joe Reams in tow, climbed into the boat through the conning tower hatch where they were met by Ludwig Kellerman, who had a tired, but proud look on his face. "What do you think of her, Herr Reichsleiter?"

Bormann threw him a bone. "Everything appears in order. How do you say, shipshape? The Fuehrer will be happy. Where is von Bittnerhof?"

Kellerman scratched his head. "I don't know. I haven't seen him since day before yesterday. No one has. He seems

Hitler's Judas

to have disappeared. Odd."

Bormann forced himself to frown, but inside, he was laughing. *He's well on his way to Italy if not already there, little man. My guess is he will be on a cattle boat to Buenos Aires within a fortnight.* "No matter, you can give us the guided tour."

"Certainly. What would you like to see first?"

"Show me where the Captain sleeps."

Kellerman nodded and led the way to the officer's quarters. Once there, he gestured both to the right and to the left. The Captain's cabin is here. The First Officer bunks across the companionway, over here. Both are actual enclosed rooms, three times the size of the rat's nests on the old boats."

Bormann opened the door of the Captain's cabin. Inside, he looked around at the Spartan, yet comfortable compartment. "It still looks like a rat's nest, but it'll do for me." He glanced at Bobby Joe Reams, and pointed across the narrow companionway. "You shall bunk down there, Herr Hauptman."

Reams, understanding hardly any German, nevertheless understood the gesture, and obeyed. Again leaving nothing to chance, Bormann crossed over, opened the door, and gently shoved Reams inside, and under his breath, said, in English. "Stay here until I return. Understand?"

Reams grinned at him, affected a silly Heil Hitler salute, and answered with one of the few German words he knew. "*Ja.*"

Bormann turned back to the Chief Naval Architect. "Now show me the torpedo room."

— 246 —

Tom Lewis

Kellermann coughed discretely. "There are two torpedo rooms, Herr Reichsleiter. One forward, one aft. Let's go forward."

On the way, Skorzeny touched Bormann's arm. "This boat is truly a masterful piece of engineering. Not a square centimeter of space is wasted. It's very impressive."

"You hear that, Kellermann?" Bormann said. "It's quite a compliment coming from a man who can field strip and put back together every weapon in use today, ours or the enemies'. Even blindfolded."

"Thank you, Colonel. Here we are."

The two tough SS guards standing on either side of the door jumped to attention, their machine guns at the ready. Ducking his head, Bormann followed Kellermann and Skorzeny inside, finding himself completely surrounded by an array of sleek torpedoes, with narrow bunks above and beneath them. "Some of the crew sleeps here?" He said in surprise.

Kellerman answered, "As the Colonel noted, not much space is wasted. The men off watch sleep quite close to their work."

Reversing directions, Kellermann led them aft, where Bormann was even further pleased with Skorzeny's thoroughness. He had not forgotten Bormann's order. There were both red and blue marks on the torpedoes here as well as up front. Under his breath, he said, "My compliments, Otto. Everything looks fine. The Fuehrer will no doubt promote you to General." Both men laughed at the joke, then, Bormann became serious again. "Your men all look capable, too. How many will be aboard?"

"Eighteen," Skorzeny answered. "Enough for three

– 247 –

Hitler's Judas

shifts, eight hours each."

"Excellent. And who is in charge of the contingent?"

"One of my best and most experienced men. Captain Joachim Kleist."

"Ah, yes. I remember him." He winked at Skorzeny. "I heard he made a pretty good American Captain, too, at Bastogne. Where is he now?"

"Keeping an eye on the men guarding the boat's crew and von Hellenbach."

Kellerman spoke up. "Korvettenkapitan Horst von Hellenbach? He's to be in command?"

"Yes. Why?"

Kellerman clapped his hands. "That's very good news, Reichsleiter. There are fewer than a handful of skippers I'd trust my baby with. He's at the top of the list."

Bormann affected a yawn. "I'm so glad you agree with the Fuehrer. All right, the Colonel and I have some private business to talk over. Leave us, now. Go and see if you can find out where von Bittnerhof went."

Kellerman saluted and scurried topsides. Bormann turned to Skorzeny. "Let's go back to the Captain's cabin, Otto. I want you to show me where the little switch is, and exactly how to turn it on. I didn't notice it when we were there before."

"You wouldn't have, unless you knew what you were looking for. It's disguised as a water valve. Come, I'll show you…"

The room Horst was given was comfortable enough, with a shower and toilet, but was nonetheless a cell. Not able to sleep, though exhausted from all the traveling of

— 248 —

Tom Lewis

the past twenty-four hours, he got up from the cot and began pacing, growing more and more irritated at the way he was being treated. Bormann and Hitler were carrying this secrecy thing too far. He'd been hustled into an airplane and flown to Trondheim by the same SS Colonel who had rousted him from his bed. He, along with the Reichsleiter and a short, mouse-faced fellow in an ill-fitting Wehrmacht Captain's uniform. None of them so much as opened their mouths during the drive from Bormann's office to Templehof, on the long, bumpy flight north, or on the drive to the secret naval complex which was crawling with SS personnel. He had then been literally thrown into this barracks room to wait for 'further orders.' It was all a bit much, and insult added to injury when the door was locked and guarded by two black-clad SS Sergeants! Where the devil had they expected him to go?

And besides all that, he was starving. He wished now he'd taken Hitler up on his offer of refreshments. Tea and sweet cakes would have been better than nothing. He didn't have a change of underwear or a fresh uniform, either, but he wasn't about to take a shower and put the same clothes back on.

Enough!

He walked to the door, banged on it, and yelled, demanding to see Bormann. No answer came. Thoroughly disgusted, Horst sat back down on the cot and lit the last of his cigarettes. It gave him no satisfaction, and after two or three puffs, he ground it out in the saucer on the table that served for an ashtray. He lay back on the cot, willing himself to think of other things, but everything melded into a mental image of Lizzle's face. Then, his mother's. *When will I ever*

Hitler's Judas

see either of you again? When will we—

The key turning in the lock jolted him back to reality. A moment later, Martin Bormann came through it, carrying a tray of food. "I thought you might be hungry, von Hellenbach." Hard on Bormann's heels was a thin man with stringy, long hair, carrying a suitcase.

Horst said only one word—"Thanks"—and like one of Pavlov's dogs, began devouring the roasted chicken and potatoes. Bormann leaned on the door, stuck his hands in his pockets, and apologized for the delay. "Permit me to introduce Chief Architect Kellermann, who will answer any questions you may have about the boat. Oh, you will find new uniforms, underclothing, and toilet items in that suitcase. I trust you've been comfortable?"

Between bites, Horst said, "I want to see the boat."

"In due time, Captain."

"No. Now. And I want Chief Knapp with me, too."

Bormann's face turned red, but he controlled his temper. "Very well. Kellerman, when he finishes eating, and has a bath, take them both to the pen." He looked back at Horst. "But if I were you, I'd try to get a little sleep. We sail in twelve hours."

Bormann hurried out, made his way to the front door of the 'barracks' and said to Captain Kleist. "Go at once to the boat and get your men out of there while von Hellenbach and his chief look around. I don't want to make him any more suspicious than he already is."

The SS Captain saluted and hurried out. Bormann then made his way to the main gate of the complex, where Skorzeny was waiting. "*Auf Wiedersehen*, Otto. Have a good

– 250 –

Tom Lewis

flight home, and become less than a shadow once you get there."

"Like I said before, Reichsleiter, I know how to take care of myself. Good luck on your voyage."

Bormann shook his hand. "Luck, my friend, doesn't have a damn thing to do with it."

Oskar's voice was an awed whisper. "It's Frankenstein's monster! Have you ever seen anything like it, Herr Kaleun?"

Horst didn't answer, but Kellermann had a ready one. "She's painted black for a reason, Chief. And since she will not be in active combat, she has no deck guns. Those davits will hold specially designed aluminum boats. Come. Let's go below."

They went in through the forward hatch. Below decks, nothing seemed to be different than the streamlined U-2512 which they had done some training in. Kellerman led the way aft. Horst, noting Oskar was lagging behind, and limping, turned to his Chief and said, "What's the matter, Knapp? Why are you limping?"

Oscar shrugged. "One of those recruits dropped the end of a toolbox on my foot the other day. It's nothing. I'm fine."

As if to reassure his commander, he forged ahead to the galley. "Look at this, sir. Two freezers! What would old Kirchner think? How many hams could you stow inside one of these —"

"Don't open that!" Kellermann shouted. But it was too late. Oskar had lifted the lid of one of the stainless steel lockers and instantly backed off. "God in heaven!"

– 251 –

Hitler's Judas

Horst looked inside and recoiled in shock and horror. Stuffed inside were the frozen bodies of two men, a Kriegsmarine officer and a rating. Horst looked at Kellermann for an explanation.

"It's Bormann's idea, Captain. They were Russian slave laborers, not Germans, and should the boat be attacked, will be shot through the stern torpedo tubes, along with oil and miscellaneous debris in order to —"

"—Make the enemy think they have sunk us," Horst finished for him. "Macabre, but probably effective. What other surprises do you have around here?"

"That's all. I'm sorry you had to see that before I could explain. Let me show you your quarters."

Horst nodded, and, shoving the shaken Chief ahead of him, followed the architect forward. Oskar, because of what he had just seen, had forgotten to disguise his limp, which was now severe. Horst reached for his shoulder, swung him around, and stepped on his foot. Oskar howled in agony, fell to the deck and grabbed his foot.

"Damn you," Horst said. "Take your shoe off and let me see that foot."

"But sir," Oskar whined.

"That's an order, Chief. *Do it.*"

Tears of both pain and embarrassment rolled down Oskar Knapp's face as he carefully removed his shoe and wool sock. Horst took one look at the blackened, swollen toes, bent down, and sniffed. The smell, and the red streaks running up the hairy leg to the knee told Horst the worst.

Gangrene. He straightened, and barked at the pale-faced architect. "Help me get him back to your car. He has to go to hospital immediately."

— 252 —

Oskar protested loudly, and Kellermann said, "Captain, Bormann will be furious. You're not supposed to leave this boat."

"To hell with Bormann. If you don't help me this instant, this boat will not ever leave this pen, at least not with me in command. Now, *move,* damn you."

"Yes, sir. But who will take his place? You can't sail without an engineer."

Horst grabbed the skinny man by the shirt and hissed into his face, "You know more about this boat than any man alive, Kellermann. If she moves one meter, you'll be aboard, or you'll be dead. Take your choice."

Oskar was still protesting when he got into Kellermann's car. Nor did he cease his arguing at the hospital. He didn't actually shut his mouth until the Norwegian doctor told Horst, "You were correct, sir. It is gangrene. We will probably save his life, but he will most likely lose that foot— up to his knee."

And so, at midnight, Korvettenkapitan Horst von Hellenbach gave orders, and the black submarine with no number painted on her conning tower — a boat that had no registry in the German Navy, a boat that, at least on paper, did not exist — moved out of her camouflaged pen into the clear, deep water of Trondheim's fiord and set a course for north of the Faeroe Islands, on the edge of the arctic circle. She sailed into the Norwegian Sea submerged, carrying a skeleton crew of only one other officer and twenty men, a furious Chief Architect, plus a contingent of eighteen hard-case SS commandos.

Also aboard was a short Wehrmacht officer who

Hitler's Judas

apparently could not speak. And, the second most powerful man in all of Nazi Germany.

In his log, Horst wrote down the date. 5 April 1945.

Exactly one week before Franklin Delano Roosevelt died at Warm Springs.

CHAPTER 25

Horst knew he had to lay a track for South America, but that's all he knew. Once the first leg was done, at the point north of the Faeroes, he reduced speed and called Bormann to the navigation station. With the tip of his calipers, he pointed to their position. "This is where we are, Reichsleiter. I think it's time to turn south. Question is, where precisely are we going? I need to lay a course, and don't forget, we have to cross the path of Allied convoys."

"Show me where they usually cross."

Horst pointed again. "Their west to east route is usually here, on one side or the other of the 45th parallel. Their ships and planes have driven practically all U-Boat activity from the North Atlantic, and are crossing now with total impunity, one big batch after the other. My hope is

Hitler's Judas

that since they no longer consider themselves in much danger, they may have relaxed their vigilance somewhat, but I'm not going to gamble any more than I can help it. What I plan to do is watch out for them, then scoot south as fast and as deep as I can between convoys. Once we're in the open Atlantic, I think we will be all right. Any contact would probably be only by chance."

"I understand," Bormann said. "Well, we are in your hands, Captain."

"As I said, it would help if I knew exactly where we are going."

"Set your course for Argentina. I'll let you know exactly where when we get close to the equator."

Horst nodded. Bormann gave him a smile of confidence, turned, and left. Horst beckoned to his First (and only!) Officer, Lieutenant Gerd Bruenner. Together, they spread the large-scale chart out and studied it closely. With his pencil Horst traced a temporary course. "We'd best go west-southwest from here to the 60th parallel. I don't want to get too close to Iceland, and I damn sure don't want to get close to the British Isles. Once we're there, we'll slow down and watch for convoys. When we get our chance, we turn due south, straight down the 35th degree longitude, fast as we can. Shortest distance between two points—"

"— Is a straight line. I agree," said Bruenner.

Horst straightened. "Very well." He turned to the helmsman. "Make your course 280 degrees."

"Two-Eight-Zero. Aye, Captain."

Horst looked next at Kellermann. "Maintain snorkel depth. Speed, fourteen knots."

"Yes, sir. Fourteen knots it is."

Tom Lewis

Horst said, "Good. Bruenner, keep your eye to that eyepiece, and sweep the horizon constantly. I'll relieve you in an hour."

"Aye, Captain."

Horst grunted, turned, made his way back to his bunk and sat down, his head between his hands. He had never felt so alone in his life. It didn't bother him much that Bormann had poached the Commander's cabin for himself, and had placed the mute Wehrmacht Captain in the First Officer's quarters, forcing him and Bruenner to share the same Second Officer's bunk space, but it bothered him a great deal that both fore and aft torpedo rooms were off limits to him, guarded by armed SS gorillas around the clock. It also worried him that he barely had enough crew for two watches. Hardly enough to sail the vessel. One day, he vowed he would have a reckoning with that son of a bitch Kellermann. And Bormann himself. He had heard rumors, from time to time, that other U-Boats had made similar voyages to isolated ports in South America, carrying cargoes of gold. But this time, Hitler's right hand man was aboard. Why? Was Bormann actually a traitor? A Judas? Well, it was useless to speculate. He first had to cross the path of God knows how many warships riding herd on their fat convoys, a feat which would require all the skill and concentration he could muster. Best to put all thoughts of everything—and everyone else—aside.

Including Lizzle.

On the Eighth, he gave orders to turn south, at slow speed. At 2100 hours, their sophisticated hydrophones picked up an east-bound convoy. Horst estimated it included perhaps

Hitler's Judas

as many as forty ships! He calculated their speed and course, gave orders to turn around and move away from them until he thought they were well out of range to the east and then reversed his own course. He waited until the last ship had to be out of radar range, then he gave orders to dive. "Take her down to 700 feet. Flank speed."

Kellermann instantly objected. "Captain! 650 is her maximum depth, and at over sixteen knots, we might tear those boats from their davits!"

Horst gave him a look of acute disgust. "Shut your mealy mouth, Kellermann. If we don't get across this path undetected before the next convoy comes by, it won't make a bit of difference anyway, will it? Depth charges drop a lot deeper than 700 feet, and unless we speed through here, we'll all be dead before those boats could ever be launched. Now, do what I ordered."

Along with the others, Horst waited, praying the new design would not be crushed like a paper cup, and that they wouldn't hear the metallic screams of those aluminum boats being torn from the fore and aft decks. An hour passed. Two hours. Three. Not a word was uttered by anyone. Midway through the fourth hour, Horst noticed Bormann, seemingly cool as a block of ice, standing next to him, also watching the clock, chain smoking.

But Kellerman's baby didn't implode. When Horst judged they had put enough distance between themselves and the convoy lane, he ordered the boat back up to snorkel depth. The men cheered, Bormann clapped him on his sweaty back, and said, "I knew you could do it, Captain."

"We're not out of the woods yet, Reichsleiter," Horst cautioned. He turned to Kellerman. "Bring us to periscope

Tom Lewis

depth. Slowly, please."

The moment Kellermann said, "Periscope depth, sir." Horst spoke to the man at the hydrophones. "Anything?"

"Nothing, sir."

"Good. Up periscope."

He turned his cap around, fastened his eye to the eyepiece, and did a 360 degree turn. Nothing was in sight.

God be thanked! "Back down to snorkel depth. We'll keep her there until dark. Then we can surface briefly and check on things on deck."

Twice daily during the next few days, Bormann came to the navigation station to ask where they were. And twice a day Horst pointed to a pinprick on the chart. On the fourth day, Horst gave orders to turn southwest again. He explained to Bormann, pointing again to the chart. "I want to give the Azores a wide berth. We now have to watch out for west-bound ships coming out of the Mediterranean. Convoys of empty ships also have escorts, though not so many."

"Understood. Then what?"

"We turn southeast again, then south to Cape Sau Roque."

Bormann said not another word and then casually walked back to his cabin.

A day later, he came back yet again. "Where are we now, Captain?"

Horst showed him. "In an hour, we turn back southeast."

"No. You are to change your course. Due west. Steer just north of Bermuda."

– 259 –

Hitler's Judas

Horst stared at the man. "What? Don't you understand where we are, Herr Bormann? Such a course would run us smack into the southeast coast of the United States!"

"Precisely. We're not going to South America. The U.S. *is* our final destination, von Hellenbach. To be exact," he pointed, "Right here. Twenty-five miles north of Cape Hatteras. Take us as close in as you can, then set her on the bottom. "I'll give you further instructions then."

Horst started to say something, then thought better of it. Bormann didn't fail to notice his hesitation, either. "Good man. Your job is to sail this boat where I tell you to and not ask questions. You've done a good job of it so far. Don't screw up now. Oh, by the way, according to my homework, tonight should be moonless, correct?"

Horst had to think. "Yes, I believe so. Why?"

"Because we have an extra little job to do."

Shortly after dark, Horst gave orders to surface. He stood in the conning tower, scanning the horizon nervously while every man on board except the cook turned to and painted the deck and the flare of the hull with streaks of light and medium brown. Perfect camouflage for a boat lying on a sandy bottom in shallow water. The marine paint was dry enough to submerge again before dawn.

On the fifteenth, Bormann called his silent partner into his quarters. In English, he said, "Bobby Joe, I'm proud of the way you have managed all this. All this way and not one single word. And now we're almost home." He reached into the suitcase beneath his bunk and handed the American airman a uniform. "Put this on. It should fit pretty well."

Tom Lewis

He watched with pleasure as the boy wordlessly peeled off his too-large Wehrmacht uniform. The money belt was fastened snugly around his waist. Bormann was pleased that the uniform of a private in the Afrika Korps *wasn't* a bad fit. Neither was the one he was wearing. "Good. It's time. The Captain tells me tonight is another night without a moon. Follow me."

They walked into the control room, paying no attention to the looks of astonishment on the faces of the crew. "All right, Captain. Bring us up."

The moment the U-Boat surfaced, Horst scrambled to the tower and gave orders for the bow deck flat-bottomed aluminum boat to be launched. Gritting his teeth, he watched Kellermann direct the boat crews on how to quietly and quickly fasten the twin, high-powered outboard engines to its transom, then saw the black painted inflatable also launched and tethered to the boat. He scanned the horizon with his glasses. Nothing, not a glow in sight, and Horst was glad the powerful Hatteras light was not in use. Their luck was holding, but for how long? They were less than ten miles from shore and with only eighty-six feet of water beneath their keel.

Bormann, the mute, Kleist, the SS commando Captain and his top Sergeant, a man named Niemans (both also dressed in bogus uniforms) were already aboard the boat, with Kellermann himself in the sternsheets at the controls. The boat cast off, and Bormann looked up at him. "We will return in exactly four hours, Captain. Go ahead back down."

Horst waited just long enough for the boat, pulling the inflatable behind, to clear, noting that the outboard motors were not very loud. "All hands below, he yelled." He turned around. "All right, First Officer, let's take her

– 261 –

down, and easy does it, a foot at the time. We could sit her right down on top of a wreck if we're not careful." Horst prayed to himself they actually were close to a wreck. They were on the edge of the graveyard of the Atlantic, and hopefully, the sonar of any ship passing near or directly over them would assume they were just another rusting hull— provided strict silence was maintained below.

Inside of three minutes, a slight grating sound told Horst they had settled onto hard sand. So far so good. He whispered to Bruenner to pass the word for total silence. No man was to so much as move. The First Officer was back in record time. He whispered to Horst, "What are they doing up there, Herr Kaleun?"

Horst spread his hands. "Your guess is as good as mine." He hung his head in thought. Have to hand it to Bormann, he mused. He had planned all this to perfection, even having a working knowledge of moon phases and weather. They had also been lucky. On the surface, there was only a gentle swell. Bormann would be able to take the aluminum boat close in, perhaps within a mile of the beach. The light southwesterly would take the sound of the motors out to sea, not onshore, and the inflatable would be easy and noiseless the rest of the way to the beach. It was a safe bet that this trip, with only one of the boats, was a recon. And, it was also manifest that whatever Bormann wanted to transfer to the beach was stowed in the two torpedo rooms. Shaking his head, he forced any further speculation from his mind.

The seconds, minutes, and hours went by slowly. So very slowly.

CHAPTER 26

Kellermann throttled back, and told Bormann, "We are within half a mile of the beach."

"We are?" Bormann answered. "I can't see a thing."

"Trust me," Kellerman said, frowning. "Best to take the inflatable the rest of the way in."

"All right. Kleist, I know you have experience with landings like this. You come with me. The rest of you wait here for us." He leaned over to Bobby Joe Reams who was sitting next to him. Bormann could smell the acid anxiety emanating from the little man's body. "You are very close to getting home now," he whispered. "Not a word out of you until we get back."

The small American airman shook his head, breathing through his mouth. Bormann knew the poor fellow's blood

Hitler's Judas

pressure was way up.

"How long will you be?" Kellermann wanted to know.

Bormann glared at the feisty naval architect. "As long as it takes."

For the first time, Captain Kleist spoke— to Kellerman. "Mind you compensate for the drift. When we start back, I'll light a cigarette. You should be able to see it with no problem." With a snicker he added, "And try not to fall overboard. I hear there are lots of sharks in these waters."

There was not a single sound to be heard in return to his gallows humor, so Kleist helped Bormann into the inflatable. Both men picked up paddles. "We're in luck, Reichsleiter. The tide is coming in."

No more conversation passed between the two of them as they paddled toward the muted sound of the gently breaking surf. Within ten minutes, they sighted the dark dunes, and soon were pulling the inflatable boat onto the pale beach, high enough, in Kleist's judgement, to be out of the reach of the flood tide. Both men drew their pistols, looked north and south, and Bormann pointed to his right. "We'll go that way first," he whispered. "According to my intelligence, there should be an abandoned Life Saving Station house no more than a kilometer away."

Kleist nodded and also pointed. "We should walk up there, on the dune ridge. Are you ready?"

"Ready."

They walked north, scanning the horizon as they went. On their right, the Atlantic was benign. A sleeping sea. On their left, the Sound was just as sedate.

Other than the lapping of small waves, not a sound

Tom Lewis

could be heard, but the experienced Captain of Skorzeny's elite Commando force was wary nonetheless. He walked in a half-crouch, pistol arm extended, like a hunting dog. A step behind him, Bormann followed, his own body just as tense. Abruptly, Kleist dropped to his haunches. A split second later, Bormann saw why, and followed suit. Directly in front of them was a tiny house; not much more than a shack. *Fishing shack?* Faint light was streaming from behind a small window, and a wisp of smoke was coming from the chimney. Kleist turned to face Bormann, his face like a broad question mark.

Bormann shrugged his shoulders in response. There had been nothing in his detailed Pea Island intelligence report about this building, let alone one that was obviously occupied. Kleist pointed again. Over the roof of the shack, maybe five hundred meters further north, they could see the outline of a much larger building— which had to be the Station House.

Bormann gave Kleist a clenched-jaw look that said, "Yes, it's an unexpected problem. So, we deal with it."

Kleist grimaced, and began crawling on his belly toward the little house, Bormann wiggling along behind him. It took a good five minutes to reach the south side of the shack, and they were as yet undetected. They had no idea how many people were inside, but Bormann knew they would have to find out, or else his entire plan might have to change yet again— to sailing directly to South America. As Bormann watched, holding his breath, Kleist raised his eyes to the left hand corner of the window, inch by agonizingly slow inch. One long peek inside apparently told him a lot. With a jerk of his head, he indicated Bormann

Hitler's Judas

should also take a look. Bormann shifted his weight so that he could repeat Kleist's movements. Squinting at the sudden light hitting his corneas, he took in the whole room. An enormous, one-armed black man was sitting at a rough table reading, totally unaware he was being spied upon. Bormann watched him for a few minutes, mainly to see if there was anyone else inside. No, the giant Negro was alone. With hand signals, Kleist indicated they should bypass the small house for the moment and investigate the larger one before doing anything else. Bormann nodded rapidly, in full understanding. If there were people in the Station House, it was possible they might come to the rescue of the black man in case he gave them any resistance or vocal warning. Together, they sneaked away from the shack and carefully made their way to the large, solidly built two-story building, which was built up over the sand. They took almost an hour snaking their way all around it, at last satisfied that no one was there, or if there was, they were all asleep. Kleist jerked his thumb south again, and they retraced their path back to the shack. It was time to deal with the one-armed *Neger*.

They crawled around to the door and examined it, both thinking it strange that it had no outside lock. "Cover me," Bormann said, and with one deep breath, he pushed it open and walked inside.

The black man looked up in complete surprise. "Who the devil are *you?*" He started to get up from the table, but then he saw the Luger in Bormann's hand, and eased himself back down in his chair. His eyes, large with fear, darted between Bormann's and the pistol pointed at him. "What y'all want?"

– 266 –

Tom Lewis

"Information. Are you alone here?" Bormann said softly, in English.

Eyeing their uniforms, the black man took a moment before answering. "Yeah. Ain't nobody here but me. You boys in some kinda special outfit?"

Bormann's lips turned up ever so slightly. "Yes, a very special unit." He looked around the shack, noting that everywhere there were bottles, jars, and clay pots filling the clean, sparsely furnished room. He also noticed that the huge Negro had been reading the Bible. "Are you a fisherman?"

The black man's face broke out in a wide grin. "No, sir. I used to be a cook, but I'm a preacher now."

With the muzzle of his weapon, Bormann pointed to the shelves. What is in all those containers?"

"Medicines. I do some doctorin' on the side."

"I see. Is there anyone else on the island? In the Station House perhaps?"

"No, sir. They's all been transferred to other places. I'm the only one on the whole island. What ya'll want on Pea Island anyway?"

At this point, Kleist said, in German, "Sorry, Herr Reichsleiter, but we are running out of time."

The black's wide eyes got wider. "You men ain't Americans...you *Germans?*"

Not bothering to give the man an obvious answer, Bormann pointed the pistol at his head. "Stand up. You will be coming with us. Behave yourself and you will come to no harm."

Urging the black giant ahead of him with their pistols, Bormann and Kleist retraced their steps to the Station

– 267 –

Hitler's Judas

House, not forgetting to extinguish the hurricane lamp the man had been reading by, and closing the door to the shack. Once inside the Station House, it didn't take Kleist more than a few minutes of searching to locate several lengths of rope. Within a few more minutes, the hapless black man was tied up, gagged with his own handkerchief, and led down to the beach. Pausing to look yet once more in both directions, Kleist casually lit a cigarette. Then they pushed off. Bormann, ever watchful, would have sworn that in the fifteen or twenty minutes it took to paddle back to the waiting boat, the black's bloodshot eyes never once blinked, and, he was sweating like a fat man in a sauna. It took some doing to get their bound prisoner transferred to the boat, but once that was done, Bormann ordered Kellermann back to the beach. "It is safe. No one is there. How are we doing regarding the time?"

Kellermann started the engines and answered, "We should make it back to the U-boat with plenty of time to spare. Why do you want to go back to the beach?"

"Not that it is any of your business," Bormann barked, "But I am leaving Captain Kleist there. I have already given him his instructions. I suggest you pay attention to yours."

At two-thirty, Horst brought the U-boat to periscope depth. After searching both sea and sky thoroughly, he gave the quiet order to surface. As soon as the conning tower breached the surface of the gentle Atlantic, Horst was through its hatch, eyes already trained to the west. They hadn't been on the surface five minutes before Kellermann, who was a better sailor than Horst had thought, expertly guided the boat back to the mother ship. Kleist, the SS

Tom Lewis

Captain was not aboard, and in his place sat a tied up, gagged, and blindfolded black man with only one arm. Bormann wasted no time climbing back to the deck. "It's all clear. We found an ideal location." With his thumb, he gestured to the SS Sergeant. "Go below and start unpacking. Captain von Hellenbach, launch the other boat. Now."

Horst complied, then told Bruenner. "Keep an eye on things up here, and watch the horizon, too. You never can tell."

He slid below and inside a minute, was halted at the bulkhead door leading to the forward torpedo room by a menacing SS guard whose finger was on the trigger of his machine pistol. Horst retraced his steps, went aft, and found exactly the same reaction at the stern compartment. He rushed back to the tower, and caught his breath as he saw Bormann supervising the offloading, through both hatches, of wooden boxes so heavy, the SS men doing the loading were straining to carry just one of them by their rope handles. But they had all been well rehearsed. Not a movement nor a second was wasted. Within minutes, ten of the small crates had been handed through the hatches and loaded into each of the bobbing boats.

Horst grimaced. Only two things could weigh that much; lead or gold, and he knew they hadn't voyaged several thousand miles to dump a load of lead on the North Carolina outer islands.

Bormann climbed down into the second boat. Sergeant Niemans, now wearing a black rubber suit instead of a uniform, jumped into the first one, along with Kellermann and the black captive. Bormann looked up at Horst. "Pick us up tomorrow night at 0300, Captain. Understood?"

"Understood," Horst replied, his voice glacial. He watched the two boats head west, laboring under their load, then gave the order to submerge. He went to his bunk, opened his Captain's case, and carefully wrote down in detail, everything that had transpired, including his grim suspicions. Finished, he closed and replaced his log, then went to the galley for some food. Trying to get any sleep was, he knew, out of the question. An idea came to him. He hurried forward to the Captain's quarters, intending to search through whatever Bormann might have left behind. It was a futile brainstorm, however. Two SS gorillas were standing on either side of the door, just as menacing as those guarding the torpedo rooms. Cursing under his breath, Horst trudged back to his bunk, and on impulse, felt under the mattress for the pistol and holster he had hidden there before sailing. It was still there. His own quarters had not been searched. So, he thought, Bormann's planning is not perfect after all. He stretched out, arms behind his head, another idea already forming in his head.

Tom Lewis

CHAPTER 27

Because of the weight, the two boats took considerably longer to reach the beach, so Bormann had time for a few idle thoughts. The first of those was ironic. He knew there was not one single SS man aboard who hadn't guessed what was in the wooden crates, yet true to their oath to the Fuehrer, not one of them would question their duty; not where they were, or what they were doing. Bormann was certain that any one of them, from Kleist on down to the lowest ranking private, would not hesitate to shoot the man next to him if so ordered— in the name of Adolf Hitler. Bormann also silently chided himself! There had been oh, so many times when he had followed the Fuehrer's criminal orders in similar fashion, but even back then, Martin Bormann had known that one day, he would reap his

Hitler's Judas

reward. And that day was now only forty-eight hours away.

Just as he had predicted back in '42, Hitler, in his madness, had all but obliterated every major city in his adopted country, decimated its population, and would soon bring down a Wagnerian *Goetterdammerung* not only upon his own head, but on the head of every innocent German citizen who was left alive. In Hitler's warped brain, if the Aryan peoples of the Third Reich were not strong enough to conquer and rule the civilized (*civilized?*) world, then they did not deserve to go on living.

Looking at the tight lips and determined faces of Skorzeny's men, Bormann felt a momentary rush of adrenaline. He knew what they didn't know. Knowledge, even negative knowledge—such as Germany's approaching doomsday—was power. *Power*. Nectar of the gods. And now, at his feet and on that beach, was enough gold to insure he would retain that power in nearly any spot on earth he chose.

What were a few minor inconveniences? Living for a few weeks or months in an American prison camp as Private Peter Reidel (who'd actually had his head removed by a British artillery shell in the North African desert) would be only a temporary nuisance, as would be an uncomfortable repatriation voyage back to Germany in the sweaty hold of an American troopship. Getting some kind of menial job, even if it meant digging ditches or cleaning up bombed out buildings would not be terrible at all for a Bormann, at least for a while, since he would more than likely be able to get his hands on the dollars he had secretly stashed in one or another of several towns from one end of Germany to the other. Money he could use to eventually buy his way

Tom Lewis

back to America— legitimately!

It would be a relatively easy thing for Mister Peter Reidel to leisurely drift down to North Carolina, dig up his fortune, ship it to anyplace, and live like a playboy prince anywhere in the world he wanted to. He glanced at the pale face of the American boy. Reams would soon be home, all right, only, it would not be at Morehead City. It would be at the bottom of the Roanoke River, naked and unidentifiable.

Borman felt the sudden forward inertia as Kellermann accelerated the boat, pushing it hard up onto the beach. He jumped out and immediately began giving orders. "Kleist, climb back up to the top of that dune and keep a sharp eye out. Niemans, untie the Negro. He looks strong enough to carry those crates despite having only one arm. The rest of you come with me."

He led them to the small shack. "Dig all around this shack, about a meter and a half deep."

Within an hour, he had supervised the transfer of the crates from boat to beach, then steadily, one after the other, to their sandy graves around the shack. He commanded Kellerman to instruct the men on how to remove the powerful outboard engines, and carry them and the ultra-lightweight boats to the deserted Station House where they were hidden beneath the building itself. He had the black man tied up and gagged again, and except for Reams, told the men they could use the old boat shed for shelter. "Try to get some sleep. This fellow and I will bunk down in the shack.

"You have all done your duty admirably. I fully expect the Fuehrer to award each one of you the Iron Cross First

Hitler's Judas

Class. As a matter of fact, I'm sure I can guarantee it. Rest here all day, but do not come out in the open. Each of you carries his own water and rations. I'm sure every one of you has seen rougher duty than this. Tomorrow night, we will repeat the same procedure, and soon you will all be on your way home. Good job, and good night, or rather, good morning. Sleep with cat's eyes."

Bormann spent most of the daylight hours catnapping himself, relieving Kleist periodically as lookout, taking Reams with him. He used his time awake to go over again his navigation plans with the young American, who assured him that with one of those aluminum boats with its nearly silent engine, they would have no problem crossing the sound and running up its south side to the Roanoke River. Reams estimated it would take only two nights to reach the area of the prison camp at Williamston.

"And after I am safely ashore, my young friend," Bormann promised, "I will give you the second money belt, and the boat. I am sure that with your nautical skills and knowledge of these waters, you can make your way home. However, I would get rid of that uniform as soon as possible."

"What am I gonna wear?" the confused Tailgunner wanted to know.

"I have provided for that. You will have to wait until our final trip back to the U-boat. That's where the other money belt is, also."

"Okay. You say so. What are we gonna do tomorrow night?"

"The same thing we did last night. I have several more crates to move ashore. Ten more of them than we moved

– 274 –

Tom Lewis

last night, to be exact. Now, get some rest. Carrying those heavy crates must be difficult."

"I can pull my own weight. Say, what's in 'em, anyway?"

"Contaminated explosives. Not to be tampered with."

Bormann was as good as his word. The following night was a precise encore of the previous one. They met the surfaced U-Boat, transferred the same number of crates to the small boats, and returned to the beach where Reams, who was eagerly anticipating his freedom, did indeed pull his own weight, sweating alongside the others, only this time, they dropped several of the crates in the black man's privy!

As the last of the crates were being hauled up the beach, Bormann suddenly felt the hair rising on the back of his neck. A sudden chill. Something seemed wrong. He glanced at the top of the dune where Kleist was standing. Kleist, the most experienced of the SS men apparently had not noticed anything amiss. His body language would have showed it. Nevertheless, Bormann quickly turned to every compass point, eyes straining. He could see nothing out of the ordinary. Perhaps his nerves and lack of sleep were playing tricks on him. With a quick shudder, he shrugged off the uncomfortable feeling he was experiencing; that someone was watching. He walked over to Bobby Joe Reams, who was struggling with yet another crate. "Relax, son. You're overdoing it. You need to save your strength. That's the last of them anyway. The negro can help with the boats and engines." Reams was grateful, and promptly sat down on the sand.

Hitler's Judas

He watched as the big black and three of the Germans carried the light boats to the water's edge and made another trip to fetch the motors. What happened next caused him to hold his breath. While working to fasten the engines to the boat's transom, the big buck took a swing at the closest man to him, knocking him backwards into the surf. Reams had seen sucker punches before, but never one so effective. Then, quick as greased lightning, the Negro kneed the next closest German in the crotch and started running down the beach. With no little admiration, Reams saw him turn to the right and try to scramble up the face of the dune behind the little shack.

Unfortunately, other eyes had also seen what had happened. The tall officer pulled his pistol and let loose three rapid shots. The first two went wild, but the third one caught the fleeing man squarely in the back, causing him to stagger, then tumble back down the dune, almost at the feet of Bormann, who had drawn his own ugly gun. Fascinated, but frozen where he sat, just like all the others who had heard the shots, Reams watched as Bormann calmly walked around the struggling Negro, who had not given up, and had struggled to his knees, trying to at least crawl. Reams would have sworn that Bormann had a smile on his face as he shot the poor giant in the face, and when he pitched forward, the German leader pumped two more bullets into his head, before turning and yelling "Los!"

Bobby Joe Reams then witnessed an even stranger sight. From nowhere, a huge dog came flying through the air, with unholy sounds coming from its throat. The animal's velocity knocked Bormann off his feet, and Reams grudgingly had to silently admit that the German boss man

— 276 —

Tom Lewis

was as agile as he was tough. Bormann twisted sideways on the sand and pumped three rounds into the dog's body. As it lay twitching and bleeding, the furious Bormann stood and emptied his entire vocabulary of profanity and his pistol into the dog's inert body.

Reams watched Bormann look around to see if there was anyone with the dog, then scream that funny word again. "Los!"

Reams joined the others hurrying to the boats. He wasn't in the least surprised, though, when the tall man who was second in command trotted up to Bormann and said something. He saw Bormann nod, then shout some more orders. Several of the men jumped back onto the beach, ran to the murdered black man's body, picked it up, and carried it to the boat. Two others picked up the dead dog and followed suit. Half a mile out to sea, both bodies were dumped unceremoniously overboard.

At 0230, like *déja vu*, Horst brought the boat off the bottom, raised the scope and swung the compass yet again, and breathed one more sigh of relief. His memory once again flashed back to the days back in '42, with the old U-119. They were between the coast and the shipping lanes; those same shipping lanes they had roamed with impunity, killing vessel after vessel. He also knew that ships, even in good weather such as this, would give Cape Hatteras a wide berth, but they were awfully close to both Wilmington and Norfolk, and some destroyer or sub-chaser could come screaming out at him at any time, not to mention the hated airplanes. Horst wondered how long Bormann's meticulous operation was going to take. Their luck couldn't possibly

Hitler's Judas

hold out much longer. Not even Martin Bormann could plan that.

With another deep breath, he gave the order to surface for the third time and was in the tower the moment the hatch cleared. The first thing he noticed was that there was a blessed cover of low clouds overhead, plus there had been a drop in temperature— which meant a little light fog for early morning, probably before dawn.

"Hallo the ship!" Kellerman's voice came from the port side, and momentarily, the black hulls of the two boats hove into view. Lines were thrown, and Bormann, rapidly followed by Kleist, Neimans, their men, and Kellerman all climbed to the deck. The black giant was not among them. "Captain," Bormann ordered, "Retrieve the aft boat, please. From now on, I will need only one."

Horst gave the order and watched while his crew shipped one of the twin boats. All the while, the SS men, like so many mindless ants, went back to their loading duty. This time, however, there were only six crates left, which were carefully loaded into the tethered boat. Bormann stood next to Horst in the conning tower, watching the final loading with a smug look of satisfaction. He turned to face Horst. "Almost finished. Only one more trip. Soon as we cast off, you may submerge again, and pick us up the last time at 0330 sharp tomorrow. Then it's back home for everybody. Got that?"

"Right," Horst dryly replied. "0330 *punktlich*. We'll be here."

Squinting at the beautiful medal Horst wore around his throat, Bormann reached for it and fingered it for a moment, saying, "Who knows, after this voyage, the

— 278 —

Tom Lewis

Fuehrer may give your another one of these pretties. Stay up here and keep an eye on things for a minute. I'm going below."

With a quick glance at his watch, Bormann went down the ladder, and headed straight to his poached cabin. He looked around, quickly ducked inside and closed the door. Bending, he reached behind the lavatory for the small dial hidden there. He felt for the knob, twisted it to the six o'clock position, and pushed the small button located on its side.

Back on deck, he saw that, as ordered, all the men, U-Boat sailors and SS crew alike, had gone below for hot food. Only the frowning Captain, Kellerman, and the First Officer remained. Another glance showed him that Bobby Joe Reams was alone aboard the bobbing boat. He climbed back in himself, ordered Reams to start the motors and cast off, looked up and yelled, "0330, Captain."

He got a silent salute in return, and nodded to Bobby Joe who throttled up, heading for shore.

Horst waited until Bormann was out of earshot, then quietly told his First Officer to summon the crew back to the deck. No sooner than they began climbing through the hatches, he yelled, "Launch that second boat again, and be quick about it."

Kellermann was at his side in a heartbeat. "What are you doing, Captain? You're supposed to—"

Horst turned on him, his face darker than the night framing it. "I'm in command of this vessel. I'm supposed to do what I want to, so get the hell out of my sight. Go

−279−

Hitler's Judas

below. Now!"

The moment the architect was down the ladder, Horst wheeled back around to his First Officer. "I'm going to follow them, Bruenner. Soon as I'm clear, take her back down. You know what else to do."

Bruenner answered dutifully. "Aye, sir. Back up at 0330."

Horst nodded at him, felt for the pistol in its holster he had strapped on beneath his uniform, then hurried down to the deck. In another second he scrambled over the side and into the boat. He cast off the lines, pushed the throttles wide open and didn't look back. He knew that Bormann's boat, loaded with crates of gold, was heavy, while his empty one was light. Bormann wouldn't be too hard to catch, probably before reaching the surf. Horst leaned forward, thanking God for not allowing the Atlantic to act up tonight. He squinted from port to starboard, looking for signs of Bormann's wake. After only a few minutes, he spotted it.

A quarter mile ahead, Bormann told the astonished Reams to throttle back. He looked once more at his watch. The seconds were ticking by, eating steadily away at the final link that held him to Nazi Germany. He wondered how much longer Hitler could hold out. Another week? Two? Surely not more. The Third Reich was, for all practical purposes, deader than that arrogant U-Boat Captain would be in about... ten seconds. He caught Bobby Joe Reams staring at him quizzically as he counted the last ones out loud, "Five, four, three, two, one—"

The underwater explosion was muffled by the ocean, but huge nonetheless, and caused a mini-tidal wave which

Tom Lewis

was half way to them before Bormann told Reams, "That, my young friend, was the sound of success. My penultimate clock. No witnesses, no—"

In his peripheral vision, he saw the boat coming but it was too late to dodge it. In reflex, he shoved Reams out of the way, and jammed the throttles forward, but the speeding boat behind him struck his transom at almost the same instant. Both boats swerved to port, nearly throwing Reams overboard. Bormann might have had a chance to escape had he gone ahead and straightened his own boat out, but for some reason, he throttled all the way back, and the second boat climbed right up the back of his, throwing him to the bottom, next to the crates which, for balance, had been stacked neatly amidships. He had time to reach for his pistol, but lying on his back in the rocking boat, had trouble aiming at the fool of a Captain who was trying to climb from the other boat to his. And, Bobby Joe Reams was screaming at the top of his voice, "You blew up the sub! Get up! I didn't sign on for no killin'. Get *up!*"

Trying to help Bormann, or at least reach him, Bobby Joe spoiled Bormann's aim, and paid for it. Bormann's first shot caught him squarely in the chest, knocking him backwards. Shot through the heart, Reams was dead before he collapsed against the crates. Bormann squeezed off a second shot, which partially found its mark. He watched von Hellenbach grab at his throat, and lean over sideways. He had been trying to aim a pistol of his own. Bormann got to his feet. There was no need to hurry now. With his left hand, he steadied himself by grabbing the boat's rail and took careful aim at von Hellenbach's head. But that shot went wild as well, because something, something powerful,

— 281 —

Hitler's Judas

had seized his left wrist, pulling down and causing him to tilt to his left, losing his balance. He was suddenly aware he was being pulled overboard— by a force he could not see! He dropped his pistol, and clawed at the rail. He missed.

Down he went. Down, into ocean water that was warmer than he would have imagined. Down, held in the vise-like grip of a brown hand. Bormann opened his eyes. All he could see was a vague form that looked female. A naked *woman?*

He looked close through the ever-darkening water. *Were those breasts?* He imagined he could see something of a neck and a face. White around black eyes. Something glinting, shining between a double row of white teeth. Waving Medusa hair. What was it? Some kind of fish creature? Sea monster? Nothing human, especially female, could be this strong. And, it was laughing at him.

Laughing!

He knew he was being dragged still deeper. His ears were popping. The water was much darker now, and his struggles were useless. Bormann saw, before his bulging eyes, a clear image of Edda's face. No, it was Gerda's face. No, not Gerda's. It was the face of his mother. He tried to call her name, but his lungs had finally ruptured in tiny bubbles of pink froth. The last thing he saw was that brown hand slowly drawing a knife across his throat, and Martin Bormann's last living thought was that he was now on his way to serve a different Fuehrer.

One he could never double cross.

The one whose Reich was Hell.

When he came to, Horst's ears were still ringing from

Tom Lewis

the shots. His throat and cheek instantly reminded him he had been hit by one of them, but the shock force of the bullet ripping into his neck, knocking him backwards against the engine, was not nearly as acute as the shock of realization that Bormann had sabotaged the U-Boat and murdered her entire crew, including his own Praetorian guard. Instantaneous fury erupting inside Horst's gut was more intense than the physical pain that quickly ensued.

Where was Bormann? In automatic reflex, Horst had squeezed his eyes shut when the bastard had aimed and fired at him, practically point blank, but when he had forced his eyes open again, Bormann had disappeared. He was *not in the boat!* Could he have lost his balance and fallen overboard? One glance at the boat's only other occupant was enough. Bormann's silent companion would definitely remain that way throughout eternity.

The scorching pain was now like blue fire. As from a branding iron. Horst reached to his cheek and felt a jagged hole. Then his fingers sought the wound in his neck, and touched the metal edge of something hot. *My medal!* Before sliding back into blessed unconsciousness, he concluded that Bormann's shot had struck his jeweled Iron Cross, which deflected the bullet just enough to keep it from passing through his throat and shattering his spine. The medal had caused the bullet to glance up and sideways, passing through his jaw and exiting through his cheek.

A sudden movement of the boat roused Horst back into semi-consciousness. Something—or someone—was pulling down on the port rail. He saw a hand appear. Then an arm. A dark face framed in streaming black hair followed. Whites of eyes showed, then even whiter teeth

Hitler's Judas

gripping a glinting knife. Horst believed he was hallucinating. Or, maybe he had already died, and was in hell. The devil's creature pulling itself aboard was surely not of this world. Through the intermittent haze of drifting fog and his own blurred vision, Horst watched as the figure climbing effortlessly aboard became— human. And, *female! A woman? Naked goddess? Mahogany daughter of Poseidon?* Even in his half-conscious state, Horst gradually became aware of several new thoughts, new *facts*, simultaneously: *He was not dead.* Renewed, searing pain informed him he was still quite alive. And if he was alive, he must also be awake, and not dreaming. What he was staring at, focusing slowly upon, was real. *She* was real. A tall, beautiful brown woman with the most perfectly formed figure he had ever seen.

And, after a quick examination of the inert body in the bottom of the boat, she had turned and was speaking to him! Horst tried to answer, but could not. As well, he was having more and more trouble simply breathing. Right away, he figured that the trauma caused by the bullet was rapidly causing interior swelling, cutting off his air supply, and getting worse by the second.

The naked she-devil-from-the-sea had also noticed it. "Gasping like a gaffed fish aren't you? Don't worry, Mister White Cap, I won't let you die."

Horst watched her move the point of her knife close to his face, and felt the fingers of her other hand touch his throat, searching for the right spot. Before he could react, she had deftly cut a hole in his windpipe. Compared to what he was already feeling, the added pain was a mere trifle, and with the immediate deliverance of new air into his grateful lungs,

– 284 –

Tom Lewis

Horst passed out again.

For the next period of time, perhaps an hour, Horst swam in and out of consciousness, unable to do more than silently watch the young woman who, in his burning mind, had become not a feminine demon from hell, but a chocolate sister of mercy. She was busy, too; first lifting the heavy, blood-spattered crates and dumping them overboard, and then, showing even more incredible strength, transferring both himself and the dead man into the second boat. She saw Horst briefly open his eyes, and said, "Well, sir, I'll say one thing for you Germans. You know how to build good boats. Never saw any like these before." Her American English accent was like none he had ever heard.

Horst became vaguely aware of yet a new sound.

Engines. She had started the engines! They were moving. He looked behind him. The other aluminum boat was gone. Instead, she was towing a different boat; a graceful sailing craft with a hull blacker than midnight. Painfully, he shifted his eyes to his deliverer, who was steering with a plainly experienced hand.

She spoke to him again. "I'll take care of you and your dead mate first, Charlie White Cap, then see if the tide has washed my Daddy's body up on the beach. You're not going to die, but I know you're hurting like hell. Still and all, don't you even think about trying any foolishness. That's right, you just keep right on staring at me like that."

Horst heard her emit a soft laugh. Like a smothered giggle. "Bet you never saw a naked black woman before, did you? Don't get yourself any ideas about that either. I want to, I can break what's left of your Nazi neck."

Horst passed out yet again, and when he awakened,

Hitler's Judas

the nude brown goddess, talking all the time, was gently pouring some strange-tasting warm liquid into his mouth, some of which trickled down his torn gullet. The effect was almost immediate. His pain began to subside, and with it, his ability to keep his eyes open. It was as if his eyelids were being pulled down by lead weights. Even so, before he slipped into a deep, dreamless sleep, he had still one more solid thought: There was indeed a God. There *was* a Supreme Being, who, in His mercy, had sent him, not to the bottom of the Atlantic Ocean, but into a promised place in Heaven. In his particular case, a sweet-smelling beach off the coast of North Carolina, in the United States of America. His promised mansion was a tiny, two-room fishing shack that reeked of herbs and roots. And his personal guardian angel was in the human form of a brown-skinned woman possessed of unbelievable beauty and strength.

This had to be nothing short of a miracle. No, a series of miracles.

His throat wound was too severe for Horst to be vocally delirious, and the drugged tea he had somehow swallowed sent him adrift between a kind of hazy awareness and blackest void. Still, in his more or less lucid moments, over a period of time he could not begin to measure, his brain managed to record a vast amount of new information. He learned that his dark angel had a name: Sunday. Sunday Everette.

He also learned that she had been raised on Pea Island by the members of the all-Negro crew of the Pea Island Lifesaving Station, and that her father had been the one-armed giant Bormann had kidnapped, and murdered. But

Sunday Everette had exacted her revenge. She told Horst that while hidden, she had seen everything the landing party had done, had followed them out to sea in her fishing boat, and that it was by her hand that Martin Bormann had died. "I pulled him overboard, drowned him and cut his throat."

She had discovered dog tags around the neck of Bormann's dead companion. Reams had probably been an American deserter who also had a money belt strapped around his waist packed with fifty thousand U.S. dollars! All this new knowledge was far too much for Horst's shocked mind to absorb in much detail, nor, at the moment, did he care. Nothing compared to the fact that Sunday Everette had *saved his life.* There would be, for Korvettenkapitan Horst von Hellenbach, some kind of future. Would it be a long one in a prison camp or a short one before facing a firing squad or gallows? Or would God grant yet another miracle? In any event, what life was left to him would surely be here, in America. With a totally new and different kind of pain, Horst knew that his own beloved country was lost. Gone. As dead as Martin Bormann, just as despised, and consigned forever to the hell-memory of history.

For each of His rare miracles, The Supreme Being had exacted a high tax.

EPILOGUE

Christmas Eve, 1946

Clem Hardison eased back on the throttle another half inch just as his fellow crew member came into the wheelhouse. "Sure is one clear night out here, Clem," Joe Freeman said, keeping his voice low. "Warm, too. You reckon we'll get back in tomorrow?"

"At least by tomorrow night. Don't worry," Clem answered, also in a soft tone. "Sunday knows what she's doin'. You'll be back home in plenty of time to play some Santy Claus with your own kids."

Joe was dubious. "I hope so. Well, at least we don't have to do no work. This one's kinda like a pleasure cruise,

Tom Lewis

ain't it?"

"Yep, for us it is. Just like the one when Sunday brought us out here for hers and Charlie's weddin'. But this one ain't so easy for her. Havin' a baby ain't no pleasure cruise. It's hard work."

Both men fell silent for a while as the trawler cruised north comfortably in the western edge of the Gulf Stream. Eventually, Joe added another comment. "You know, I didn't mind a bit bein' a witness back then, and I'm sure glad it's Charlie's down there helpin' her, but I don't know about this godfather business. What's a godfather supposed to *do?*"

Clem showed his teeth in a wide smile. "In our case, not a whole lot. Sunday and Charlie are both healthy as horses. Most likely live a long time, but if anything did ever happen to them, it'll be our responsibility to look out for the kid."

Joe absorbed this with a frown, waited a beat or two, and remarked, "Sunday said it's gonna be a girl. How does she know?"

"Don't ask me. Sunday just *knows* things like that. She says it's gonna be a girl, that's what it's gonna be. That's all there is to it." Clem tried to change the subject. "Say, this new diesel runs real good. Smooth as an eel's back."

"Yeah. Sunday's got herself a mighty fine vessel here. I reckon you and me are pretty lucky to be her crew. Work's hard, but her and Charlie are downright generous with our shares of the catch. I got more money in my pockets now than I ever had."

"Me, too. Hey, you didn't forget to bring that rockin'

Hitler's Judas

chair aboard did you?"

"Naw, it's down there." Joe snorted. "Ever think you'd see the day there'd be a rockin' chair in a fishin' boat?"

"No, but this one ain't no ordinary fishin' boat. It's also Sunday's and Charlie's house. Their home. You know something, I ain't never seen her so happy or Charlie so nervous. You'd think that all they went through last year, havin' this baby would be a piece of cake. She tell you what she's gonna name it?"

"I heard her when she told you. Susan. Right nice name, ain't it?"

Clem didn't answer right away. He wasn't much on names, and if Sunday wanted to name her baby after old Susan Bearclaw, it was her business. That old woman had taught Sunday everything she knew about healing folks, which was a lot, and he knew that Sunday thought of her as the only mother she had ever known. "I reckon she can name that little girl anything she wants—"

A tiny, high-pitched cry below their feet stopped him in mid-sentence. "Hear that, Joe? I do believe it's here! What time is it?"

Both men glanced at the ship's clock simultaneously. Three minutes after midnight. Christmas Day.

An hour later, Horst von Hellenbach, now known throughout the Outer Banks and beyond as Charlie Everette, came up the companionway, arms raised above his head like a victorious prizefighter. Clem and Joe watched as he walked forward to the prow. He did not want them to see the tears streaming down his face. Tears he could not remember shedding since he was a small boy. Not bothering

Tom Lewis

to wipe them away, he lifted his eyes up to Orion's belt. As a young cadet, studying stars and constellations, he had always whimsically thought of those few stars as three diamonds in a box. Mutely, of course, he gave thanks to the God he knew was watching, exulting over His latest miracle. "That is what we are now, for sure," he silently mouthed. "Three diamonds in a box—or rather, a hull."

He heard, over the pleasant, almost reverent rumble of the powerful engine coming from beneath his feet, a different sound.

Humming.

He cocked his head and listened to the faint tune of that silly song Sunday always sang while she worked.

Old Dan Tucker was a fine old man
Washed his face in a frying pan
Combed his hair with a wagon wheel
And died with a toothache in his heel.

Only this time, it was not the boisterous work chant she had learned from her father. It was a lullaby. The loveliest one he had ever heard.

AUTHOR'S NOTE:

HITLER'S JUDAS is fiction, and most of its principal characters are totally fictitious. However, many of the other characters in the story are (or were) actual persons, including Adolf Hitler, of course, plus Martin Bormann, Himmler, Hess, Goebbels, Goering, and Otto Skorzeny, to name a few. Anyone who has studied World War Two history knows these names well, and a great deal about the monstrous deeds they combined to commit during the brief avalanche of horror that was the Third Reich.

The man closest to Hitler was Martin Bormann. Always careful to stay in the background shadows, Bormann was in a position to know Hitler's every move, his mood swings, his decision-making— and his insanity. The most important thing to remember about the relationship between Bormann and his Fuehrer was that Hitler trusted him completely. In fact, after Rudolf Hess defected, Bormann was probably the *only* man Hitler trusted. As his increasing paranoia advanced, Hitler relied more and more on his faithful personal secretary, which only increased Bormann's power; to such a degree that Martin Bormann quietly became the second most powerful man in Nazi Germany. He was most likely the only man who had no fear of Himmler and his dreaded S.S. Other leading Nazi figures and military leaders were highly jealous of his closeness to Hitler, and most came to fear him because of it.

Tom Lewis

It is inconceivable that, given his intelligence and cunning, Bormann would opt to also go down in the flames of Hitler's *Goetterdammerung* like a blind sheep. He was an opportunist above all else, and extremely patient. Many historians now believe that Bormann did not die trying to escape the Hitler bunker at war's end, and in fact, the consensus is that he indeed survived, eventually making his way to South America. He no doubt had the means, the opportunity, and certainly the motive to do so, and very well could have conceived of such a scheme of betrayal and theft that I have fictionalized in this book.

PUBLISHER'S NOTE:

We hope you have enjoyed "Hitler's Judas", which is the second installment of the Pea Island Gold trilogy. Book Three, "Sons Of Their Fathers"' continuing the saga of Sunday Everette, will follow.

Please visit Tom Lewis online at www.tomelewis.com for further information about Tom and his forthcoming works. The website also has short stories, and a link to contact Tom directly. You may also register to be notified by E-mail when future volumes are available. If you do not have web access, you can send a postcard to VP Publishing at the address below to be notified by mail when future books are available.

Copies of "Hitler's Judas" may be ordered from your favorite bookstore, from Amazon at www.amazon.com, at www.tomelewis.com, or directly from the publisher at the address below. "Sunday's Child", which began the trilogy, is also available.

VP Publishing, LLC
PO Box 4623
Rocky Mount, NC 27803

Direct pricing:
Hitler's Judas $14.95 plus $4.00 shipping and handling
Sunday's Child $14.95 plus $4.00 shipping and handling

For quantity orders inquire at:
orders@vppublishing.com